NO ONE DOES IT BETTER THAN
THOMAS TRYON!

THE OTHER

W9-ASD-601

Other Books by Thomas Tryon:

THE OTHER
HARVEST HOME
LADY
CROWNED HEADS
ALL THAT GLITTERS

THOMAS TRYON

THE OTHER

A DELL BOOK

Published by
Dell Publishing Co., Inc.
1 Dag Hammarskjold Plaza
New York, New York 10017

THIS BOOK CONTAINS THE COMPLETE TEXT OF THE ORIG-
INAL HARDCOVER EDITION.

Dell ® TM 681510, Dell Publishing Co., Inc.

ISBN: 0-440-16736-1

Reprinted by arrangement with Alfred A. Knopf, Inc.

Printed in the United States of America

November 1987

10 9 8 7 6 5 4 3 2

WFH

FOR
MY MOTHER AND FATHER

ONE

How old do you think Miss DeGroot really is? Sixty, if she's a day, wouldn't you say? She's been around here as long as I can remember—quite a *old* stretch, if you calculate it—and I know she goes back a good many years before that. Which should give you an idea of how old that spot on the ceiling must be, because she says it's been there as long as *she* can remember, Miss DeGroot. See it, that damn blotch up there in the plaster? It's from seepage. The rain drips in through the roof, see? Only they won't fix it. I've been after them for years, but you can't get them to lift a finger around here. Miss DeGroot always says they're going to, but they never do. Miss De-Groot says that, to her, the blotch—it's a water stain, really—has the outlines of a country, someplace on a map—I can't remember which, but some particular geographical location she's got in mind. She has a good imagination, don't you think? Maybe it's an island. Tasmania, perhaps? Or Zanzibar? Madagascar? I can't remember, really. I heard recently they'd changed the name of Madagascar. Can that be true, I wonder? I must ask her—Miss DeGroot, that is. Hard to picture a world without a Madagascar, isn't it? Well, that's no large matter. *CRAZY*

The mark on the ceiling grows bigger and darker year by year. Big ripply rust-colored stain. Like that other stain, the one over *his* bed. Odd, how I recall

whose?

that, isn't it? You never saw it, probably, but—well, confidentially, *this* one in *this* room reminds me of *that* one in *that* room. Only to me it doesn't look like any place on a map, as Miss DeGroot suggests, to me it seems to be—you'll think I'm crazy—but to me it resembles a face. Yes, actually—a face. See the eyes, there, those two dark round spaces? And then the nose just below? And there's the mouth, there—see how it curls slightly at the corners? Rather benign, it seems to me. I am reminded of—never mind; you *will* think I'm crazy.

Unseasonably dry this year. No rain in months now, so the blotch hasn't spread much lately. But it will, I suppose. It's inevitable. Death, taxes, and that damn stain. I guess if it were up to Miss DeGroot they'd probably do something about it, but Miss De-Groot, I've decided, doesn't wield a great deal of influence around here. What's one more water mark on the ceiling to *them*—for the likes of *me*, The *dislikes* of me, I should possibly say. I do dislike this place. Why? Ask Miss DeGroot; she could tell you. Funny cheery hopeless Miss DeGroot. (How old must she be? I don't even know her first name—is it Hilda? Olga?) I guess some day the whole ceiling will be one big brown stain, if I live long enough. And then it will all cave in on me. Except for one thing—I won't live long enough to see it. Not that that would matter to anybody. Lonely, isolated

It's evening. Can you see that bit of sky through the window? (As if anyone could see through the window—it's too dirty.) But I can, kind of. Lilac, amethyst, mauve . . . indigo, perhaps, that bluish-purple hue, but of the palest shade. Any one of those,

possibly a mixture of all, the color I can see beyond
the clouded glass, carefully, geometrically divided BARS
into nine oblongs by those rigid black muntins, while
I lie here on my bed, staring out at that one small
piece of sky visible to me. (Miss DeGroot tells me
I'm lucky to be living up among the roofs and chimneys; it's quieter, she says; maybe she's right. And
you can see the moon when there is one. Yes, I think
possibly there'll be a moon.) Lilac. Amethyst. Or lavender; rose, almost. Lying here, I can see how the
light is fading slightly, already deepening, a trembling, opalescent light. The crepuscule, if you care for Niles
the poetic. No, I'm not poetic, particularly. He was, HOLLAND
of course; not that his imagination was any better ELT
than mine, to be truthful. Soon it will be dusk, then Niles
dark again. Always the loneliest part of the day to
me, that painful, slowly descending interval before
the night ultimately comes down. What the French
call l'heure bleue, a time of rare conviviality, gaiety,
bonhomie—things all lost to me in this place—people
eagerly planning, over apéritifs, their evening rounds
—carousal, rendezvous, dalliance—bright lively figures, tingling with anticipation, surging forth upon
the boulevards, shimmering in the purple dark, their
reflections wavering in puddles of light.

I know what you must be thinking: Madness.
You're thinking, He's never been to Paris. You're
right. I never have. But there's a TV downstairs in
the community room, and sometimes in the news-
reels—the six o'clock news; they never let us stay up
late enough for the eleven o'clock—I see scenes of
Paris. And I've read a lot of books, oh yes, watched
some movies. The rest is all my imagination, true.

Miss DeGroot has nothing on me, nor does _he_, for that matter. No, I have never been anywhere; nor ever will. Will never, I fear, leave this small, very precise world I inhabit. A lonely place, you are doubtlessly thinking. You're right there, too. Yet, what should I do about it? I miss—what? What _is_ it I feel, what do I _sense_ that I miss? This vague distress, this malaise? I think, in some strange, awful way, I miss—_him_. Niles misses Holland who misses Niles

This is a terrible place. I hate it. The steam clanks in the radiator, the sink taps abound with rust, the ceiling, as I have noted, is stained. It has been colder this month, cold, cheerless, shabby; an inhospitable season. And quiet. Once there was a time when, even from this height, you could hear the streetcars; they are all gone now; the buses today are less noisy. I used to watch for the streetcars; I recall that little song that always made me think of them. I miss them. There is not much for me to do here. If I join the others they laugh at me, make fun of my name, and there is often trouble. No, not violence, at least, not _all_ the time. But as a result, I keep to myself; a tedious existence, you will agree, but Miss DeGroot says it is better so. Trust Miss DeGroot. (She has promised to bring me some tobacco for my pipe— Prince Albert, a brand which I have been smoking since I was eighteen; that's over thirty years now.) 48+ years old

Later. Still lilac, the sky. No—clover; yes, more than clover shade. I remember there used to be a patch of clover that grew beside the well behind the house, the clover she loved so much—it was her wedding bouquet, you know—and she would stand and stare at it, and you would ask yourself why? And for how long? How she loved the clover! Did she plant it there beside the well, I wonder, or had it sown itself wild? I don't suppose anyone else ever gave it a second thought.

Do you know about the well? That dark and secret place where the accident happened—one of the accidents, I should say. The hanging. No, not *that* kind, but in its way nearly as horrible. Can you hear it, the noisy grating of the pulley as the rope travels through, spinning the rusty wheel, dropping its burden down, down into the blackness? The savage cries; terrible, shocked, outraged cries of fury, of horror. No. I *said* it was not *that* sort of hanging, not one of those state executions—well, yes, execution of sorts, but only because Holland didn't like cats. Hated them, in fact. Yes, it was a cat; didn't I mention that? Trouble, the old woman's animal, her pet. Got this rope around Trouble's neck—he could make a noose with ease—dragged it across the drive and hanged the cat in the well. For spite. The trouble was—excuse the pun—he darn near hanged himself. Poor Holland.

Niles, the brother (he was playing cowboys and Indians near the pump), saw it all, heard the caterwauling—miaow! miao-o-ow!—ran to help.

A frightful scene, as you can imagine, the cat clawing, spitting, Holland chuckling—fiendishly, as it were, and now, amidst the horrible caterwauling, crying out as his body tumbled over the brink of the well, the animal with him—*miaow! miao-o-ow*—and there was one who thought, for a quick moment, that Holland was—but no, he told himself, no, he's only hurt. "Help! Somebody help! He's hurt! Holland is *wishful illusion*

hurt! Help!" And surely there was time yet; the well was dry; the cat, poor creature, was dead as a door-nail, and there was the end of that. But Holland—a patch here and there and he'd be fine, though sore for a week, which is what comes of hanging cats in wells. ("Are you sore, Holland? Does it hurt?" "Sure it hurts, what didja think?") But accidents, he said, will happen. Funnily enough. And, for action above and beyond the call of duty—What? A present, you fool. Behold a gift! From Holland; no, I take it back, *gifts*, not gift.

And beware of Greeks; an eminently suitable maxim in this instance. *allusion*

Poor cat.

You don't remember the Perry place, do you? It's gone now, they tell me. All of it, gone. The well has been filled in and sown over with grass, but it might just as well have been salt, for all that remains. The outbuildings—the barn itself, the apple cellar beneath, the icehouse, the spring- and carriage-houses, the corncribs, the cider mill, all those are gone. Sad to contemplate; they say I wouldn't recognize the place today. The Lutherans bought the property and for a time the house served as a church but even that has since been demolished and replaced by a newer, larger building. There is a television antenna on the roof. The bogs have been drained, the meadows sub-divided into tracts, and where we used to wade the brooks, streets are now laid out, with light poles, sidewalks, chain-link fences, and two-car garages. Of what was, nothing is left. *except N/H*

It was an ancient house, two hundred years or more old, built on a sweeping breadth of land dipping from Valley Hill Road down to a cove on the river. Back in the old days of course it had been a proper farm—both Granddaddy Perry and his father before him having been known thereabouts as the Onion King. That was before my time, but you could picture how spidery carriages with cracker-thin wheels would come whispering along the gravel drive; how Yankee captains navigated their boats upriver to load onions at the landing, prosaic, field-grown onions by the ton, in sacks of red string for all the exotic ports of the Caribbean: Jamaica and Trinidad and Martinique. And in Pequot Landing didn't the Perrys prosper!

Pequot Landing—I'm sure you know what that's like, a typical Connecticut river town, small, unpretentious, elderly. Splendid elms forming shady aisles over the streets—before the Dutch Blight, this was—spacious, well-kept lawns, promising in June, scorched by September, houses of wood or brick or stucco, sometimes all three. The Perry house, stalwart, large, rambling. Once-white clapboards grimed to gray, paint blistered on green shutters framing tall windows, the glass pitted and watery, the patinated gutters pocketing last October's leaves. A comfortable house: veranda, pillared portico at one end, fireplaces in most of the high-ceilinged rooms, everywhere lace curtains, even the attic dormers. Watermarks on the plaster overhead.

The barn was venerable, swaybacked, lichen-spotted, musty, sitting on a small rise beside the icehouse road. Up on the rooftree was a cupola, a four-windowed affair where pigeons were housed. This was the highest point anywhere around, and on this small peaked roof sat a weathervane, a peregrine falcon, emblem of the Perrys, commanding the view.

With the passing of Granddaddy Perry—just after the First World War, that was—the farm had ceased altogether being a farm. Except for one hired man, old Leno Angelini, all the hands were laid off, the livestock disposed of, the plows and harrows sold or left to rust. Neither Vining nor his younger brother George entertained notions about onions, nor about husbandry in any shape or form. The earth lay fallow, the farm moribund, while each working day Vining left his family—his wife, the boys, Holland and Niles, Torrie, his daughter—and drove his Reo to a successful insurance business in Hartford. The Perry place had by this time become home for that quiet and most purposeful tower of strength—Ada Vedrenya, who, as the children grew and their demands increased, closed up her own house in Baltimore and came to live in Pequot Landing, to relieve her daughter, Vining's wife, of all household burdens. George had moved away to Chicago and by 1934—the year of Vining Perry's death—you could tell that the place had a decidedly rundown air; the icehouse was an abandoned shell, the barn below the house was empty, the stables, too, except for a pair of horses, the chickenhouse tenanted by only a derelict rooster and some laying hens, the implements hung away in Mr. Angelini's tool shed, and the cider mill alone remaining in operation, pressing each autumn the orchard fruit that was too bruised to be marketed or used at home.

Perhaps you read about the accident, that cold November Saturday when Vining Perry, father of the

12

twelve-year-olds, Holland and Niles, met his death while moving the last of the heavy baskets from the threshing floor of the barn down to the apple cellar for winter storage. Everyone considered it a great tragedy. And in the eight months following Vining Perry's funeral you weren't allowed to play down there. But come June, after school had let out, with discipline relaxed and the history and geography books put away, when Daylight Saving Time had commenced, with the grown-ups occupied elsewhere, and the afternoons pleasantly long and perfect for apple cellar doings, there were those who ignored the interdict. How cool and dark and silent it was! And secret, too. The room held a strange fascination— you could positively feel it, and not only because it was down there that death had shown its face.

I've told Miss DeGroot all kinds of stories about the apple cellar. She says it's a spooky place; she's right. Buried deep in the heart of the barn, with thick walls of New England traprock, and no electrical illumination, the room was a marvelously clandestine place. For six months of the year, October to March, the bushel baskets stood in rows, brimful with apples; onions dug out of the kitchen garden swagged from the rafters, and garlands of dried peppers, and along the shelves lay bunches of beets, parsnips, and turnips. But during the remaining months, its store of provender spent, the apple cellar served for other, more devious, employment. Shut away from the light, free from intrusion, you felt it was such a place as could be peopled by a boy's imagination with all the creatures of his fancy, with kings, courtiers, and criminals—whatever; stage, temple, prison, down

which boy?

there seeds were sown, to grow magically overnight, like mushrooms. A place whose walls could be made to recede into airy spaciousness, the ceiling and floor into a limitless void, wood and stone and mortar dissolved at will.

But in June, with the whole of the summer stretching endlessly before you, the apple cellar was forbidden and you had to be close and cunning not to get caught. You had matches hidden in a Prince Albert tobacco tin and a candle butt stuck in a Coca-Cola bottle for light. All was dead secret; you listened carefully, one ear cocked, fearful of discovery; you envisioned every sound a Betrayer, a Giant, a Walking Horror . . .

I

"Stop!" Niles cried, and the music stopped, stopped precisely and immediately, that twanging sound that rang in his ears and made him nervous. "Listen! Somebody's up there. Do you hear? Listen!"

"You're crazy."

"Holland—*listen!*" he insisted, his voice ecstatic with horror. He had hastily put out the candle, flatting his hand against the flame, knocking over the bottle the candle was stuck in; its empty clatter still echoed up and down the room.

There *was* Somebody walking around up there, you bet. Somebody trying very hard not to be heard, Somebody being a sneak, Somebody out for trouble. Almost soundless they were, the footsteps, so soundless you had to make a face to hear them, but there they were all the same. Somebody crafty up there, crafty enough to be barefooted, or to be wearing sneakers. *He's not there*

"You're nuts. Jeeze. It's nobody." Niles was unable to see him, but Holland's voice had that familiar, well-honed edge of ridicule. Unconsciously Niles rubbed the palm of his hand, greased by hot wax.

"Somebody's *up* there," he rigidly insisted. "Somebody—" Somebody *human,* he had meant to say; at least he imagined it human.

"Crazy as a bedbug."

"No sir!" Niles retorted, grimacing with suspense, eyes roving the floorboards above. There they went again, surreptitious, creepy, sneak-up-on-you steps. He waited for the grating protest of iron hinges he knew must follow.

Silence.

The footsteps neither progressed nor receded, they merely stopped. There followed a faint double thud on the trapdoor and he could picture Somebody kneeling on the floor overhead, hand cupped to ear, ear to floor, listening . . .

He held his breath. Now Somebody moved away, went tippy-toeing back across the trapdoor; a board creaked; Somebody must have gone outside. Phew. Niles inhaled the terror like exotic incense, his thin frame rippling with fright.

Nyang-dang-ga-dang—drumm-drumm—dang-ga-dang—

Cripes, there he went with his harmonica again, that idiot Mother Goose rhyme. Niles had heard it so often he knew the words by heart.

> *How many miles to Babylon? Threescore*
> *   miles and ten—*
> *Can I get there by candlelight? Yes, and back*
> *   again.*

A mocking, lilting refrain, perfect for blowing on a harmonica. On it went, the tripping refrain:

If your heels are nimble and light, You may get there by candlelight . . . nyang-dang-ga-dang—

Damn Mother Goose.

Next, Holland's hateful crooning: "Ni-yuls

——Ni-yuls Al-ex-an-der Per-ry." Cripes. The Alexander was by way of <u>Alexandra, his mother,</u> and had,
Niles felt, sort of a sissy sound. "Ni-yuls Al-ex-an-
der—"

At last, defeated: "What?" he answered Holland.

"What?" They were sitting there in the dark; some
light, you fool! Niles groped for the bottle, righted it.
He fingered a kitchen match from <u>the Prince Albert
tin hidden in his shirt</u> and swiped it against a damp
stone in the floor. Its phosphorus head crumbled
away to nothing.

"Can't can't can't," came the chant.

"I can do it with two." Fumbling out a pair, Niles
scraped the heads together. They sprang to life with a
fizz. He dropped one and nursed the other to the
candle stub. The scarf of flame burned uncertainly at
first, dimly bluish, then gradually turning orange as
the oxygen reached and fed it. Increasing in brilliance, it shone through the flesh of his hand translu-
cently, gilding the edges of his fingers and dyeing his
palm a deep vermilion. Briefly his figure cast a wavering shadow across the dirt floor, gigantic as it
climbed the mottled wall, the <u>whitewash there flak-
ing away</u> in leprous patches. Beneath his knees the
stones felt agreeably cool; in his nostrils the acrid
odor of phosphorus mingled with the smell of dust
and mold and withered coppery fruit scattered about.

"There," he said, pleased with the candle effect as
he hunkered back Indian fashion and rubbed his
knees. Towering ominously in a corner was a pale
segmented beast: an <u>irregular stack of empty bushel
baskets climbed the wall like a huge caterpillar.</u>
Overhead, an arm's span apart, solid hand-hewn

beams ran the length of the low ceiling, supported by thick Y-shaped joists, adze-marks on their surfaces eagerly catching and tossing back beads of amber light. Between the two center beams a narrow wooden stair-ladder rose at a sharp incline to a trap-door let into the rough planking of the threshing floor twelve or so feet above. On the lower floor level was a smaller door of whitewashed wood, called the Slave Door, which gave entrance from a passage between the wagon room across the way and the apple cellar itself.

Frowning slightly, Niles carefully removed from a pocket a chameleon on a fine silver chain. He dropped it inside his shirt with the tobacco tin, then scrambled across to an upended crate partially hidden by the baskets. A divider in it held a pile of dog-eared magazines. He dug one out, then returned to the pool of light, holding it up to the flame. On the cover a man was struggling against a pack of vicious wolves, their fangs dripping gore onto the snow as they attacked a dogteam hopelessly entangled in the harness of a sled.

" 'Doc Savage and the Winter Kingdom of the Akaluks,' " Niles read aloud. He peered expectantly beyond the candlelight into the dark. "Holland?"

"What?"

"I've got this idea, see? For snow."

"Snow." Holland sniggered; was always sniggering.

"Sure. Like Doc Savage and the Winter Kingdom. Remember the frozen tundra? Well, with snow we could have our own Winter Kingdom down here."

"How?" He sounded mildly curious.

"Easy. With cattails."

"Cattails? You mean *bulrushes?*" Guffaws.

"Sure—bulrushes. It's a good idea, no kidding. If we went down to the river and got cattails, we could shred 'em up and have snow all summer. A Winter Kingdom—huh?" He watched Holland's face while he gave it thought; somehow he was always the one to make the decisions. Certainly Niles was pleased to be with him, pleased with his company, pleased they were not only brothers but friends as well. Only, truthfully, they weren't—not really. Not that Niles didn't desire it—they just weren't close. Niles found Holland strange, unpliant, distant. Often secretive, brooding. Of a *dark* nature. Holland was his own person, a loner, and who was there could do anything about *that?*

Watching, Niles saw Holland's solemn wink. The Winter Kingdom was pronounced as having possibilities. He felt elated; clever, Holland had called him. In the flickering candlelight he considered how little their contemplation of each other across the dimly lighted space did to bring them closer together, though he passionately wished it. Holland was wearing his favorite pink shirt and khaki shorts rolled at the thighs. His eyes shone remote and glassy like a cat's in the night. Gray like all the Perrys', sober and deep-set under a shock of sun-whitened hair, they were oddly tilted at the corners beneath dark slanting brows, giving occasional random expressions a curiously Oriental cast; sometimes it seemed he must have come riding with Genghis Khan across the steppes from Tartary.

Niles returned the magazine to the crate and re-

sumed his place. Absently he considered the fingers
of one hand, which, as though directed by a life of
their own, crept to the front of his shirt. He
scratched where the lizard's feet had tickled his
stomach, and lightly whistled through his teeth. He
felt inside his shirt for the tobacco tin, withdrew it,
and spilled several objects into the circle of light:
among the matches a carved horse chestnut, a fasci-
nating-looking blue tissue paper packet—that which
contained The Thing—and a gold ring.

He spit on his finger and with difficulty slid the
ring on and held it out admiringly. It was a pippin, as
Father would have called it. How brightly it gleamed
in the light, how heavily it weighed on his hand! A
jewel, worthy of a Midas. Its broad face bore an inta-
glio crest: a savage-billed falcon. Niles turned the
ring, examining microscopically the tiny silver seam
in the gold band where it had been cut down to fit a
smaller finger. "Everybody thinks it's just a plain
hawk, but it's not, it's a peregrine." He absently fingered the blue tissue-wrapped packet. "Peregrine for
Perry. It *is* my ring, isn't it?" As though seeking reassurance.

Holland nodded. "It's yours. We made a pact."

Niles caressed the gold on his finger. Yes indeed,
the pact; the ring was his. That was part of the Secret.

Cripes! Look out—there they went again, the same
footsteps. Only now they were right there, skulking
along on the other side of the wall in the passageway.
Niles froze. "He's coming!" he whispered. "I can
hear him! Quick—hide!" Scooping up the things
from the floor—the blue packet, some of the

matches, the horse chestnut—he fumbled them into
the tobacco tin, then slid it back inside his shirt.
"Hide!" he urged, scrambling to duck behind the baskets where he'd seen Holland disappear. Wait—the
candle! He was reaching to put it out when with a
rush the Slave Door flew back and an intruder appeared on the threshold. Niles's look traveled up
from a pair of U.S. Keds to two round eyes blinking
at him behind steel-rimmed glasses.

"Ah—*ha!* Caught in the act!" is what a person
might have said, given a discovery of such moment.
But not this person. Standing in the doorway, Russell
Perry said only, *"Ooh,* you're playing in here! You
know you're not supposed to—no one's supposed
to!" Cousin Russell had a tendency to squeal *"Ooh!"*
the way fat little pigs did. Niles ventured a glimpse at
the baskets where Holland had disappeared. Holland
had always called Russell "Piggy Look-a-doo," a
porker in one of their storybooks, that greedy one
who ended up on a platter with an apple in his
mouth. Poor pig. Russell had a pudding face, at present unattractively peeling from sunburn, and under
his shirt his titties showed pointed and pudgy like a
girl's. Russell—cripes.

When Uncle George and Aunt Valeria had come
back for Father's funeral, they brought Russell with
them—and then they just stayed, all of them, Uncle
George and Aunt Valeria in the choice corner room
at the front of the house, Russell in a spare room at
the back. Fifteen his next birthday, Russell *("Ressell,"* Aunt Vee pronounced it, *"Ressell* dear, don't
forget your rubbers." *"Ressell's* got a bit of a temper-
ature today, I'm going to keep him home from

school.") was a pale and limp city boy. He missed
Chicago and he hated Pequot Landing, and made no
bones about either. He hated the kids at school and
the people of the town, hated all his relatives, and
most of all hated his cousins. In December he
stabbed Holland's finger with a pencil (the point left
a definite blue mark under the skin when it healed)
and in February bit Niles's hand so badly that
stitches were required. Ubiquitous and eternally underfoot, making mischief, snooping and spying, Russell Perry was nonetheless in residence.

Just now the gleam of his glasses hid his eyes but
you could tell that behind those thick lenses his
squint was taking in the apple cellar at a glance: the
candle stuck in the Coke bottle, the magazine-filled
crate, the burnt matches, the ring—

The ring!

Quickly Niles turned it on his finger and enclosed
it in a fist; not, however, before Russell had had a
chance to see it.

"What's that?" he demanded.

Niles made no answer; suggested Russell beat it—
"if you know what's good for you."

Though formidable, Russell's defiance, in the light
of events, proved foolhardy. "You can't make me! If
you can be in here, I can be in here too!"

Niles's smile was affable enough. "Okay. Russell,
suit yourself. C'mon in, then."

Warily the newcomer stepped back. "Nosiree you
don't," he said. "I know what you'll do. You'll get
me in there and you won't let me out. Like Holland
did that time." Blinking with alarm, he retreated to

the safety of the passage; Niles wondered if he had guessed Holland's hiding place.

"Then you better scram."

Woe to Russell, who only craned his neck and timidly returned to the doorway. "Where'dja get that ring?" he said, a suspicious glint behind the glasses.

"I sent away for it."

"Ya did not. That's not a *box*top ring, that's *real gold!*"

"Then why'd you ask, if you're so smart." The corner of his eye on Russell's U.S. Keds, Niles found himself wondering why his cousin favored those blue lisle socks—with clocks on them. Cripes.

Russell lifted his chin and sniffed. "You shouldn't have that—it's a grown-up's ring." He covered his mouth with a fat hand, his astonishment ill-concealed. *"Ooh!* That's—" Wide-eyed and agog, piping his delight, he danced out of reach, describing with relish the consequences of his intended revelations about the ring. "Wait till my dad gets home. Just *wait!*" In a second Niles had leaped for the door, only to have it slammed in his face; on the other side, amid fat chortles, the hasp was snapped onto its staple and apparently secured, for no amount of banging or jiggling could budge it.

When Russell's footfalls had padded back through the passage and up the stone steps to the barn above, Niles, whistling soundlessly, went behind the stack of fruit baskets, where he found Holland sitting on the floor casually inspecting the blue-black dot showing beneath the flesh of one of his knuckles.

Niles raised his eyebrows. His silent question and the indifferent shrug he received failed to dispel the feeling of dread that was blotting his mouth dry. With little difficulty he could guess what would happen if Russell squealed to his father. Uncle George was okay most of the time, a big red-faced bear of a guy, until you crossed him—then look out. He worked down on Church Street at the Fenstermacher soda pop plant, a dingy red brick factory next to the railroad tracks where Rose Rock carbonated beverages were bottled. His wife, Aunt Valeria, when not coddling her son, was busy down in the basement doing tie-and-dye cloth on a two-burner stove next to the furnace. You didn't have to worry about Aunt Vee, but watch out for Uncle George. Bears could attack. Rose Rock let out at five; detection was inevitable. Niles tried to rouse his spirits by telling himself that Russell couldn't know, that there hadn't been time for him to put it all together, that he wasn't bright enough. Only he was; Russell was shrewd. But what business of his was the ring, anyways? Niles was obliged to guard Holland's secret against anyone's prying, and though it was a family matter, Russell wasn't exactly family.

The ring—Peregrine for Perry—had been Granddaddy Perry's. He had had the weathervane emblem copied in gold, and when he died—the engine of his steam automobile had exploded—the ring had passed by primogeniture—like a king's crown, that was, from father to eldest son—to Vining. But the ring, people said, must have been jinxed, for no sooner was Granddaddy Perry dead than first the well went dry and a new one had to be dug; next, Grandmother Perry was taken away under strange and sorrowful circumstances, which left Father to head the family.

madness?

Then Father himself died, in November, and the ring went to Holland, not to wear of course, for this he might not do until he had reached the age of twenty-one, but it was his to keep, hidden away in the chest at the foot of his bed. There it remained until March, the month of his birthday, when Holland, determined to wear the ring, and unbeknownst to everyone in the family but Niles, pocketed the piece of jewelry and nefariously transferred it by streetcar to a jeweler in Hartford who for a price was inveigled into reducing its size to accommodate Holland's finger. The ring, however, now seemed almost too small, for Holland had to soap his knuckle to force it on. But sure enough, come his birthday, there he was, secretly sporting Peregrine for Perry practically all day; after which time, as a result of the pact, the ring found its way into Niles's Prince Albert can; though this too remained a closely guarded secret. Till today, that was. Russell Perry, Spy. Ruefully Niles twisted and tugged at the ring until it came off and he returned it to the tobacco tin in his shirt.

Holland rose and stretched. "Don't look so worried, little brother." Though his tone was reassuring, Niles could see the muscle in his jaw twitch. It came and went like a winking light, signaling some disorder.

"What will we do?" Niles asked.

Holland's expression was enigmatic. "I don't know. But I said not to worry." He treated Niles to a smile. Well then, if Holland said so, he wouldn't worry. But why, when trying to overcome his thoughts, he suggested their going to the river, why did Holland ignore him and remain where he was, staring into space as though moonstruck? Holland's spellbinder look, he called it.

"Well, what *do* you want to do?"

"Let's go up and see the pigeons," Holland replied with a sly look. Sometimes he reminded Niles of Achilles—very crafty, he could be. He had brought something out from his pocket, some small pellets which he thumbed around in the palm of one hand. Carrying the light, Niles headed for the door in the wall. "Cripes," he swore, remembering Russell had locked it from the other side.

Holland chuckled to think that Russell imagined the Slave Door was the only way out of there. With a last worried glance, Niles put the ring away with the other things in the Prince Albert tin and held the candle up while Holland went to the stair-ladder leading above to the trapdoor.

"But what *can* we do?" Niles's hiked shoulder was mute but eloquent appeal.

"Russell is a jerk." Holland's voice, Niles noted, was stern and cold. Head tilted slightly downward, gray eyes flinty, gazing out from under gable-shaped brows, his expression was one not unknown to Niles: stark, flat, implacable; and holding the candle high, watching him climb the ladder to put a shoulder to the trapdoor, Niles felt a queer chill, like a slowly growing stain, spreading through all the walls and membranes of his stomach.

II

"Eee-yaiee!"

Listening to the scream, Niles smiled as Russell tumbled from the loft in counterfeit glee, hurtling through the air, his arms pinwheeling, his body arcing into space and dropping out of the light into blackness, his voice ricocheting from the recesses of the barn as he landed with a thud in the haymow twenty feet away across the threshing floor.

"I'm the King of the Mountain!" he heard Russell shout, wading kneedeep through the remains of last year's fodder to the mowstead, where he clambered onto the ladder chained against a vertical timber and, puffing, hand-over-hand ascended the rungs to the loft above.

Russell, Niles suspected, did not really enjoy jumping in the haymow, for he'd said he found it a little like falling in a dream, down down down into nothingness, and no hand there to catch you. His heart was in his mouth each time he leaped, Niles could tell. He did it, not because he was a daredevil, but because he had nothing else to do; poor Russell, he was so bored, and this dumb imitation of Holland and Niles's game was all he could think of to take up his time. Poor fat old four-eyed Russell, he should know better than to come snooping around. Once, last year, having caught him sneaking into the apple cellar, Holland had tied him up and threatened to set fire to his feet; had in fact pulled his shoes off and actually lighted matches—scared the hell out of Russell. Russell ought to stick to his rats. The whole family of them, white rats, which he kept in a pen up in the cupola where the pigeons nested. With a rabbit, a dumb old Belgian hare who thought she was their mother.

Niles lowered the trapdoor into place and stepped away from it, standing shoulder-to-shoulder with Holland in the shadows, watching Russell squinting through his chaff-covered glasses. He wiped them and set them aside—so they wouldn't get broken, probably—and hung on a pulley rope to peer over the countryside. Poor Russell. He hated the country, too. Hated it all, hated the flowers that bloom in the spring, hated the smell of the grass, hated the animals (except his rats), hated the outdoors. Hated his father for selling his soda pop business and coming to Pequot Landing to cap damn old sarsaparilla bottles.

Silence. Niles stole a glance at Holland. What was he thinking about, with that same strange, almost glazed expression on his face? Hardly to be heard in the abandoned emptiness came the sound of a field mouse, scurrying somewhere in the hay, the acoustics of the barn amplifying each shy rustle.

"Eee-yaiee! I'm the King of the Mountain!"

When Russell began climbing the ladder again, Niles stepped into the light, a wide pillar of gold surrounding his figure in the cathedral-like spaces of the barn, his hands clasped thoughtfully under his raised chin. He looked like an acolyte assisting at Mass. Then he turned and, his eyes on Holland's back,

crossed to the great sliding door let into the side of
the barn. *Father's death*

FB

Through that door, on that November day last fall,
Father had come, bringing the apple baskets to store
below. A dark sullen day, he remembered, not bright
as today was, though all the rest was as it should
have been. He had been down in the cellar with the
lantern, looking up at the patch of light through the
trap. With one foot over the edge, Father started
down with a basket. Both feet now, and he was halfway down when, hearing a noise, he looked up to see
the door, the heavy, iron-bound trapdoor, come
crashing down onto his head—the screech of the
hinges, the explosion of iron and wood—slamming
him down onto the stone floor. Cries of agony. And
when the door was raised he lay there at the foot of
the ladder, spilled fruit all around, and blood . . .
oh, the blood . . .

"*Eee-yaiee!*" On the other side of the threshing
floor Russell bounced in the haymow. Exchanging a
look with Holland, Niles followed him outside. He
stood in the small yard outside the granary, and fer-
reted out the tobacco tin, unconsciously rubbing his
thumb over the face of Prince Albert. What *was* it?
He could not get the niggling worry out of his mind;
it buzzed around in there like a bee. Apprehensively
he recalled his cousin's face in the apple cellar. It
spelled trouble. Well, if it came to that, then tell the
truth. But who would believe him if he did? He having come to Holland's aid, who would come to his?
No one. It was all too far-fetched, too grotesque. And
that feeling in his stomach, he knew, was fear.

The granary, a ramshackle attachment to the main

barn, overhung a forebay under the cupola, which was the highest point anywhere around, and on its small peaked roof perched the peregrine weather-vane.

Coo-coo-coo-eee. Niles could hear the melancholy sounds of the birds and the brisk rustling of their wings. *"Coo-coo-ee,"* he answered through cupped hands. Entering the granary, Niles ran up the rickety stairs and stepped into the four-windowed cupola; about him from all sides fell the soft contralto cooing of the fantail pigeons and the brush and spread of their ashy feathers as they waddled about on coral-colored feet.

He raised a window and looked out. In the upper meadow Mr. Angelini, the hired man, a patch of burnt umber against the yellow grass, was tossing hay into the back of a wagon, his pitchfork catching the sun on its tines. Sally and Old Crow, farm horses older than himself, stood in the field, switching tails against ropy flanks.

It was premature for haying, but spring had come early this year, billowing up through the valley, melting the snow on the stubble, the ice in the cove, greening the shoots as fast as they popped through the March-thawed earth. And what a spring, the color of lettuce, with early birds everywhere, generous with song. April came dripping forsythia and pussywillow, May saw pink dogwood and the orchard surfeited with bloom, by June the grass was already high and ready for first cutting.

Niles looked down beyond the orchard to the river, which reflected the clear span of vernal sky. At the bank, under a parasol, a familiar figure bent, gathering flowers into a basket. Along the water's edge were the cattails, bending to meet their reflections. He thought what an exciting prospect the Winter Kingdom was, if they could just pull it off—and they could, he was sure. Snow in July, snow all summer long, right through until school, when the apples would be put down again. A secret snow. Secret by necessity. *what necessity*

"I hate to think how many it'll take." Holland, lolling at another window, humming on his harmonica, and it was as though he had read his mind.

"What?"

"Cattails. Isn't that what you were thinking, little brother?" His grin was wide and crooked.

Bravo, Holland—mind reader! Great feats of legerdemain! Niles wasn't surprised. Holland could more often than not tell what he was thinking; and vice versa. But when would they start, he wondered? With the cattails? As in all things, he would defer to Holland's decision (Shall we—? Will we—? Want to—? Holland, Columbus, Niles the crew; Holland, Fu Manchu, Niles, trusty henchman; Holland, Charlemagne, Niles, never Roland, but the groomsman, the page, the varlet). Niles stole a look at him surveying something out the window, once tapping the spit from his harmonica into his hand and wiping it on the seat of his pants. Holland? Nothing doing; he was riveted. Niles rambled on by himself. Sure, it'd take a lot, and they'd have to sneak them in, but it'd be worth it: Winter Kingdom in the apple cellar. And all from shredded cattails.

Holland? What was he thinking? Funny, he hadn't noticed before, but this year he'd lost that chubby look. His face had narrowed—wolf? No, fox? The chin line had a sculpted flow, the skin turned in flat spare planes over the thin cheekbones, across the broad forehead, the mouth curved and curly, faintly smiling. What's the joke, Holland?

Still no reply. Niles made a face to himself and knocked his chin to his shoulder. He went and opened the wire cage that housed Russell Perry's family of pets, gently lifting one of the white rats into the palm of his hand. He could feel the warm creature quiver as he held it up to the window and lightly fingered the soft downy fur on its back, tickling the pink nose until the whiskers twitched.

"What about it, Holland, the cattails, I mean?" No; Niles could see he wasn't really interested, not in *that*, anyway. Something else was on his mind. Strange, because (watching Holland step across the floor and relieve him of the rat, hold it close to his face, fondle it) usually any new idea would provoke the utmost of his imagination, take Rasputin and the Czar for example. After hypnotizing the Czar (Niles), Rasputin (Russell, enlisted especially and given the starring role) had been dispatched by a Russian noble (Holland), a happy homicide entailing not only pistols but clubs and poisoned cakes as well; poor old Russell had to run and upchuck, but that was the whole idea, wasn't it, of letting him play? And summer in the apple cellar always saw some such drama. It was good to let young people act out such gruesome pageants; it assured calmer, more healthy minds—or at least so the doctor had declared —that same doctor they had sent Holland to. Murder most foul? By all means, the fouler the better.

Fascinated, Niles observed the brown hand stroking the furry white rat, then slipping into a pocket to produce a tidbit for it to nibble on. What was he feeding it? Oh, vitamins? He was joking. Yes, just a joke—Gro-Rite pellets, actually. Gro-Rite for stronger healthier rats. Haw haw. Feed 'em, step back, and Bam! A woolly mammoth at least. Russell would be getting 4-H ribbons for his rats. Well, Niles said, he'd never heard of *that*. Gro-Rite? Oh sure, he'd found it next door at Old Lady Rowe's. A whole bag, in her garage. Only she caught him crooking it, chased him out; Holland called her a dirty name.

He chuckled wryly. "And she says she's going to tell Father—how about *that*." He tossed an amused look over his shoulder, down to the meadow where Mr. Angelini was haying.

"But what about the cattails?" Niles persisted, his mind on the Winter Kingdom. "You said it was a good idea."

"It's good," Holland said laconically. "But—" He cocked an ear. From down in the hayloft came the cry of Russell Perry at play. *Eee-yaiee! I'm the King of the Mountain!* "How do we sneak cattails in with him jumping around down there? If he sees us—"

"—He'll squeal." Niles nodded, ruminating. "We could bring them in through the wagon room. We'll open the Slave Door from the outside."

No reply. The rat continued feeding. Niles gave up. Holland was preoccupied. And stubborn—if he didn't want, he didn't want, and that was the end of it. In a while the rat stopped nibbling and lay faintly panting, as though exhausted from its meal. Idly Holland watched it. The pigeons were quieter. Niles tried to dream up something of greater interest than picking cattails. Fishing was no good—Holland got bored sitting around waiting for perch to bite. Was the root beer all gone? Maybe Winnie would let them bring out the enamel tub and mix a batch in the kitchen sink. Or churn some ice cream. But, jeeze, that was work, Holland would say; besides, ice cream was Sunday treat. Or they could go up in the store-room and play Granddaddy Perry's old records on the Victrola. Or practice some more magic tricks. Though that morning had already seen secret practice in this regard. Next month was the Firemen's Fourth of July Carnival. Chan Yu the Disappearing Marvel. With who knew what latest feat of prestidigitation!

"What's a hermaphrodite?" Niles asked out of the blue.

"What?" Holland, who collected big words as others collect stamps or money (though there were collections of these as well), was a million miles away.

"A hermaphrodite. There was this poster at the drugstore this morning that said they're going to have a real live hermaphrodite this year. All the way from Malta."

"I don't know what that means. Look it up." Holland stooped and opened his hands out onto the floor. The rat crawled from his palm, dragging itself to the center of a panel of light where it lay beside a knothole, belly down, tail limply curled, quiescent and scarcely breathing. What was wrong with it? Niles looked down at the lime-speckled planking where the sun melted in a syrupy flow of red and gold around his feet and around the still, white form.

Bending, he gently and carefully lifted it up, feeling the faintly throbbing heartbeat across the palm of his hand and wondering, cripes, what could be the matter with it. Water . . . it must need a drink . . . the water in the pan in the cage was stale. Turning to bear the rat away to the pump, he stopped in the doorway, struck by Holland's cryptic smile. Then his brother had turned his back, stood idly staring out the window, watching where Mr. Angelini worked among the windrows of fallen hay, gathering them onto his fork and tossing them into the wagon. Niles left then, cradling the rat between spread fingers and, a dry whirring of feathers behind him, ran quickly down the stairway, his heart in his mouth; but even before he reached the bottom he felt quite certain that however much water might be provided, it would not be sufficient to restore the rat. The animal would never touch water again.

Poor rat.

III

God damn you, Holland.

He slammed across the granary yard to the breezeway. In the tool shed he found a Sunshine Biscuit box in the trash can. He laid the rat inside and put the lid on, then took a trowel from a nail on the wall —the one hanging between Mr. Angelini's red-handled rose shears and the rubber hip boots Father used to fish in—and went to the kitchen garden. Close by, an outside stairway with wooden steps and a white railing rose to the house's second story. With the trowel he dug a hole, buried the box, and, meditating, slowly covered it over. *Oh Holland, you bastard. What a heartless thing to do.* Those pellets from Mrs. Rowe's garage—they weren't Gro-Rite at all. It was as bad as the cat. Involuntarily his look shifted to the well across the drive. The pulley gear under the peaked roof was rusted with disuse, the bucket hung cracked and leached. Inside, the spring had long ago dried up and there were only puddles around the mossy rocks at the bottom. That and blackness, for now it was covered with a cement slab where toads would sun themselves and garter snakes slough their skins undisturbed, where summer weeds grew tall around it and clover sprang in patches of bright lavender. It looked like an ancient tomb, decaying.

He thought a moment. Yes—he knew what was needed—flowers for the grave, a memorial for the dead rat. Quickly he ran and gathered a suitable bunch of clover. He had started back to the tool shed to find a jar to put them in when his eye was attracted by a movement at an upstairs window. A curtain fluttered. Behind it he glimpsed a figure partially hidden by the shadow of the half-raised window; two dark eyes in a dim face peered indistinctly back at him. Like a pale lily a hand bloomed there for an instant, then wilted, a gesture as gossamer as the curtain immediately obscuring it.

Raising the clover bouquet in front of him, he made a low comic-courtly bow and presented the flowers to the window. Then he started across the

lawn to the stairway. At the bottom he looked up to
the screen door on the landing above and saw the
same lily hand. A figure darted out. Bright slippers of
embroidered silk flashed overhead as a slender figure
hurried down, looking above and below, now eagerly
rushing, now hanging back, reluctant, trembling a
little, a light, lilac-colored dressing-gown trailing as
she descended to sweep into her arms the astonished
boy and to bury her face in the clover he offered.

"Niles." Tremulously Alexandra Perry raised her
wet eyes from the blossoms to receive her son's kiss.

"Oh Mother," he said, smiling and gently touching
the tip of a finger to a tear as it rolled downward,
"don't cry."

"Oh darling, I'm *not* crying!" Chestnut hair be-
comingly framed the pallor of her face, a spot of
color brightening each cheek. The heavy eye makeup
was not unattractive and he delighted in her cool
fragrance. A bittersweet, will-o'-the-wisp light flick-
ered in her expression, a faintly gleaming mixture of
pain and pleasure as she repeated his name, her red
lips brushed with a smile. "Are these for me?"

"Yes," he lied bravely with scarcely a glance at the
newly covered hole in the kitchen garden. "Clover
for you." He touched her cheek, lingering a while in
her embrace, making the most of their closeness. He
set his head back and looked at her. "Mother!" he
exclaimed delightedly, "you came down! You came
downstairs again." Reclusive

She laughed. "Yes, darling. It's not—not so terribly difficult. I was watching you, so busy you were
with your trowel, I know, don't tell me, another bird,
wasn't it, another of your funerals, a robin or an ori-

ole maybe? And then when I saw you picking the clover—"

Clover, he thought, clover for the rat. He felt like a rat himself, a dirty rat. He looked at the flowers clasped in her trembling hand. If that was all that was needed to bring her from her room, she could have all the clover he could find, bushels of it, bales, wagonloads.

"How are you, Mother?"

"Fine, darling, I'm fine." Putting a finger to her lips she took him by the hand. Together they stole under the horse-chestnut tree where a double-seated glider stood, sheltered by a tattered bit of awning, she sinking languidly onto a creaking slatted seat, he taking the one opposite and leaning in order to hold her hand, his gray eyes fastened on her brown ones, already restless travelers up and down the drive, her mouth moving in nervous, disjointed sentences, her mind veering from subject to subject.

"What have you been doing today?" he asked, trying to stroke her hand to calmness.

"Oh." She waved vaguely. "Reading."

"Did you start *The Good Earth?*"

"Yes. Pearl Buck. It's all about China."

He nodded. "Miss Shedd thought you might like it. And she'll be sure to save *Anthony Adverse* for you next time it comes back. She said it'll take you a month to read." When he paused to smile again she adored his sweet, shining look.

"Niles dear, you're so thoughtful to be going to the library for me all the time." There was a huskiness in her voice which he found pleasing, a hoarse, rather

actressy sound, quite different from that of most
mothers.

"I don't mind," he said. "I like doing it. Miss
Shedd says we do more reading in this family than
any other in town."

"What is Ada reading?" Ada, her mother, his
grandmother, was never called anything but Ada by
anyone in the family.

"She's not, this week. Until she gets the cherries
canned. I got another Agatha Christie for Torrie."
Torrie, his wonderful sister, lived here at home with
Rider Gannon, her husband of less than one year,
and both read a lot of books each month, she ad-
dicted to mystery novels while she awaited the birth
of her first baby, he studying methods of agriculture
with an eye to rejuvenating the family onion business.

"And you, darling, what are you reading now?
Still Richard Halliburton?"

"Yes. I took *Royal Road to Romance* back and got
The Glorious Adventure. But, Mother, Miss Shedd
says—" He bit his lip.

"Yes, dear?"

"She says, please, if you wouldn't tear off the corners of the pages as you read them."

Her look faltered. "I don't do that. No one should
treat books like that. It's destructive. Sometimes—
sometimes I'm a little nervous, I imagine." Her eyes
darted to the drive, where the cement slab blocked
the mouth of the well, where the weeds were tasseling
like ears of corn and the clover rioted. " 'A good
book is the best of friends, the same today and for
ever.' As the poet says," she laughed, embarrassed;
and in her lap her hand flitted like a caged thing.

"Come into the kitchen," he suggested, "we could have some root beer if there's any left, or Winnie could make some iced tea."

"That's all right, dear, Winnie has enough to do." She looked up to the washline. "Well, I imagine I must go up again now—"

"Wait—" He thought quickly, grasping at straws, anything to keep her from running back upstairs. "When are the aunts coming?" he asked conversationally, speaking of his grandmother's younger sisters who arrived each summer from New York for a country visit.

"Oh ye-e-s-s," Alexandra answered, thinking, "now what did Ada tell me? I think they plan to come just after the Fourth of July. And it will be so good to see them, won't it? Who can that *be*, so noisy in the barn? Such a rowdy voice." *Botticelli,* she was saying to herself, her mind veering again as she looked at his face. *Botticelli angel.* She brushed his hair back from his eyes. Incredible. They made her catch her breath every now and again. Had she really produced such a child? She leaned to kiss him. "Niles, if you don't stay out of the sun, I swear your hair is going to go pure platinum, like Jean Harlow's." She laughed at the notion and for an instant he glimpsed a flash of her old gaiety.

"How are Granddaddy's roses, darling?" she said, veering once more as she looked at the ramblers near the grape arbor at the edge of the property.

"Mr. Angelini sprayed again. I picked practically a whole jar of June bugs off them. But they're really bad this year. I bet there's a zillion."

"Really. I hope you put them in the trash." She sat musing. "Tomorrow's Friday, isn't it?"

"Yes."

"We must remember to have Leno set out the ash cans."

He was perplexed. "But it's June, Mother. We haven't had the ashes go out since April. *June* bugs, remember?"

"Oh. Of course. I'd forgotten. Somehow—March —how *asinine.*" Another vague gesture belittled her memory, describing some faulty conjunction there. "Your birthdays are in March, aren't they?" Her fingers drifted across her brow, pushed nervously at her hair, arranged a pin, fell back in her lap exhausted, then swept across her knees, and the clover fell about her feet. He gathered the flowers up, reassembling for her the bouquet and laying it back in her hands. One bloom had escaped his eye and he leaned again to retrieve it; the tobacco tin slid from his shirt onto the platform of the swing. He looked down quickly to see the lid spring open and amid a shower of matches, behind the horse chestnut, the little blue packet popped out, with it the brief gleam of gold.

"What's that?" she asked, with a too-bright smile as he scooped the things back into the can.

"Just a tin box. Prince Albert. It was Father's. I keep some stuff in it." *Hello, Pilgrim Drugs? Do you have Prince Albert in a can? Well, let him out. Haw haw.* "Mother—are you all right?"

"What? Yes, yes dear, certainly. Just for a moment I thought—" She shook her head, and the word her mouth had fashioned died stillborn on her lips. Again

her eyes darted as though trapped; some dreadful
thing . . . lurking . . .

"Hoo-oo, Ni-yuls? Are you thay-*urr?*" That was
Aunt Valeria, Russell's mother, calling from the basement hatchway. Quickly Alexandra pulled herself
up, teetered for a moment on the swaying platform of
the glider, at the same time rescuing her hand from
Niles's. "Mustn't see me," she murmured with a lost,
pleading look to him. "Mustn't tell, will you, you
won't tell that I came down."

"No," he said stolidly, helping her to the ground.

"That's my darling. Let it be our secret," she
called back to him as, clasping the clover to her
breast, dropping a trail of stems, she fled wraithlike
away over the lawn, disappearing up the stairs, the
lily hand trailing the banister, and with never a backward look.

The screen door slammed above while, below, here
came Aunt Vee, out of the hatchway, lugging a large
copper washtub by its wooden handles. Niles ran to
help as she set down the tub and proceeded to flap
out wet pieces of tightly wrung fabric, hanging out
the squares and rectangles of tie-and-dye chiffon
which she had bound in places and dipped into pans
of color. But somehow, Niles observed as she pinned
the muddy-hued pieces up, Aunt Vee didn't quite
seem to have the knack.

"Golly, isn't it a *scrump*tious day? Makes one feel
good just to be alive," she sang. She wore rubber
gloves and her housedress was protected by a tan
plaid apron. "Seems like I've been down in that cellar
just for*ev*er." Batting aside a wet sheet, she stooped
for another piece of fabric. "My, just smell those pies!

Honestly, where does Ada find the time? And crullers, too, I'll bet. The air is absolutely *red*olent! Honestly, Thursdays around here, it's just like a bakery! *Ohh* dear-r-r. Why, will you look at the clover! No, there, hon, on the grass. Somebody must have dropped it." Niles said not a word. "Can't *look* at clover, hon, without thinking of your dear mother and father's wedding and how I ran my stockings jumping over that fence into that pasture to get it. Stepped right in you-know-what, too. Why, they thought I must of been crazy. *Ohh* dear-r-r." Niles had heard that Aunt Valeria's Chicago friends called her "Chickie" and he could understand why: she never spoke, she cheeped, like young poultry.

"Niles, hon"—she was talking around a pair of clothespins in her mouth—"if you're going down to the Center today, will you—"

"I already went, Aunt Vee."

"Ohh—I wanted some more dye. Perhaps Ressell could—" A dubious remark at best, and Niles caught her shaking her head to herself. You didn't stand a chance of getting Russell to do anything, let alone leg it to the store, and no one realized it better than his own mother. "Perhaps he could borrow your bike," she suggested hopefully, and Niles offered the use of his machine with all the good will in the world. "But it's got a flat," he felt bound to add.

"Oh. Well, perhaps it would be all right if he used Holland's, then."

"Sure, Aunt Vee. He can. It's in the shed." Holland wouldn't mind. Much.

Her work hung out, she stripped off her rubber gloves with a wet snap and began turning them right side out. *"Ohh* well . . . never mind." She sounded fatigued. "I don't think I'll do any more tie-and-dye today. Tomorrow, maybe—they're just for Christmas presents. Your uncle can pick me up some Tintex while he has the car. I hate bothering Ressell." She blew out the fingers of her gloves and went to upend the dye dregs behind the bed of lilies-of-the-valley in the laurel shade. "I'm sure he's busy," she cheeped, plucking two dishtowels from where they hung drying on the snowbush by the back entryway into the kitchen.

Niles contemplated his dirt-stained hands.

When the old well had dried up, water had been discovered nearby and a pump installed. It stood in the center of the circular gravel drive under the horse-chestnut tree. The long, gracefully curving iron handle fitted Niles's palms comfortably and felt cool as he plunged it up and down. He filled and drank from a copper cup whose rim tasted sour-bitter, the way marigolds smelled.

Russell would sure find out what was what if he went tooting off down to the Center on Holland's bike, Niles reflected, his head thrown back, the water dribbling down his chin, over his knuckles, along his bare arm. The cup empty, he set it down and plied the handle again, watching where the water spilled into the cement curb that formed a pool under the spout. He washed his hands, bits of earth breaking apart and filtering to the bottom. Gradually a mosaic of glassy fragments formed his own image in the shallow depth. He watched it shimmer, draw together like the pieces of a puzzle, yet not quite, never quite, forming an undistorted reflection. He put his

TWIN IMAGE

hand out, thoughtfully, abstractedly, as though to touch that other, similar boy who peered back at him with such a longing expression. Did he seem hopeful, perhaps? A little wistful? Who was it, that figure there? Friend or foe? What did he think? If he, Niles, spoke, would the other answer? He watched silently and shortly pulled away the bleached leaves caught in the bronze drain at the bottom, saw the water disappear, with it his image, saddened now by the parting, the face so familiar, though not because he often sought its reflection in a glass; so pleasant to see, though not because of any personal conceit; so cherished, though not for any sake of its own, but because in each small particular it was the exact and perfect twin of Holland's.

The sun was already drying in patches the cement under the spout when Niles scampered back to the shed to replace the trowel on its proper nail between the red-handled rose shears and Vining Perry's old rubber fishing boots.

IV

Half an hour later, Niles, feeling better, sits at the end of the landing, spine curved against a post, his line hanging in the back eddies, his eye following the lead sinker as it twinkles an instant, then drags the filament from sight. Along the river, among the willows, the afternoon is spread lavishly, like a picnic on a checkered cloth of light and shade. Overhead, faces

in the clouds—that one there, look—two eyes, a nose
. . . Phew, it was hot; Holland was right—fishing is
a bore. Why wouldn't he come pick cattails for the
Winter Kingdom? Why get mad at Russell, do that
to his pet? Now he was sulking, up there in the loft,
independent Holland. Still and all, he'd flash that
grin and you'd forgive him. By supper time, sure. At
least he, Niles, would. He couldn't speak for Russell
but Russell wasn't susceptible to grins, however engaging.

The line yanked; he reeled it in. Breaking the stillness, shattering the mirror of water, a catfish leaped
into the air. Niles jumped up and swept his rod back.
The fish flopped onto a plank, its scaleless pewter
body jerking in spasms. He put a foot on it, carefully
avoiding the barbels on either side of its mouth as he
extracted the hook. Again the fish jumped; he pulled
his hand away and a drop of blood appeared on its
tanned downy surface.

Sucking the injured flesh, he cast his line again,
and saw the stream draw it toward a half-submerged
rowboat; a strip of red along the curving gunnel wavering in the water resembled a wound. His line
drifted through a rusted oarlock, a thread through
the eye of a needle. He sighed, made himself more
comfortable, dug out the ring from the tobacco tin,
and, crossing one leg over his knee, slid it onto a toe.
He raised his foot against the sky and watched the
gold sparkling against the blue above. Peregrine for
Perry. Nibelung gold.

He daydreamed for a time, then put the ring away.
His eyelids felt heavy; he could not keep them from
drooping . . . closing. The hour itself was drowsy,

the air hushed, an atmosphere of quiet thrills . . . in his ear he heard the maidens splashing . . . enticing Rhine maidens with flowing hair and lovely sinuous bodies . . . romantic creatures, hoarding their river gold . . . he dozed . . .

"Douschka?"

He jerked his head up, his eyes blinking in the sunlight. She was standing a short distance away, on the planks of the landing, observing him quizzically, a flower-laden basket on her arm, her face shadowed by the parasol. Ada; weathered and lined face, grizzled hair pinned in a careful, old-fashioned knot at her neck, baked-apple skin still drawn taut across high cheekbones, in places almost translucent, with the effect of a fine teacup held to the light. Spare but strong, she held herself erect, the still-supple core of her body springy, like her step—she never walked but moved with long strides—her shoulders set and determined. Keen brown eyes, amused, lively, authoritative, heavy-lidded like a hawk's, with edges that held the colors of certain seashells—bluish, with a tinge of purple, even silver in them. Hands large, gnarled, brown, capable-looking, and an air of magic about them. Like everything about her, an air of magic.

She came closer, her chin outthrust, and in her smile was a soft, childlike innocence, which is sometimes the way with grandmothers. Her dress, a modest bouquet of printed flowers, whispered around bare tanned legs; at her breast a pin, crescent-shaped like a new moon, catching the sun's rays between golden horns.

Niles reeled in his line and ran to meet her. *"Dobryĭ den',* Madame."

"Dobryĭ den', grazhdahnin." She smiled at his greeting and hid her nose at the catfish he waved, trophy-like.

"Think it'll bite you?"

"I do not care for fish," she laughed. "Here all the fish have bones. The shad—nothing but bones."

"But the roe—you like shad roe. With bacon?"

"The roe I like, yes. Fish eggs—"

"Ick!" He wrinkled his nose and dropped his catch. "They look like pollywog eggs. You eat them and they'll grow into frogs and jump around inside you like Mexican jumping beans. Like this." Letting go his pole, tongue lolling, he hopped up and down, hugging himself and making ludicrous faces.

She pressed her hand below her heart as though to be mirthful hurt her. "Oh, *douschka,* such nonsense."

"It's true! And cherries—you swallow cherry seeds and they'll sprout out your ears. Or your—"

"Niles."

"Ass me no questions, I'll tell you no lies." He gave her his innocent look. "I didn't say anything."

"Niles," she said, humoring his superb glee, "Niles, you are a clown. A clown in a circus. Ringling Brothers will come and get you and put you in their show."

He giggled. "Like Mr. La Fever?" Mr. La Fever, Arnie La Fever's father, worked in the circus sideshow.

"Hush, do not say such things. You have an imp

sitting right there"—she touched his shoulder—
"who provokes you." Holland

He shifted his gaze upwards. "See that cloud?
Doesn't that look like Holland's face, a little?"

She peered up under her parasol, cocking her head
one way and another, scrutinizing. "Why yes, perhaps it does," she said, indulging his whim. "The
nose, however, is wrong. Do you see—it is too long.
More Cyrano than Holland."

"But see how tilty the eyes are—almond-shaped,
like a Chink, aren't they?"

"We say 'Chinaman,' not Chink," she gently
chided. "Chinks are found in walls and usually get
plastered."

"Like Uncle George," he said, capering.

"Niles."

"Well, I heard Aunt Vee say that's what he was
last—"

"Child, don't be impertinent." She tried to sound
severe, but he could tell she didn't mean it, which is
also the way with grandmothers.

For a while they amused themselves making out
interesting faces and shapes from the procession of
puffy clouds overhead: an elephant, a ship with sails,
a buffalo, three fat ladies "with *hu-u-uge* behinds!"
Niles described arcs in the air with his arms.

"What have you done to your hand now?" She
took it and inspected the injury. "We must put some
Listerine on that." Listerine was her panacea for all
the maladies of life.

"No, it's okay, honest." Resisting her ministrations, he sucked again, then spat.

"Is that the only shirt belonging to you?"

"No."

"And you have tennis shoes of your own. Why do you persist in wearing the old ones of Holland?" *Ach,* she thought with amused dismay, how far apart were children and old ladies. How could she think to try to bridge the gap? While she squeezed his finger to make the blood flow, he looked past her bent head where, up in the meadow, he saw Mr. Angelini under his straw hat, working along the windrows, saw a flash of red as he paused to wipe his face with a bandana. At the barn there were other glimpses of bright color: at the pigeon loft up in the cupola a bit of pink at the west window where Holland was lingering, mouthing his harmonica; lower down, at the hayloft hatch, Russell Perry in blue, pausing in his solitary pastime to hang again on the pulley rope.

"And what have you been up to, this day of days?" she asked.

"Me?"

"*Yah,* you."

"Nothing."

"I see. God gives us a glory of a day and you do nothing with it. Since school is out shall you dawdle away the summer? I have sewed name tapes in all of your things and Winnie has bought you that nice celluloid soap box and soap—"

"Lifebuoy, ick."

"—yet you will not go to camp. And you know it takes money to send boys to camp."

"Yes." But no, he meant, no camp. There was one on a nearby lake and Mother had said there would be money enough, but no, Holland didn't want to go, didn't like the games, the groups, didn't care much for playmates. Holland liked staying home, liked playing in the apple cellar, in the pigeon loft. There was going to be a show—"And the proceeds will go toward sending another child to camp," he explained, "some more unfortunate child." *irony*

"Sometimes," she laughed, "I do not think such a child exists."

"What d'you mean?"

"I mean children who can go to camp but don't choose to may spend some of their vacation time in the hands of Mrs. Jewett."

Horror struck! Mrs. Jewett tutored arithmetic, in which subject Niles had been floundering ever since long division. "Oh cripes—"

"Must you use such expressions, dear?" Ada said sweetly, her face adamant behind her smile. Ada meant business; Mrs. Jewett loomed. "Now tell, what have you been doing today?"

"Well, I did lots of things. I went down to the Center and got your corn plasters—"

"Thank you."

"Welcome. And your pills are over the sink in the kitchen. You have one more refill on the prescription."

"Thank you."

"Welcome. And I practiced."

"Your piano?"

"No, my magic. For the show. With Holland."

"Ah? Yes, Holland's tricks." She pressed the tips of her fingers to her mouth and spoke behind them, her tone a little wistful. "What sort of tricks, then?"

"A card trick. It's called a Royal Marriage—you do it with all the picture cards."

funeral images

"Court cards, yes."

"And then there was a funeral. Another funeral. I had it. I did the digging. Remember last month when the bird died? Well, today—"

"Child." She urged him to calm himself, for excitement had crept into his voice and she saw that his face was flushed.

"Yes, another funeral. It was sad. A rat died."

"Died? How?"

"It just—died. Holland told me to get rid of it, so I did."

She interrupted him with a look. "Holland did?"

"Yes."

"And?"

"And so I did. Buried it. That was the funeral—I found this cracker box and I put the rat in it and took Mr. Angelini's trowel and buried the box in the aspergrass. Then I wanted to put flowers on the grave, only I gave them to Mother instead."

"To Zan?"

"Yes. Clover. It was clover, the kind she likes, so I gave it to her. She—"

"Yes?"

"Nothing." He had started to confide Alexandra's secret. He sat down on the landing and patted a plank beside him. Disdaining the hand he offered, she removed her canvas shoes—the fabric over the little toes was cut with X's to ease her corns—and sat beside him, feet dangling, one toe making ripples. Careful that the moon pin shouldn't prick, she brought his head close to her breast and took fistfuls of his hair and commenced gently tugging it. To keep the scalp limber, she insisted; no bald heads among the

Vedrenya menfolk. He remembered how she had practiced this exercise on their scalps ever since he and Holland were youngsters.

"And the rat? How did it die?"

"I . . . I don't know." How could he tell her of Holland's cruelty. "It was one of Russell's pets. Maybe it was the heat."

"I see. Tch. Poor creature. I hope the rabbit won't miss it too much. Fancy a rabbit mother to a rat."

"I think they were a happy family at least."

"Meaning?"

"Well, our family—" He groped to express himself.

"Is not happy?"

"Not that. But families should be thick."

"Yes, of course. Like soup."

"But ours is broth," he said with a droll look. "Why does Mother like clover so much? It's just a weed, isn't it?"

"Clover is one of our most common wildflowers; it is not, however, a weed. And you know the story of the clover, surely. It was your mother's wedding bouquet."

Yes, she knew he'd heard the story, a favorite of the family, especially with Torrie, the new bride; but to hear it now would avoid further talk of rats and funerals and death. So she told it again, how there was the World War and Father, stationed at Fort Dix, and Zan, his mother, had decided hastily to marry before he sailed. How Uncle George and Aunt Valeria were present and how at the last minute Aunt Vee had remembered there was no bouquet for the bride and had hopped a fence into a nearby field where she picked the clover.

"And stepped in cowflops," he was quick to remind her.

"Yes. In the cowflops, if you must have them. And so," she finished, "your dear mother is charmed her life long by clover. And you, you are planning some flower arrangements yourself?"

"No'm."

"What should those be?" She pointed to a pile of still-dripping cattails lying close by on the riverbank.

"Cattails," he said; another innocent gaze.

She was used to his little strategies. "Yes, I know they are cattails, young man. And what will you do with them, these cattails?"

"Oh—nothing," he said evasively, in the manner of thirteen-year-old boys. "They're just for—nothing."

She took his chin in her hand to plumb him with eyes ancient and humorous and wise, her expression thoughtful, half smile, half frown.

"Well?" she said, waiting with her sibyl look, and he looked away, feeling transparent, knowing she knew he lied.

With certain evasions he explained about Doc Savage and the Winter Kingdom of the Akaluks. A fantastic imagination, she thought, brushing her fingers against his cheek.

"What's a hermaphrodite?" Niles asked.

"A hermaphrodite is supposedly a creature half man, half woman, though I don't expect one actually exists. It is more mythological, half Hermes, half Aphrodite, do you see. Why?"

He explained about the Firemen's Carnival and the Maltese freak. "How're your hands?" he asked, watching her gingerly press her swollen fingers.

She dismissed the subject with a wave. Never had he heard her complain about the pain that nagged her joints. For her amusement he reached into his shirt and extracted his pet on its silver chain, laying it between them in the sun.

"That chameleon will perish inside there," she told him, thinking how continually enchanting she found him. *Crouie*

"He can breathe okay. I like the way he tickles. And he's not a chameleon, he's a basilisk. See—he has a diamond for an eye. Don't dare look at it or you'll turn to stone."

"Ah, a lizard Medusa, no less." Such whimsy. *rory* What to do with the boy? But where had he learned of basilisks, if not from her? And unicorns and Rhine maidens, those water creatures hidden there in the depths, his secret that he had pledged her to keep. She shook her head and drew wet moss over the flowers in her basket: sunflowers, black-eyed Susans, devil's paintbrush, spotted lilies, and buttercups.

Taking one of the latter he held it under her chin. Yes, she liked butter. But her favorites were the sunflowers. He lifted one up and blew at it, dispersing a little cloud of powder into the air.

"*Yah*, here all the sunflowers get dust." But it was pleasant to see them all the same. They reminded her of St. Petersburg, where the wind sweeping across the Russian plain kept them fresh and dust-free.

"Is it really true that sunflowers follow the sun all

day?" he asked. She had read this to him from a book.

"I think it is only superstition. But all Russians are superstitious, you know. See?" She took his cheeks between her hands and lifted his head upwards, turning his face to the sun.

"Sun*flower!*" he shouted, grinning proudly and squinting against the light. She let her eyes rest upon his face for a moment; ah, the freshness of his features, the flower-soft skin with the golden fuzz below the hairline. This was her *podsolnechnik,* her sunflower now; gone were all the sunflowers of Russia, but in their place grew this one, this prize flower of her heart.   *why not Holland*

irony

"Why are you smiling?"

"*Ach,*" she said, "I was remembering that day we played the game on the sunflowers, and you cry because of that damn crow. My *douschka,* such a crybaby you were."

"Was not," he protested, pulling away.

"It's all right. Everyone should cry sometimes. It's good for the digestive tract. *Yah.* When your uncle gets home, shall you come with me to take the flowers down?"

He paled, looked at her blankly. Uncle George? Home? "The flowers down?" he echoed, voice shaky, a sick feeling in the stomach.

whose burial

"To the cemetery. When Uncle George comes with the car, Winnie shall drive us and we shall put decorations out. We go in secret and say nothing so your mother shall not be upset, yes?"

He stole a look to the barn and Russell's form in the hatch. *Wait till my Dad gets home!* "Yes, all right.

pB

I'll come with you." He took a deep breath, expelling it slowly, carefully, that she should not see his fear. Oh the secrets he must guard . . .

"How is it you do not caddy for Uncle George today?"

Reprieve! He'd forgotten Uncle George was golfing after work. If he played the second nine out he wouldn't get home until seven, and he always stopped for a drink at the nineteenth hole. Niles's look aroused her suspicions. She gave him another piercing stare. "Yes? Well?"

Well, he explained to her, he couldn't caddy for Uncle George any more. Why? Well, this morning he'd been barred from the golf club. Why? Well, he and Holland had gotten up early and had taken the trolley car (riding on the back of the cowcatcher no doubt, she surmised) out to the second nine fairway looking for yesterday's lost golf balls and the greens-keeper had caught Niles and now he was barred. "And we had to give him all the golf balls we found. Almost two bucks worth. Cripes!"

"Niles," she chided.

Grabbing up a handy stick, a diversionary tactic, he dropped to one knee and sprayed her with lead. "Rat-tat-tat-tat-tat!" Machine-gunning her, sweeping the stick about in an arc. "You're dead. You're Dillinger and you're dead! You're Mad Dog Coll and you're dead! Dead dead dead!"

"Stop that this instant," she ordered. "Throw that stick away." She could be very stern; he obeyed promptly. "The idea. Where do you children learn about such things? Mad Dog Coll indeed!" *Beware of mad dogs lurking, for lurking, they shall bite.* "And biting—" She was half muttering to herself, but he knew what she meant.

"Well, you're supposed to fall down when you're killed," he informed her. Dejected, he shoved his hands in his pockets. Gosh, when the Feds got Dillinger last year in front of that theater, *he* sure fell down dead. Think of getting lead poisoning because you took in a movie, for cripes sakes. Clark Gable—ick!

"Don't frown so, child."

He looked up at her. "Ada?"

"*Yah?*"

"How can you always tell?"

"Tell what?"

"About what's true and what isn't. How do you always know?"

"I do not always." She looked down at him. "But you do, child, don't you?" IRONY

He frowned. "Well," he said gravely, "sometimes I do." He stretched to her ear, asking conspiratorially behind his hand, "Can we do it now?"

She smiled, showing the strong white teeth which were still hers. This was their game, of course, and accordingly she rose and, moving from the landing, drew him with her, holding him slightly to one side, his head a little lower than her shoulder, pointing out a dragonfly darting at the patch of goldenrod. He looked up at her with questioning eyes.

"No, look there. Look at the darning needle. Look hard."

The insect hovered above a frond and he stared silently, intently, for a long time, his gaze transfixed. Sun waves shimmered and even from a distance he became gradually aware of the harsh weedy scent.

Now the dragonfly darted once more, hovered, darted again, all at once soaring aloft, now diving, now hanging suspended. Still he observed, never for an instant taking his eyes from it. In time he felt her light touch.

"What is it like?" she asked, a kind of expectation in her voice. "What does it feel like?" *THE*

"Airplanes. It feels like airplanes." *GAME*

Ah, she thought, airplanes—rather perceptive.

It *was* something of that nature, though not a machine, a—what? Creature, he supposed. Carefully he examined the longness of it, the slenderness, the—airiness. Lighter than air, and as thin; segmented body, metallic wings veined with silver and gold, iridescent like fairy-tale wings, inaudibly humming, beating faster than eye can see. Head loosely jointed, turning every which way, exquisitely sighted eyes avid for prey. Delicate, ferocious little beast, swifter than a swallow, flushing insect game from the clover preserves, devouring, devouring, devouring . . .

Now the dragonfly wafted high into the air and Niles felt his own being lifting away from the earth, felt his corporeal self go soaring up over the meadow in company with the creature, compound eyes taking in, grasping, everything; to the west along the pastures running to meet the Avalon ridge across the river, and dimly in the distance, the Shadow Hills blanketed in haze. Away to the east, beyond the house, over billowy green treetops, down to a cluster of roofs and spires: the Center. At his own backdoor he saw into the kitchen garden, saw Winnie the hired girl taking in the laundry, saw the trolley car running the Shadow Hills route, up from Talcotts Ferry, up past Knobb Street and past Packard Lane, out through the city on the north, and on to Babylon to the west; Babylon, End of the Line. It lay all before him, like a miniature playtown, the houses diminished, the barn a toy, the people on the sidewalk only make-believe. Saw, down there on the ground, Ada, standing alone, a speck.

All this he described for her in precise detail. "That's what it feels like," he said, ardent and breathless from his flight.

She agreed; it must be all of that, surely. And between them they savored like forbidden fruit the secret of the game.

He smiled. "Did I do it good?"

"Yes, child."

"Good as Holland?"

Beneath the moon pin the delicate lace at her throat was trembling in the breeze, the smile elusive. *"Ach,"* she said at last, and her voice was pained, "as good as Holland. As good as me, as any." Shading her face with the parasol, as though to obscure her feelings, she peered out across the river.

"Another," he begged, tugging eagerly at her arm, but she only smiled and said, "That is enough for today"—which is also the way with grandmothers.

"Pajalsta, just one more?"

She raised her basket. "I must gather some watercress to bring to Winnie for salad tonight."

"Just one more," he pleaded, not to be put off. *"Pajalsta, pajalsta?"*

He was irresistible. She tousled his hair and scanned the field, moving the parasol against the sun. "What shall it be?" Her eyes roved from object to object: a red-winged blackbird flitting on a twig, a dilapidated fence post, a rusting oil drum, a worn-out tire.

"There," she said at last, "look there. Tell me what you see." He followed her eyes up the meadow to where Mr. Angelini continued his haying. "But," he protested, "it's too far. I can't—"

"Look," she insisted. "Do as I have taught you. Concentrate. Tell me what it is like."

Compelled, he looked. Perceived bright plumes wafting through the sunlight, the hay sailing in yellow forkfuls against the sky. His eye fastened upon one, saw it scooped from the ground, watched it trace a pattern, a delicate, almost musical figure, *swis-s-sh,* sliding from the fork, *swissssh,* into the wagon. Now, distracted, his eye followed the path of the pitchfork through the air as it reversed itself, completing its movement, the curving tines, their tips like sharp fingers, beckoning the sun, waiting to catch it, glinting like cold fire—stabbing—a pain—*ohh*—

"Niles, what is it?"

(connects to Russell)

He was clutching his chest, fingers stiffly arched, his face contorted. He hunched over, his breath coming in short gasps. "Ada—it hurts—"

"What, child?" She bent in alarm, trying to examine him, enfolding him till the pain subsided. Racked, he shuddered, held himself very still. Then he looked up at her, gray eyes wide, wondering at the strangeness of the pain. "It's gone," he said in time, his breath coming irregularly. He managed a smile.

She felt his forehead, his chest. "Niles, what was it? Are you all right?"

He nodded, fingers retracing the mysterious path

of the pain. Was it his heart? No—the span of his fingers told her the pain sprang across the width of his chest.

"Tell me what it was like."

"I can't. It was just—a pain—all sharp, pointy, here." He touched his chest again. "But it's gone. It's all right, Ada, honest." Butting his head against her, he nuzzled his face in one delicate hand while her fingers caressed the golden pelt growing along the nape of his neck. Unabashed, he said simply, "I love you."

Her heart leapt. *"Ach, douschka,* I love you too."

He picked up his rod. "I'm going down the river a ways and see if I can get some pickerel."

"Perhaps," she suggested before he went, "Russell might like to go fishing too. Surely there must be more fishing poles somewhere." She caught his look. "You don't care for Russell very much, do you?"

He shrugged noncommittally. "Oh, he's okay, I guess."

"After all, he is your cousin. And a guest. You boys should play together more. The trouble is, you just have him in the wrong throat," meaning Russell was apt to go down the wrong way. "It is important to make guests feel at home, do you see? And when Aunt Josie and Aunt Fanuschka come, Russell must move into your room—"

His puckish laugh cut her off as he ran through the marsh grass into the field, where he quickly gathered a bunch of goldenrod, returning to lay it in her basket with the other flowers.

"For you, Madame, to take to the cemetery."

"But what about the hay fever?"

"Dead people don't sneeze. And no mayonnaise jars, okay?" She was always putting her wildflower arrangements in any old kind of glass.

"But did you hear me?"

"What?"

"Russell will have to move into your room."

He sighed. "I know. I don't mind. There's plenty of space. And he has to go somewhere, I suppose. But he *is* hopeless," he said with engaging candor. She had opened her mouth to commend his artlessness until his next words made her start. "Holland won't like it though," he said darkly, and when she replied her voice was sharper than she intended.

"Why, how's that?"

Cripes, he didn't want to get Holland in dutch. He shook his head and obstinately said, "He's just not going to, that's all."

"Stop making faces, child, and tell me why."

"Because he isn't. Because—because he doesn't like Russell. That's what it was, with the rat. That's why there was a funeral."

Abruptly, as if she could no longer stand, she sat down again on the landing. By chance a cloud passed across the sun, gray, with a gold edge, like a huge doily, casting a mournful shadow. A sudden breeze scalloped the surface of the water. She shivered.

"Are you cold?"

She shook her head. *"Nyet.* A crow was walking on my grave, is all."

A crow. The crow's name was Holland. He knew what she was thinking, how worried she was about him, how she tried never to show it, tried not to let on that she knew things . . . she'd have guessed, anyway, he bet, eventually, about the rat. And he was supposed to go on protecting Holland, covering for him, keeping his secrets, the ring, the packet, the blue packet which contained The Thing He sighed. No—one of these days Holland was going to have to start fending for himself. Niles was going to forget he was a twin. *IRONY*

The cloud passed. She waved him off. He ran to the riverbank, where he stalked along beside the sedge, waving back at her, still seated on the landing. She watched him go, tugging his khaki shorts rolled above tawny thighs, his shoulder blades protruding at the back of his gay shirt like incipient wings, the halo of tow hair which topped the slender neck flashing in the sun. Then he was lost behind the screen of willows, and, her eyes lingering on the spot where he had disappeared, it came to her mind that he was not a human at all, not her grandchild, Holland's twin, but instead some wild woodland thing, a faun perhaps, carrying a fishing pole in place of pipes.

How was it that she felt chilly? She lay back against the boards of the landing and let the sun-drenched wood warm her bones. She hated the cold. Russian to the core, still she hated it, loved the hot summers. The sun was for her a blessing. In the old days, even after the cold winters, the great ladies, spending the summers in the country, stayed out of the sun to keep their skins fair, stayed behind shades or under big umbrellas in the afternoons. Not she. Ada would have followed the sun all day long if she could, skirts caught up above her knees, running barefoot through the sunflower paths.

When the sun had dropped further, when she had

gathered her watercress from a nearby spring, and squeezed out the hem of her dress, she slipped back into the canvas shoes. They were very comfortable, with the X's cut into the tops to let her corns breathe. But it was not only the corns which gave her trouble. One leg, badly mangled by a dog when she was much younger, still gave her pain sometimes, causing her to limp slightly.

Suddenly she was startled by a movement in the grass. She laughed to herself. A tramp cat—one she had not seen before—peered through the weeds and, tail curled like a question mark, strutted across the swale toward her.

"Ah, *zdravstvuĭte, zdravstvuĭte,*" she said, crooning to it in her native tongue. *"Podoidi, koshecka."* As she bent to it, the animal bounded to pounce on Niles's catfish. It seized it in its mouth and scampered off to the meadow. Up at the barn Russell stood in the loft door fanning his face, his glasses glinting in the sun. Mr. Angelini was no longer in view.

Ach. Ada shook her head again, thinking about her own cat—Pilakea. Pilakea was a word Holland had collected from somewhere; "trouble," it meant, in Hawaiian. Trouble indeed. But of course there wasn't any more Pilakea; that one had come to a bad end, back in March, right after St. Patrick's Day. On Holland's birthday. Died horribly, poor *koshecka;* Holland had hanged it in the well. Holland . . . what senseless, what tragic destruction. She could weep. And all those years of pain he had caused, all the things preceding. The day he set fire to the Joacums' shed. The day he ran away, went and hid in the freight car behind Mr. La Fever's costume trunk, and the circus got all the way to Springfield before he was discovered, and the family half out of their minds. Yes, she could weep for Holland.

So alike, yet so different. She remembered the way they reacted to "doing the game"; this almost mystic "transference" she had discovered as a girl and taught them. So different, Niles a child of the air, a joyous spirit, well disposed, warm, affectionate, his nature in his face; tender, merry, loving.

Holland? Something else again. She had always loved them equally, yet Holland was a child of the earth; still, guarded, bound within himself, fettered by secrets unshared. Craving love but not able to give it; so mysteriously withdrawn.

Holland's very birth—his body struggling, rending the womb, emerging dead. Slapped into angry life by the doctor. Twenty minutes later, when midnight had come and gone, Niles appearing with miraculous ease. *Smoothest delivery I ever saw,* Dr. Brainard had said, delicately removing the caul. Imagine, born with the caul.

"Twins? With different birthdays? How unusual." Indeed, for identical twins, very. Oh yes, there were the mixed signs, on the cusp, as one says—they should have been more alike; nevertheless, the difference. Holland a Pisces, fish-slippery, now one thing, now another. Niles an Aries, a ram blithely butting at obstacles. Growing side by side, but somehow not together. Strange. Time and again Holland would retreat, Niles pursue, Holland withdraw again, reticent, taciturn, a snail in its shell.

It hadn't always been so. As twins should, they

had been inseparable to begin with. Why, they had
shared the same cradle, head to foot—that old wicker
cradle, still in the storeroom—until they outgrew it,
and then they slept in the same crib. You would have
thought they were Siamese twins, so close they were;
one being housed in two forms. What had happened?
Whose fault? She could not tell. Always the same
question, over and over . . . *what quest*

Yes, for Holland she could weep. *Give him his mind*

"Why, Niles would give that boy the shirt off his *NILES*
back." *I expect he would. It is his nature.* Generous to *Gives*
a fault, that was Niles. Half the things given him had *up*
found their way into Holland's possession. Give cach *HIMSELF*
a tin soldier, Holland would end up with a pair; some
cars, Holland would have a fleet. And a sorcerer
when it came to money. Niles—born with the caul,
naturally he was lucky with money—found a dollar
bill tucked between the pages of Granddaddy's Bible,
a piece of old-fashioned Civil War currency. Finders
keepers, Vining had said; but turn around and Holland had the money, squirreled away behind the picture roll of the Chautauqua desk. Alexandra had
found it later, dusting. *She knows hiding place*

And Holland's nature? There was the day, for instance, when he was sent home from school. "I'm
sorry," informed Miss Weeks, the Principal, seated
stiffly in the parlor, "we're all sorry, really, Niles is
such a good pupil; however, Holland—" She turned
red.

"But what has he done?"

"Holland is a disturbing influence . . ."

"How? What do you mean exactly, a disturbing
influence?"

Her stringent, tight-lipped report was more than disturbing: shocking. *No Detail*

"Nonsense!" They denied the stories. But the facts were there.

"Perhaps a psychologist—" Miss Weeks had suggested.

So, Dr. Daniels: "High-spirited boy. Boisterous, but with no defects, unless an excess of spirits. Not unnatural in young boys. Keep him busy. Lots of exercise."

Holland

But there was more to it: stormy, fretful, surrendering himself to blind rages, torn by tantrums, this was Holland. Rash, sulky, proud by turns. "Holland," she would say to the scowling imp-face he put on, "you can catch a lot more flies with sugar than you can with vinegar. Holland, smile—you don't want your face to freeze that way." And in time the smile would come, reluctantly at first, then dazzlingly; afterward, an extravagance of affection. Dear Holland, she could weep. She lowered her head and her hand moved past her face as though to brush away, like a cobweb, some painful memory, then, raising her eyes again, she stood motionless for some moments, her parasol tilted against the sun, her figure oddly turned, held as though awaiting some event while the breeze rippled the slight fabric of her parasol, causing it to shudder.

And up in the barn, moving from the open door, out of the sunshine, stepping back into the shadow of the loft and once more laying his glasses down, Russell Perry blinked into the dim void and took four long steps to the edge of the loft. Arms flung wide, he

leaped. *"I'm the King of the Mountain!"* Down and
down and down. Hardly soaring, but dropping
merely, the smell of fresh-cut hay in his nose, holding
his breath and dropping into the cool dark nothingness, rushing as though late for an appointment, hurrying to where, only a blur at first, then more clearly,
clearer than anything he had ever seen, astonishingly
clear, reaching for him with cruel beckoning fingers,
waiting to catch him as he fell, he saw in the blackness the glinting silver prongs, sharp, sharp, and fire-
cold . . . *"Eee-yaiee!"* As the steel tore through his
chest, shattering flesh and bone, his scream sent the
mice scurrying with fright, and hot blood, all red and
frothy, with little ruffles like ghastly lace, spurted
into the yellow hay, and in another moment Winnie
and Mr. Angelini had come running from the pump,
and, at the landing, her parasol quivering, Ada stood,
her body rigid, her head slightly averted, listening as
the cry reached her ears, with it, on the breeze, the
lazy thrum of a harmonica, while the fingers of her
trembling hand pressed ever more fiercely against the
sharp points of the golden crescent moon pinned at
her breast.

V

Russell Perry is in the parlor, in his coffin, open to
view. It is from the parlor that the Perrys have always been buried. In the parlor they are christened,
are betrothed, are married; dead, in the parlor they

are laid out. It has always been so: the shades drawn,
the casket on black-draped trestles looped with cords
and tassels; sighing, whispery, shadowlike forms slipping in silently to mourn, to regret or—secretly, as
some will—to savor, laying warm lips against cold
unyielding flesh in last farewell. This is the Perry's
way.

There are sprays of gladioli and a pair of Sheffield
candelabra, one to a side, their smoking tapers lend-
ing the room an eerie feeling in the late morning
light. Mr. Tuthill, a dull, eulogizing man, stands to
one side, while seated to the left of the casket, in
folding chairs from the undertaker's, are the family;
opposite, a few others: Dr. Brainard and wife, and
Simon and Laurenza Pennyfeather, friends from farther up Valley Hill Road.

While the minister speaks of how often they have
gathered in the parlor for this same sad purpose,
Niles stares at Holland, spruce in his blue suit and
white collar, wearing one of his father's ties, his hair
neatly combed, shoes shined, standing just behind
Ada's left shoulder and looking straight ahead, inex-
pressive gray eyes fastened on nothing.

Beyond him sits Winnie Koslowsky, behind her,
Leno Angelini, the once-handsome immigrant, still
hardy and manly, but bandy-legged and bowed, with
brooding eyes, complexion the color and texture of
old leather, his columnar neck corded, his hands sin-
ewy, the iron-gray mustache below his long, veined
nose obscuring the expression of his mouth. He had
been the first to reach Russell, with Winnie close behind, she having been cleaning radishes at the pump,
he washing up and in a hurry to get home when the

scream was heard. They found Russell still moving in the hay, writhing with pain, and trying to pull from his chest the pitchfork which had gone clean through him and out the back, and when Leno had yanked it free, the blood came pumping out with the boy's heartbeat in a pulsing red tide. A shocking accident. With one curious sidelight: Mr. Angelini was always so careful about his tools. He was sure, swore, in fact, that he had hung the pitchfork back in its accustomed place in the tool shed right after he stabled the team.

By stretching his neck slightly, Niles could see past his sister Torrie and her husband Rider Gannon to Uncle George and Aunt Valeria. Poor Aunt Vee— what a transformation—overnight from chipper chickie to sad sparrow. You had to feel sorry, all she could do was cry and blame herself for having let Russell play where it was unsafe, where children ought not to be allowed. Uncle George had given strict orders: no more jumping in the hay; had given Mr. Angelini a padlock to put on the Slave Door. But it was too late now. *Why?*

Niles looked at his grandmother. She was sitting in her black dress, the gold moon pin on her breast, hands folded quietly in her lap, her head making faint, almost imperceptible nods, and her eyes resting, not on the minister, nor even on the open coffin, but on the painting beyond. It was as though she were trying to solve some enigma hidden in the faces of the three subjects: her daughter Alexandra, striking-looking in a long black dress, her figure slim, elegant, against the gray stripes of a chairback, a large amethyst-colored flower held negligently in a hand.

Hair piled like a smoky cloud on a finely shaped head, a long curving neck, a captivating smile, the eyes dark and arresting; Holland on one side of her, a boat in the crook of his arm, Niles on the other with a stuffed animal, their features uncannily similar, all three gazing out of the gilt frame, sharing some undisclosed but amusing secret. Mother and Her Boys, the family called the picture. It made her ache to look at it.

Speaking of her sister-in-law, Valeria used to say, "Just a bit theatrical looking, don't you think? Seems absolutely *stalked* by tragedy. Something about the eyes, I expect. *Deep—ter*ribly deep. *Haunt*ed, actually." Aunt Vee always selected her words as she might fruit, squeezing each for ripeness and juiciness. But an apt description: Alexandra leading her secluded existence, remaining upstairs for many a mournful month, sitting up there in the chintz-covered chair reading books brought her from the library; unwilling, unable, to come down.

The minister's monotone unabated, Niles's mind wandered farther afield, in time abandoning altogether his cousin's funeral while his thoughts strayed to earlier, happier times. It was like looking at the photographs in an album: the corners tidily stuck down, the images preserved and captioned, a bit of dust on one, another slightly faded. Mentally he thumbed the pages, pausing to review familiar scenes.

 At the Pump: Holland and Niles, naked, in the pool under the spout. The pool filled, their broken images doubled in the water, duplicated precisely as jacks on a playing card. In one moment of sheer delight, bursting with unreserved joy, their arms reach out to each other, hands clasp in a mirthful flash. Their connection seems not only physical, but spiritual as well. Each smiling, each expressing a deeper delight in his human reflection, there is evidence of a profound sort of union. Father records the moment with his Kodak.

The Pony Cart: Holland and Niles, grinning crookedly from a wicker cart with skinny red wheels; the pony's name is Donald. Father leads him along the drive. Father wears a crewing sweater and smokes a pipe—Prince Albert. He is a giant of a man, stronger than Atlas, wiser than Solomon (richer than Croesus, alas no), more virtuous than Galahad, his eyes alight with humor, a tolerant smile on his mouth. Father, A Man Much Admired. He can do everything—well, practically. Anyway, Niles thinks so.

At the Pictures: An enormous movie cavern. Silvery giants leaping on the screen. Niles goes for a drink; returning he becomes lost; cries. Holland comes, takes his hand, leads him to his seat.

The Riverboat: Holland and Niles are standing on a sandbar in the middle of the river. The last of the paddlewheelers goes by. The pilot waves. He smokes a corncob pipe. As the boat passes, a marvelous thing happens: Niles discovers *money!* He finds, half-sunken in the sand, a silver dollar.

Niles Discovers Money—Part Two: Leafing through Granddaddy Perry's Bible, he comes across a large green bill. Civil War currency, Father explains. Sure, finders keepers. Looks from Father to Holland. Later, conniving. Money ends up in Holland's pocket, thence to a hiding place, thence, discovered, to the bank account. Niles—rooked again.

The Poverty Party: Saturday night, a baked-bean supper on trestle tables set up in the barn. Holland and Niles hidden overhead in the loft, watching the country club crowd getting drunk on the gin Father stirred up in the set-tubs. Everyone costumed and dancing on the threshing floor. Great fun until Niles laughs too loud at Father's outrageous garb and they are banished to bed.

Then, *The Apple Cellar:* Saturday morning, last November. Holland is above on the threshing floor, steadying the baskets for Mr. Angelini and Father, who carry them down the stairladder where Niles waits with the lamp. Mr. Angelini goes up the ladder, Father starts down through the trapdoor with another basket. Holland's legs may be glimpsed through the opening. With Father halfway down, the door starts falling . . . falling . . . The cry . . . the blood. "Father!" The door raised, Holland rushing down. Taking his twin out through the Slave Door into the wagon room . . . When Niles sees Father again, he is lying there, where Russell lies now . . . before the fireplace . . . a casket . . . a quilted bed of silk . . . drawn shades . . . flowers and candles . . . the lower body hidden by the closed part of the lid. Niles looks down at the face on the pillow, hears the same minister, repeating those same words . . .

"—forever and ever, Amen." In unison the mourners, led by Mr. Tuthill, were finishing the Lord's Prayer; in another moment Russell Perry's service was concluded. Next, the drive to the cemetery behind the church, where Mr. Tuthill would read—inevitably—the Twenty-third Psalm and commend

Russell's spirit to Life Everlasting. Then would come
the last part, the burial, the sexton's shovel tossing
back the dirt into the hole. But for this people seldom
lingered. Niles glanced again at his twin—noted Holland's expression, dreamy and far away, that same
moonstruck look, his eyes obscured by a filmy glaze.
Beads of perspiration lay across his upper lip, moist
and slightly parted from the lower. What was he
thinking? Certainly it was not a worried or perplexed
expression: now his thoughts were not on the ring in
the tobacco tin—or the blue tissue packet. No,
clearly, he was not worrying. His face, both dim and
vacant, was inscrutable, with that curiously Asiatic
cast to it.

To jolt him from his reverie, Niles found it required a vigorous nod on his part, and he jerked a
hand up in an abrupt flashing gesture to indicate the
way past the casket, while Ada, clasping her pocketbook in her black-gloved fingers, caught the movement over her shoulder and revealed her disquiet as
the last of the mourners filed from the parlor.

Upstairs in her room, Alexandra's slippered feet nervously paced the flower-patterned rug, gliding to the
door, to a window, past a bedpost, the dressing table,
pausing before a mahogany pier glass, then continuing back and forth across the rug until, at the sound
of an approaching motor in the driveway, they returned to the door, where they contrived to linger. In
time she opened the door a crack. A step sounded
along the hall. She threw her arms wide and drew
Niles into the room.

"Hello, Mother." She was quite tall and he had to stretch to reach her mouth.

"Is it all over?" She dropped into the chintz-covered chair, while he, taking the dressing table stool, watched her wan face, easily detecting the strain. She was wearing her cologne, a fresh, flowery fragrance he liked, but one that failed to mask the other smell, though she kept her scented handkerchief close to her mouth.

Over. Yes, it was over. Russell was buried and Aunt Valeria was shut in her room, unable to stop crying. Niles was struck by the clarity with which he could identify his own reflection in the dark center of his mother's eye; how easily he recognized the pain there. Like the lens of a camera, stopped down to a single vivid image, this gleaming iris doggedly focused for him the picture of Russell Perry's round body tumbling out of the loft, down onto the cold steel jutting in the haymow.

Her eye was flitting again, coming to rest periodically on the drawer of her dressing table, while he toyed with the silver handles of her vanity set. Arranged around the brushes, nail buffer, and button hook were silver-framed photographs: Niles and Holland under the pump; the family bathing at the seashore; Ada wearing moiré and a fashionable string of pearls; Holland and Niles again, sailor-suited in the pony cart; Torrie in her wedding gown; the poverty partygoers with Mother wearing Father's tuxedo and Father in Mother's red dress and his old rubber fishing boots.

"I guess the aunts won't be coming now." He had picked up a snapshot of two ladies in navy bloomers, smiling shyly on either side of a tennis net: Ada's sisters, the great-aunts, Josie and Fania.

"Yes they will. They thought they might not come because of the—situation—but I insist, I *insist,* we're not going to have any more long faces around here, and they are to arrive as planned. Though I think they want to postpone until after the middle of next month. A suitable waiting period, they feel."

He beamed. "Then there's lots of time."

"For what, darling?"

"For the show!" he exclaimed gaily, an effort to perk her up. Each year, while the aunts were visiting, there would be a show in the barn, all proceeds to charity. Lantern slides and colored postcards projected on a sheet, Charlie Chaplin silents and Aunt Jo performing "Yes, We Have No Bananas" or "Don't Bring Lulu"; afterward, her Betty Boop or Mae West. Then, *pièce de résistance,* magicking, with Holland got up in cape and top hat and Niles stooging for him in the audience.

"And Chan Yu's coming again," he added, recalling for her the Fourth of July Firemen's Carnival and the magician who last year had performed an amazing trick: had seemingly hanged himself, but at the last minute the cloth covering him had dropped, the noose was revealed as empty, and presto! there was Chan Yu in the aisle, alive and smiling! Chan Yu the Disappearing Marvel. Viewing the remarkable performance, Holland and Niles had played their game, concentrating to discover the secret.

"And?" prompted Alexandra, who had forgotten, "what was it?" Niles described again the way it had

been accomplished, how they had solved the mystery
of the hanging.

"Yes. Yes, dear. That will be nice, I'm sure. Your
tricks . . . always wonderful . . ."

She was drifting off. Placing her book in her hands,
he rose. "There. Finish *The Good Earth* so you can
start *Anthony Adverse* when it comes in."

"Yes, dear. Thank you. Be sure to change your
clothes."

He pressed her hand and bent to lay a cheek
against hers and exchange kisses. To forestall him,
she pressed her handkerchief to her lips; turned her
head away; shammed a cough.   DRINKS

Oh Mother, poor dear Mother, he thought. *I know.*
What could he do for her? How could he help her?
What could he say that would free those thoughts
imprisoned inside her head, those unspoken things he
knew she would never say. He looked down at her
tiny slippers, pretty things Father had brought from
Gibraltar, those and a tortoise-shell comb too, when
he came back from overseas. And a monkey of
carved coral—they ran wild in troops all over the
Rock, he said—which she wore when she got dressed
up. Such pains she took: never went farther than the
corner without stockings. Always, before taking the
trolley car upstreet, selecting her costume with care,
gloves and bag to match, and a hat with some frivolous bit of veiling in front. When she passed, heads
turned, all nods and smiles and friendly inclinings.
"Oh that Alexandra Perry," he would hear people
say, "she's got a gleam in her eye." It was true. She
had a rainbow laugh, and displayed it liberally for
her family.

"Mother?" he said lightly. She made a garbled, half-sound in her throat, and shook her head.

"Nothing, dear." She tried to laugh. Again her eyes skidded; in the afternoon light her face shone pale and incandescent. She fidgeted with her robe, started to get up, then, changing her mind, leaned back as though the effort were too much. Her look went unobserved by him as he kissed her again, feeling the veins in her wrists beat when he leaned to squeeze them a final time. "Bye, Mother. I'll be back later."

"Yes, darling, of course. Please do. And we must try to keep the house quiet, for Aunt Vee's sake, please?" Languidly she kissed her fingertips away. When he had gone, she rose and drifted about the room at length, clasping and unclasping her hands, pressing them to her temples as if she would seal in certain broodings which lay hidden there. In time she returned to the dressing table where, from under the scarves in the left-hand drawer, she drew forth a bottle. Pouring some cool water from the carafe thoughtfully provided by Winnie, she added the whisky and, resuming her chair, once again let her eyes roam toward the lavender patch of clover by the well.

At the rear of the house the Perry roof had difficulty encompassing both a north and south wing as each rambled patchwork-like in its haphazard additions: dark passages, unexpected turnings, oddly located stairways, and eccentric, surprising spaces. One of these, over the kitchen with its own back stairway, was a pleasant and sunny bedroom. Once it had been

INSTITUTION

the "invalid room" set aside from the rest of the
house for a peculiar aunt ("mad as a hatter, Old
Aunt Hattie") whom the family had wished to care
for themselves, rather than entrust her to an institution. Cheerful with yellow paint and white trim, the
place was known now simply as "the boys' room."
More sleeping porch than bedroom, it had two
matching beds with spool-turned posts; at the foot of
each, wooden chests, carpentered by Father, identical
except for the "H" on one, the "N" on the other.
Overhead, tissue-and-balsa airplane models; and
spilling over shelves an array of boys' miscellany:
lead soldiers, rock crystals and schists, a stack of
trolley transfers, a stamp collection, jumbled books, a
world globe, a fold-down desk with picture scrolls—
the kind known as a Chautauqua desk—hanging on
the wall. Added touches both humorous and bizarre:
a sun-bleached hawk's head, a red bicycle reflector
stuck in one eyesocket; a plaster bust with antlers
attached; the mandible of a fox on whose teeth was
latched a turkey wishbone. To the north the windows
overlooked the other wing; south, out along the
drive; west, past the barn, down to the icehouse at
the river.

Niles undid his tie, removed his jacket and pants,
and hung them up. He took his shoes off, undoing the
laces thoughtfully, some unintelligible dismay jarring
his consciousness. What was it? A picture had
formed in his mind; at the center it remained blank, a
space he was unable to fill. Something to do with
Russell. It bothered him. He threw the lid of his
chest back: neatly folded underwear, socks, all with
name tapes Ada had sewn on; belts and moccasins, a

sweater, some shirts freshly laundered by Winnie. He put one on—his favorite—buttoned it and tucked it in. Seated on the chest at the foot of Holland's bed, he emptied out the Prince Albert can into his lap and one by one returned the items inside, the carved horse chestnut, the matches, the ring, Peregrine for Perry, the blue tissue paper packet, this last—The Thing—of an intriguing shape, approximately two inches long, narrow, only slightly thicker than a pencil, and the paper, well worn by frequent undoings, a bright robin's egg blue. He dropped the can with its contents inside his shirt, went to stab his finger at a word in the dictionary, and left the room.

The shocked gloomy aftermath of death pressed a heavy hand upon the house. In the hallways the shades were pulled, the darkened staircase sprawled into a shadowy limbo. Lugubrious crying came from behind Aunt Valeria's door. Downstairs the bell rang; Niles, pausing on the top landing, glimpsed a face beyond the screen: Mrs. Rowe from next door. Ada would go to answer; she would be there to see to all the formalities. A man in black, a flower in his lapel, tiptoed across the hall carrying folding chairs to a second, similarly dressed man: Mr. Foley the undertaker, and an assistant; and there went the trestles, the funeral draperies. It was all so forlorn, so sad, so empty; such a feeling of finality to these events. A termination. The End. Born 1921—Died 1935. Poor Russell.

Mr. Foley, speaking to his assistant. What was that he was saying? *What?* Holland—? Niles's ears buzzed; he could feel his face flush; was forced to restrain himself from running downstairs, shutting up Mr. Foley—big-mouthed Mr. Foley, like the Fish Footman in *Alice in Wonderland. Shut up, Mr. Foley* . . . *what did Foley say*

The grandfather clock at the head of the stairs was a perverse timepiece: *tock*-tick, it insisted upon, *tock*-tick. Today it sounded pervasive and excessively loud, making the silent house seem more dolorous than ever. Standing stockstill, Niles listened and watched, measuring the silence.

From the hall closet beside the clock he took a wooden milking stool and opened the door of the clockcase: the weights were unwound almost to the floor. Strange; never had the clock been allowed to run down. It had accompanied Ada and Grandpapa Vedrenya to America and for years had stood in the hall of their house in Baltimore. When Ada came to Pequot Landing the clock came too.

Niles drew down the chains, pulling the brass weights upward, still thinking of Russell in the hayloft. He touched the weights to stop their swaying, set the pendulum in motion, and closed the door. He stood on the stool and, using a rigidly extended finger, moved forward the minute hand to coincide with the one on his watch. It *had* been an accident. In his rush to get home that afternoon, Mr. Angelini had left his pitchfork in the hay. And Russell must have taken off his glasses and—wait a minute—*there it was,* the missing blank: Russell's glasses. *That* was why he hadn't seen the pitchfork; he had taken his glasses off. And, strangely, no one had been able to discover what had become of them. He'd had them on in the hatch; Ada had noticed them shining; but they weren't in the loft and they weren't in the hay.

Afterward, the mow being thoroughly searched, the hunt failed to turn them up, and Mr. Blessing, the town constable, investigating the accident, had declared it a puzzling thing.

It was.

"Slow, huh?" Unmistakably Holland, the throaty timbre, the slightly mocking tone. Leaning indolently against the newel post, twirling Father's necktie in one hand, still wearing his Sunday suit. To Niles's "You forgot to wind it," he replied, "No, little brother, your turn last week."

Niles returned the stool to the closet; closed the door. Warped, it refused to shut all the way and he pressed his back against it, trying to get the latch to click. "You forget sometimes; it's not good to let the clock run down," he told Holland, "it's very old. Old things should be treated with care."

Holland put on a prissy face and, miming an aged person with a cane, recited, " 'Who touches a hair of yon gray head dies like a dog—march on, he said.' Okay, Barbara Fritchie." He laughed and blew on his harmonica.

"Cripes—cut that out!" Niles looked askance at the breach of decorum; quickly Holland adopted a sober expression.

"Jeeze," he whispered, "I'm sorry—I forgot." His contrition was unavailing, for in a second George Perry's red face appeared at the door, crew-cut hair, gray and spiky like a sea urchin, eyes pale and haggard. "Hey, pipe down out here, can't you?" he whispered urgently; Niles thought Holland looked (and properly so) sheepish as he shoved his instrument behind his back and, chastened, scuffed a toe at the carpet.

Appropriate apologies were made, the door closed again and, over Uncle George's helpless pleading came the louder sobs of Aunt Valeria.

"Please, Vee, don't. Chickie? Please don't cry any more. Try, can you—for me—for Russell? Please?"

"Who touches a hair of *that* yon gray head," Holland breathed, joking as he stole along the gallery and listened at the door. "Aunt Vee's going away."

"She is? To a hospital?" Niles came to stand beside him.

"No, she's going on a trip. I heard Mr. Tuthill say the change would ease her."

"I guess it would. She's very unhappy." He wondered what might be done to cheer her up. Not much, he supposed; when people died, people cried a lot; but that's what death seemed to be, always crying, hurting, remembering . . .

Niles went to the hall window and raised the shade, feeling the sun stream through the lace curtain. "I've got a word for you," he said; saw Holland prick up his ears.

"What?"

" 'Asinine.' "

"*Ass*-inine." Holland chortled. "Sounds dirty."

Niles's look was superior. "Means 'stupid' or 'silly.' Like a jackass."

"Where'd you hear it?"

"Mother."

Holland remained pointedly silent, and Niles, looking across the street, thought how much the leaves on the Joacums' sassafras tree resembled mittens, his eye somehow unable to avoid the shed at the back of the house where Holland had bundled up the oily rags and started the fire. The clapboarding was still burned black. Sassafras mittens, three-, four-, five-fingered leaves. *Sassafras albidum,* according to the Chautauqua roll.

Up in the topmost branches, the arrow—his arrow; no, Holland's, really. But what matter? The bows were gone. Under the tree—not that one, the horse-chestnut tree behind the house, Father had daubed a target. Their birthdays, three years ago; bow-and-arrow presents. Holland's lot with one particular beauty, its shaft banded in bright stripes, the feathers hawk, not hen. His lucky arrow, he declares. A volley at the target. "Wait, guys, let me show you." Father helps them gather up the scattered arrows, patiently shows them proper stance and how to knuckle the shaft with one hand, guide it with the other.

"I hit it—I hit it!" Niles pulls his arrow from a ring; Holland scowling blackly at his own wild shots. Mother from the kitchen: "Dear, telephone—the insurance office." Father goes in while fresh fusillades pepper the target.

"Jeeze!" Holland's arrows continue to miss. Nocking the last to his string, the color-banded one, he watches while Niles, on tiptoe at the tree, reaches to pull out his shafts.

Thwang!

From Holland's bow flies the arrow, wobbling through the air; turning, Niles catches it in the throat.

"Accident!" Holland swears after Dr. Brainard has

gone. "Give the arrow to your brother," Father orders. Enraged, Holland dashes out, sends the arrow flying across the street into the topmost tip of the sassafras tree. And there it is, still, three years later.

And since then? Since the arrow, Holland has somehow ceased caring. Now, more and more, the mocking smile, the Mother Goose rhyme . . . Holland had a Secret, Niles was sure.

Er-roo-aroo-a-roo-o-o!

His train of thought was broken by an aged banty rooster who came pecking hopefully at the gravel down the drive, lifting his legs high off the ground as he strutted along. Holland stuck his head out the window and softly called, "Chanticleer." Ignoring the voice, the bird made husky half-crowing noises in its throat and continued on its way. "Chanticleer!" Holland leaned out, lightly repeating the name and Niles distinctly caught his oblique look, at once quizzical and amused, making a critical study of him, looking from boy to bird and back to boy, his mouth open as though to speak; but in the end he only smiled his lazy crooked smile and shook his head, implying his thoughts were of small consequence. For an instant their looks fused, then Holland shrugged and, his expression unfathomable, left him, went away to change his clothes.

And, holding his breath for the longest time, Niles, his eye again on the rooster, remarked to himself how the stale, faintly scorched odor of Winnie's last ironing still clung about the yellowing folds of the lace curtain.

VI

To Niles, the storeroom was the most glamorous room in the house. Tucked away in the north wing, adjoining Torrie and Rider's bedroom, it was a dusty and cobwebbed museum crammed to overflowing with sheet-draped trunks, boxes of clothing, oddments of costumes and uniforms. Near the door was the twins' wicker cradle, beyond it a dress dummy, a wheelchair, a gilt and painted rocking horse, a tangled marionette dangling on the mirror door of a wardrobe; old friends, all.

Straddling the horse, Niles rested his head and arms along its neck, rocking while the Victrola—Granddaddy Perry's antique machine with the morning glory horn—sounded the crashing chords of *Siegfried's Rhine Journey*.

From the corner of his eye he caught a shadow as it fell across the floor. Quickly he sat up to discover a figure standing in the half-open doorway, watching him.

"I have been everywhere looking for you," Ada said. She had changed her black things for a house dress and tidied her hair. "I might have known you come in here. Are you having a Rainy Day?"

"No. Yes. Sort of. I was listening."

"Ah—*Götterdämmerung*." She came and looked down at him, her brow furrowed. "Are you all right, *douschka?*"

"Sure."

"Uncle George is going to drive your Aunt Valeria up to the station and wonders if you would like to ride along."

"No thanks." Sliding off the horse, he went to take the needle from the record and select another.

"But maybe he don't want to be alone today. Maybe it would be nice for you to ride with him. Besides, you like to see the trains, don't you?"

"Yes. Sometimes. But not just now." He looked steadily at the gouged flooring under his feet. "If Holland comes back, maybe he could go."   *wrong*

He could feel her eye intent upon him. "Has Holland gone away then?"

He sighed. Supposed so. Didn't know where, though. Had he sneaked down to the cave he frequented at Talcotts Ferry? Or down to the freight station to watch the trains? Up to Knobb Street where the tough gang lived? Was he hanging around at the Pilgrim Drugstore? Or had he gone off riding the trolley cars on the Shadow Hills route, a trip out to Babylon, the end of the line?   *fine*

He went to roll up the wheelchair for her to sit in, a sturdy, ugly thing whose rubber-rimmed wire wheels were cracked and hard as rock. Guiding it to a spot opposite the rocking horse, ignoring her set expression, he gently took her hands and tried to press her into the chair (why did she resist him?), where she might sit comfortably.

"Guess what? The clock was slow. I wound it. It was practically run down."

"Indeed. Someone forgot, did they?"

"Well, you know how he gets mixed up."

"Who?"

"Holland. It was his turn."

She put his hands from her, lightly and in no way reprovingly, and in another moment went to lift the window curtain. He came to stand beside her, looking down at the lawn, the pump, the well close by the grove of firs at the edge of the drive. The way she held the curtain aside, it was as though she exhibited for his perusal a landscape: sky, grass, river, trees, a cow or two. Her hooded eyes gazed out across the meadow, the river, and up along the fields on the farthest side, up to the Avalon ridge, beyond, even, across some vast untraveled space, and he could tell she had gone farther yet, even to that farthest point, that faraway place where no one might accompany her, beyond the ridge, beyond the Shadow Hills, to a place where she was alone, aloof, a solitary, pondering—what? witch, perhaps? no, something grander, a goddess, he thought—Minerva, all serene, imperturbable, benign, sprung full-blown from Jove's brow.

Again the record ended; he turned it over and wound the machine. Following introductory scratchings came the rich sonorous notes of a soprano. *Hoyo-to-ho*—Brünnhilde's battle cry.

"Yah," said Ada at last, turning from the window, *"Die Walküre."*

When he had led her back to the chair and gravely seated her, she said, "Niles, don't you think sometimes you blame Holland for things that perhaps are not his fault?"

"Maybe, but it *was* his turn. Well, it *was*, honest to—"

"Niles."

"Gosh." He grinned back at her look. "I remember, don't I, when it's my turn?"

"Is that so much to be proud of?"

"No." He turned this over. " 'Pride goeth before a fall—' "

" 'Pride goeth before destruction and a haughty spirit before a fall.' "

"Have I a haughty spirit?" His query, coming after further consideration, as though acknowledging the possibility, made her laugh.

"Gracious no." She smoothed his hair down and kissed it. She reached for the marionette hanging on the wardrobe door: poor tangled king with its cardboard crown, costumed by her from scraps of velvet and lamé left over from a dress Zan had made for herself, and a saturnine face painted by Holland, the eyes not quite straight: King Cophetua. And where, she asked, working to untangle the strings, was the beggar-maid he loved? Niles dug out a hatbox, rummaged, produced a raggedy, woebegone figure, tried to make her bow at the waist, and laughed when she slipped through his fingers to drop into a broken heap in the corner.

"What did you say?" he said, returning to her and the marionette dangling before her.

"How's that? Did I say something? Why, I must have been talking to myself, mustn't I? That is a sure sign of age, I expect."

"You're only as young as you feel, that's what Mr. Pennyfeather says." A smile, both spontaneous and disarming, broke across his face briefly, then dimmed, clouds before sun.

"I went in to see Mother."

"*Yah*, I looked for you there."

"She's nervous today."

"I know."

"I guess it's because of the funeral and all."

"I am glad everyone remembered to speak a word to Mr. Angelini after the service." She shook her head. "That poor soul, he is being made to suffer so for his carelessness. We must remember to try to smile him up so he does not feel quite so guilty. Accidents will happen."

"That's what Holland said. Is Aunt Valeria really going away?"

"Yes. For a visit. She has a friend in Chicago, one she went to school with."

"That'll be good. Doesn't she have folks?"

"No, dear. Mr. Russell and his wife went down on the Titanic over twenty years ago."

He had forgotten. That was why Granddaddy Perry had generously arranged for them to be married in Pequot Landing, right downstairs in the parlor with the minister saying the do-you's in front of the fireplace and the stair banister garlanded by Grandmother Perry with laurel and apple blossom.

"Aunt Vee's very unhappy, isn't she?" Niles said after a while.

"Yes."

"Mother is too. Tomorrow I'm going down to the Center and buy her a present to smile her up." He paused to review the available merchandise. "Do you think she might like some Mexican jumping beans?"

Ada hid her amusement. "I don't see why not. I imagine jumping beans might be very cheerful. And shall you please ask at Miss Josceline's if the tube of crimson lake I ordered has come in? I should like to do a painting of the roses before they go by."

"Yes'm." The music ended and he got up to change the record again. In a moment the high tenor voice of John McCormack filled the room.

"Isn't that 'The Minstrel Boy'?" she asked. "I haven't heard it in years. It used to be a favorite of Daddy Perry's, I remember." Bemused, she hummed a snatch of the Irish air; "Strange, how one forgets the words."

"Ada?"

"Yes, dear?"

"Why did Brünnhilde ride into the fire?"

"My, what made you think of that, the Wagner music? Why, in those days, that is what the women did. It was called immolation. They offered themselves on the pyre of the beloved."

"Yes, but why?"

"For love, I imagine. When one's love of the beloved is greater than one's love of life or of one's self, one sometimes prefers death. It is not so much an immolation of the body, I think, of one's *physical* being as—" she paused to select her words.

"What, then?"

"As an immolation of the heart."

He thought this over, then; "Was that Mrs. Rowe at the door before?"

"Why, yes. Wasn't that nice of her, she come to bring us a dish over." Their nearest neighbor, Mrs. Rowe, was an elderly widow who lived with a house-keeper-companion, Mrs. Cooney, who "did" for her.

"What did she cook?"

"A meatloaf. Now none of your icks, young man,

meatloaf is perfectly nice. And it was thoughtful of her to bother. She don't have to do things like that." Niles winced: sometimes she sounded so dreadfully "old country." "Yah," "Yas," "dat damn bird." She handed him the marionette, the strings freed at last.

"There; there's your King Cophetua, good as new." She rose and looked at the figure on the floor. "Alas for his beggar maid. Will you stay and listen to some more music or come along with me? I'm going to visit a while with your mother before supper."

He blinked up at her, eyes troubled. "What is it, Ada? What's wrong with Mother? Sometimes she seems fine, just like she used to be. Then she gets—" he shrugged a child's bewilderment—"funny. She gets the time all mixed up. And she can't remember things. She asked if the ashes were taken out and the furnace hasn't been on since April."

"The record, child," she said, nodding at the Victrola, where the end of the disk scraped under the needle. He got up and put the arm back to the beginning again. "You must be patient with your mother," she told him. "She will be all right again, in time—please God"—here she made a cross of her thumb and forefinger in the Russian way and kissed it fervently—"she has had a shock. Her mind—her mind wants to protect itself against pain. And sometimes it takes longer for some people to get over things than others, do you see."

"Yes." Though from his tone it was not clear if he did or did not.

"Also, you must remember that your mother does not rest well. Often she walks the floor far into the morning. Sometimes she does not sleep at all; the light shows under the door until dawn. And this is very bad, because sleep is a most holy thing. It is while we sleep that we get our mind and our imagination filled up again." She shaped a bowl with her gnarled hands. "It is like a deep pool, this imagination, and during the day it gets used up, like water, and when we sleep at night the water we have used during the day gets replaced. And if it is not replaced, if there is none to drink of, we are thirsty. It is from sleep that God gives us our strength and our power and our peace, do you see."

He nodded, impressed by the gravity of her speech. Not to sleep, he decided, must be a very bad thing. "I wish I could help," he murmured, with a turn to the Victrola handle.

"We help one another by understanding one another: that is the only help there is. And the only hope as well."

"Hope." He took this in, turned it over, accepted and, like so much of the rest of the product of her mind, stored it. Listening to the song, he wandered far away, across some darkened landscape where another mocked him and fire failed to warm his body. Out loud he added a final word to all that had preceded.

She turned swiftly and gaped at him. "How's that, child? Death, you say?"

"Yes, it's death," he repeated decidedly, "it's death that Mother can't get over." Dancing the marionette along in the air, he walked back to the window. "That must be awful. Do you think Father felt any pain when he died?"

"We do not know. Hopefully he did not."

"Yes. Hopefully." He hooked the strings over the window latch and lay the puppet on the sill, crossing its arms over its breast. "Russell did, though, I guess." *(The glasses; where were the glasses?)*

"Did what?"

"Felt pain. I mean, falling on a pitchfork, that must really be painful, don't you think?"

"Yes, surely." Another thought. She faced him again. "Niles."

"Yes'm."

"Do I imagine to have been hearing a harmonica?"

He laughed. "No, you hear it. That's Holland. He plays it sometimes." He did not say how he had just made him quit, how it upset Uncle George.

"Where did Holland get the harmonica?"

"Oh—from a friend."

"Who is this friend?"

"Just a friend."

"And this—friend—gave it to Holland?"

"No." Reluctantly. See? See how she can tell when he's lying?

"Then?"

"Well, the friend didn't exactly *give* it to him. Holland—"

"Yah?"

"—crooked it from him. Or, well, it wasn't exactly a 'him,' it was a 'her,' and it wasn't a friend, it was—"

"Yah?"

"Miss Josceline-Marie."

"Shoplifting? Oh!" she exclaimed in exasperation. "I did not raise any boys to become thieves." Standing at the sill, where the marionette lay, a tiny corpse, she observed a bleak, protracted silence, seeming to have shrunk further within herself, her eyes closed, lost in thought, apparently not at all aware of the tenor voice singing again the old Irish melody.

Nor, leaving the room with a look, did she in any way acknowledge the words:

> *The min-strel bo-oy to the wars is gone,*
> *In the ranks of dea-a-ath you'll find him . . .*

Now there: that's what he meant. Something was bothering her, though she tried to keep it hidden. Something on her mind. A faintly puzzled air—why was she asking questions about the harmonica? It had to do with Holland, he felt certain. All these looks going around: Mother sorrowful (Aunt Vee, ditto); Uncle George, helpless; Winnie tearful; Holland, mysterious; even Mr. Angelini (looking, Niles thought, sort of like a tribal elder, his dark brows lowered—how long the hairs in his eyebrows were— his look hardly ever leaving the back of Holland's head as Mr. Tuthill droned on about blasted buds on the family tree). And now Ada. But you never could tell, with Ada. Her looks were often the strangest of all. Russians, being happy, the happiness oozed out of every pore; it was all around them, like the sun. Unhappiness was hidden, as though it didn't exist. Well, of course she was unhappy about Russell's getting killed on the pitchfork (no sense in hiding that). Everyone was unhappy; Holland too. Holland . . .

And what, Niles asked himself again, had happened to Russell's steel-rimmed glasses that were in the loft?

Alone, humming along with the Minstrel Boy song, Niles looked down to see his hand again drawn, as though by some other, some magnetizing, outside force, to his shirtfront, where it crept inside and removed the tobacco tin. He regarded the face of Prince Albert thoughtfully (even *he* had a Look today!), then unsnapped the lid, raised it, and drew forth the packet of worn blue paper. He unfolded the layers of wrapping—how like the crumpled petals of a rose they were, a blue paper rose—opening it oh-so-gently, that he might not tear the paper further; and for a long time he stared down at its contents, The Thing. The Thing given to him by Holland, that which lay there at the center of the corolla-like layers of tissue, that Thing of shriveled flesh and bone and cartilage that was a severed human finger.

TWO

Getting darker. Little by little the light is waning. Imperceptible changes. I'm actually feeling a bit drowsy. Even after that dinner. (Imagine, *standing in line* for what they throw at you down in the cafeteria!) Later on I won't be able to sleep at all. Never do. If I sleep, I dream. No, not always the same dream, as some do. But, awake, I don't even like thinking about the dreams I have. Hard to see the face on the ceiling. Or Madagascar, whichever. I'm going to be sure to ask Miss DeGroot about that when she comes. (She should have started her rounds by now.) I've been wondering what place it is she thinks it looks like. Maybe it isn't an island after all; maybe it's a country. It does look a little like Spain and Portugal together, don't you think? If you turn your head this way? The whole Iberian peninsula? If you use your imagination a little. Even though Miss De-Groot is Pennsylvania Dutch—big hands, big feet, big nose, the horsy kind—she's got a lively imagination. I suppose if she looked long enough at that spot she'd probably see it as the Abominable Snowman or something.

I think imagination's a healthy thing. Makes so much more possible to one, doesn't it? I know; you're probably saying Holland never had that sort of imagination; but you're wrong. He had imagination all right. Lots of it. It isn't all Niles, you know. Not by a long shot. Do not imagine I am predisposed in his favor as a simple matter of course; if you think this, then I have led you up the garden path.

Given your druthers, which of the pair would you prefer? I am more inclined to identify with Holland; his stamp seems, to me, to be the less counterfeit. My predilection for the underdog, no doubt, and every underdog shall have his day, to coin a phrase. Believe me, Niles is not entirely the paragon he appears, nor Holland quite the knave. People like Holland are, it seems to me, by far the more engrossing; that is to say, endearing. Their ways are winning indeed, but who is unwilling to be won by such charm? Consider: I have described for you a Niles warm, sympathetic, innocent, virtuous, a little droll—fine, to a point—a child possessed of a certain, clear sentience, and certainly a most genuine one. On the other hand, the picture painted of Holland is nearly villainous: aloof, independent, mocking, a cold, wintry boy, and as we have only a moment ago seen, a thief. But here a question arises: why then does Niles engage in such emulation? Such imitation? Why wear his sibling's shoes? Wonder at his whereabouts? Miss him? Why lie, not on his own bed, but on his brother's, staring at that face, up there in the plaster, the watermark face, like this one here, in this room?

Ah, you may say, but Niles is lonely. Agreed; and who then are Holland's friends? The Knobb Street gang? The older boys whistling at the girls outside the Pilgrim Drugstore up at Packard Lane? Do not believe it. Why does Niles watch Holland off to ride the streetcars? And, more to the point, why does he not ride, himself? And, what, I wonder, is the particular significance he attaches to those streetcars as they rattle past the house, the house that was pulled down even before the advent of the buses on the Shadow Hills route? Discovering this would, I think, unravel much of the mystery.

Niles is generous, you say. Agreed. But what of the gifts he has received from Holland? The ring, the blue packet? Admit it—taken by and large, Holland is an entrancing character. Surely he is. And that smile—nonpareil; who could stay mad at him for long?

Not Niles, assuredly, whose smile is no less celestial, and Niles, who knows his twin better than anyone, will defend Holland to the death.

See if he doesn't.

You have perhaps observed, as I have, how the Hollands of this world are sometimes moved by a depth of passion unlikely to be found in the average child of like age. How their hatreds seem scarcely less ingrained than those to be found in the more mature personality. Yes, you say, you have heard of that shocking business behind the schoolhouse with the little girl, but who of us has not engaged in such frivolous investigations; moreover, the girl was older than he and should have known better. And if Holland did burn down a shack, who was hurt? Not much harm was done, and Ed Joacum was known to have been insurance-poor. As for that much-talked-about business concerning the Talcott boy, assuredly Holland *was* there (he himself admitted it) and assuredly the boy *did* drown, but one ought to discredit—as I have always been inclined to do—any oblique allusions to the ac-

cident, except for the fact of the boy's limp, that one
shorter leg which for somebody of Holland's discrim-
inate and sensitive nature must have seemed monstrous enough. He detested the ugly and the grotesque, I will admit; though, for him, as for most of
us, it exerted a certain macabre fascination.

Which brings me to the Firemen's Fourth of July
Carnival, grotesque enough in some of its aspects,
and which, in a manner of speaking, is a beginning—
this at a time when Russell had been buried for several weeks and already most of the family's thoughts
of the death had faded into an increasingly dim past.

Oh—I should mention that there was at that time
a new girl in town. She boarded with some people on
Church Street and worked at the Ten Cent Store,
demonstrating the latest song hits on an upright piano. She was called Rose Halligan but, though she
had only been in Pequot Landing a few months, the
boys already had a sobriquet for her . . .

I

"Hey Roundheels!" ← Prostitute

Dressed in a tight skirt and a blouse the color of dried blood buttoned over a sparrow chest, Rose Halligan ogled the cars on the Ferris wheel. Star-pricked with lights, the contraption turned fitfully, dipping couples out of the dusk and ladling them high into the air. A loudspeaker braying "On the Isle of Capri" vied with the tinny mechanical clatter of the merry-go-round calliope and the electric splat of ladycrackers and cherry bombs.

At the series of hot whistles greeting her from one of the cars, Rose wiggled a shoulder in disdain, tossed her head, and looked away. Rose Halligan didn't mess with the young fry. With a wink to Holland, Niles waved, called "Woo-woo," while the ground rose in a flat plane and quickly receded.

"Carmen Lombardo sings through his nose," he remarked of the music while the car jerked spasmodically, moved, stopped, moved again, then all at once lurched to the topmost position of the wheel, others below dropping to disgorge their loads and board new ones. He looked down at the crowd milling about the postage-stamp lot where a small, tawdry carnival had been thrown together, offering under the sponsorship of the Pequot Landing Fire Department thrills and excitement for one night only. On either side of a narrow avenue carpeted with a debris of strewn popcorn and crumpled Dixie cups, booths, shabby, faded, limp, furnished third-rate amusement: Win-a-Doll; Madame Zora, Stargazer; Chan Yu the Disappearing Marvel; Zuleika, the World's Only True Half Man-Half Woman. *Hermaphrodite*

Bang! Whoosh!

Somewhere a rocket exploded; now and then a Roman candle showered gorgeous rain-light on a lawn; a child sliced crazy zigzags out of the night with a Fourth of July sparkler. The wheel creaking, Niles put his head back and took in the expanse of black sky.

"That's Gemini," he said, picking out a constellation.

"You're crazy," Holland told him.

"Sure it is—see? That's Taurus there, and that's Cancer over *there,* and right there, between those two bright little stars, that's Castor, the yellowish one, and Pollux. The Twins."

Holland slanted a look at him, then, impatient for the wheel to move again, began rocking the car and while Niles continued his survey of the sky—over there was Ursa Major, and see that seedlike cluster? Cassiopeia's Chair—the thrum of the harmonica made a pleasant accompaniment to the moment.

"Holland?" Niles said, when the music stopped. *not when Holland just playing*

"Mmm?"

"What did you call Mrs. Rowe?"

"Hm?"

"What did you call Mrs. Rowe that day—when she found you in her garage?"

Holland chuckled; repeated some words that shocked even Niles. "Did you, honest? What'd she do?"

"I told you, she chased me home." This time his chuckle was a little more than wry, a little less than savage. "But just wait."

"Wait for what?"

"Wait till Old Lady Rowe gets it." And Niles noted how, as Holland made the remark, the flushed exuberance of his face evened out, leaving him with a placid, introspective expression, his narrowed eyes thoughtfully examining some private phantom. Niles considered his profile against the dark sky: Holland, he thought; Holland. He needed him—they needed each other. That was the thing. He was—what?—dependent on him. Without Holland, he felt some unidentifiable part of him had been lost.

"Look! There's Arnie La Fever." Niles pointed down at the ground. "And look—that's Torrie!"

Arms about each other's waists, Torrie and Rider stood at the Win-a-Doll booth, beguiled by the spinning wheel. Torrie was not really a Perry at all. After three childless years, Alexandra and Vining had found a four-year-old to adopt; twelve months later the twins arrived. Everyone liked Torrie. Her pixyish features were in direct contrast to the Perrys', who had always managed somehow to look regal. (Grandmother Perry was given to Queen Maryish toques and carried a walking stick before they took her away.) More petite, with thinner, less fleshed-out bones, Torrie had reddish hair and brown eyes and lots of freckles. *Gamine,* as the French would say, charming and gay and lighthearted, with both spirit

and humor, determined to make Rider Gannon a
good wife. Eight months pregnant, she was showing
rather full, though Dr. Brainard expected her to go
full term.

Rider laid two coins on numbered squares, and the
operator spun the wheel again. The leather flap,
clacking in and out of the wheel's perimeter, gradually slowed. Niles, perched on high, could see that
Torrie hadn't won. She stood for a long moment,
yearning at the row of prizes ranged behind the
counter while Rider generously dug again in his
pocket. She shook her head and drew him away from
the booth—and temptation—and back into the
crowd.

"Too bad," Niles said glumly, thinking how, with
her awkward flat-footed gait, Torrie walked like a
penguin carrying a watermelon. "But she's going to
have a pretty baby."

Holland tossed a scornful look down at the depart-
ing couple. "Is she?" he said mysteriously, and the
Ferris wheel began to turn.

When at last it had completed its prescribed number of revolutions, ending the ride, Niles ran down
the ramp and pressed through the throng behind
Holland. Someone jostled him: Arnie La Fever,
whose fat and limp features evoked a picture of Russell Perry, his face shoved into a bobbin of spun
candy; bits of the stuff came away on Niles's arm,
looking like some unnatural fungus growth. He
touched his arm, felt the sticky confection dissolve,
leaving an uncomfortable residue glistening like snail
tracks on his bare skin. He sucked his fingers and
wiped them on a handkerchief. "Hi, Arnie," he

called, but Arnie had disappeared in the crowd. You didn't see him much; mostly he was sick and his mother kept him out of school.

"Try yer luck?" the man at the Win-a-Doll booth was calling, "tin cints is all it takes folks just a thin dime win and you get a dollie fer yer girlie." Niles inspected the dolls: funny-looking things, they had round brown kewpie-doll faces garishly painted with idiotic, implike expressions—more leer than smile, a row of cheap duplicate countenances attesting to the inept workmanship of some would-be artisan. Below the waist was a full skirt of peach-colored fabric, forming a lampshade, with an electric cord running underneath. To demonstrate, the man stuck the plug in a socket and the doll lit up, the skirt glowing a warm orange.

"Here we go folks here we go," he cried, banging on the counter of numbered squares, "ev-ree-body try yer luck." He zipped the wheel and as several onlookers chanced their money, Niles laid a dime on number 10. His eyeballs spiraling in their sockets, he tried to follow the blurred path of the numbers on the revolving wheel. Eventually he could make out his numeral; it slowed and stopped on the opposite side; again he tried; and yet again, with no success. On his fourth attempt, when the wheel had almost stopped, the pointer crawled into the 5 sprocket, then, at the very last, as if by magic, pushed its way into number 4. *The game? or rigged?*

"There y'are, kiddo," the man said, handing him his prize. Niles carried the lamp over to Holland, who stood eyeing the proceedings from the shadow of a dilapidated tent. Cripes—the Look.

"Jeeze, what d'you want *that* for?" he said.

"I won it for Torrie." Niles held it up, arranged the skirt.

"Took you forty cents to get it." Holland reached and turned the doll upside down. "Nothing," he said, looking up under the dress. "Who wants a sissy doll, anyways." Niles took the lamp and watched his twin as he walked over to the entrance of the tent where a poster displayed the picture of a yellow-faced, mustachioed Chinese, his hands hidden in his sleeves, his body resting vertically in an open mummy case.

"Laze 'n gennamin," a voice bawled, "las' chance t'night t'see Chan Yu, the Disappearing Marvel. Twenny fi' cents t'see the Disappearing Marvel Chan Yu, hurryhurryhurry, show's just beginning—"

In the darkness of the tent people had gathered in front of a small stage hung with velvet curtains; from somewhere at the rear issued the scratchy sounds of a phonograph record: an Oriental dissonance of cymbal, bell, and flute. On stage, a spotlight fell upon a large, highly lacquered red cabinet, and on Chan Yu the Disappearing Marvel, standing beside it. Slant-eyed and trying hard to look exotic, wearing long black mustaches and a little cap with a pigtail, he was grandly bowing to thin applause. Producing an ivory-tipped wand, he rapped with it against the cabinet, simultaneously slipping a concealed latch and opening the front panel. Inside was a duplicate cabinet, slightly smaller and lacquered green, which he displayed with flashy magician's gestures. He turned the box, rapping again to reveal a third, blue, a fourth, black, and finally a fifth, gold.

Hands folded across his chest, the magician

stepped back into the cabinet. After a short pause, during which the needle was raked across the record as an invisible hand restarted the music, a girl glided onstage in kimono and stiff black wig. Chan Yu, his eyes closed, a red light making a weird mask of his impassive features, his makeup and mustaches obviously fakes, appeared to be dead. The assistant closed the panel; there was a click and she rotated the cabinet; next, the black panel shut, the box turned again —blue, green, red.

The music increased in volume and in the dim light the audience waited, hushed and expectant.

Niles looked at Holland for a moment, then whispered, "Let's try it."

"What?"

"The game. Let's *do* it—see if we can figure the secret." Satisfied that Holland was concentrating, Niles began mentally examining the nest of boxes. What does it feel like? What is the mystery of it, the truth? The magician seems to be in the cabinet— that's the appearance of it; but he isn't, at least not for long, that's the reality. Boxes; shiny, smooth, lacquered surfaces, brass-banded, escutcheoned. Incense, some exotic fragrance. A box within a box within a box. Another and another. Gold, black, blue, green, red. A nest. A riddle. A trap? Let's see. Hold your breath inside the box, in the dark; wait for the moment. Cymbals and bells and flutes flourishing to mask the noise of a wire being tripped, while below a trap is sprung. Now drop flat in the dirt beneath, roll from under the stage, behind the tent, strip off the mustaches and pigtail, fling away the cap and robe. In their place a suit of black paper, shoes, hat, everything paper: a Chinese funeral suit. Out at the back of the tent, in at the front, mingling in the audience. Chan Yu the Disappearing Marvel.

Again the light, the music doused, the girl assistant clicking the latches, smiling as she opens the panels, each in turn, all the boxes empty, one after another; cries of astonishment and applause as Chan Yu is discovered lounging casually among the onlookers: he lifts his hat and bows. Hurray, Chan Yu!

Lights up to full signaled the end of the show and the audience chattered their way from the tent. Outside, Niles took a deep breath and, nodding with a professional air, said, "So that's how he does it."

Holland was silent and looked at the ground.

"Right?" Niles prodded.

After a while, a grudging "Yes," but Niles could see the way it was—Holland turned away, his expression hostile, eyes sullen. They exchanged a long look, then Holland stepped out of the bright swarm of papery moths and walked away, leaving a solitary Niles, alone with the tinkle of bells and cymbals, the whisper of a flute floating in his ears.

A light wind chased a flurry of soiled rubbish end over end along the patchy ground, flapping tent canvas as it went. The hum of the crowd seemed far removed. In the darkened space between two tents, like the deserted alley off a main thoroughfare, two figures huddled: Rose Halligan, the piano player from the Ten Cent Store, and a man Niles recognized as the operator of the Ferris wheel, both lolling against a guy rope, his neck hunched, his hands working at her, fumbling at the buttons of her red blouse, running across her front, eagerly meeting her own frantic fingers.

Niles could hear her low amused laugh as he moved away. He overtook Holland at the freak show tent, where, under faded, gaudy posters shrieking of meretricious and unbelievable sights to be discovered inside—"Sexational—Shocking—Seductive"—a muffin-faced man, cigar butt plugging the corner of his mouth like a cork, leered while he barked his spiel.

"Laze 'n gennamin, stip right up! See the Wonder Pig, Bobo the Wonder Pig, five feet, not four but five, the fifth foot right where it does the most good, see the great colossal-headed baby, before your very eyes, Nature's mistake, the hideous horrible hydrocephalic monster! Watch Mister and Missus Katz, the Arkansas Little Folk, lovers even as you and I! Marvel at Zuleika, the Maltese morphadite, she has somethin' for everyone, laze 'n gennamin, a gen-u-wine morphadite, half-man half-lady, shows you the works, real sexy!" Swiveling his cigar to the other side of his mouth, he poked a cane and said, "Beat it, pretty boy, you ain't old enough fer this here show. You Boy Scouts keep yer minds above yer belts and none of this here sort of stuff." After a brief and obscene pantomime, he commenced his spiel again. "Stip right up, laze and gennamin—"

Holland glared and put his tongue out at the man's back. With a grin, Niles followed him as he ducked out of the moth-infested light. Through an alley between two tents. At the rear, the chrome gleam of a pocket knife; a slit in the canvas panel. Down on all fours. Inside, the air was smoky and stale; on the trampled sod gobbets of hawked spit glistened.

Several feet directly ahead was the back of a platform, hung with grommeted canvas curtains on a wire forming a three-sided cubicle with one wall open. From within came the sound of a child speaking. Holding his breath, Niles moved cautiously in the direction of the voice.

"Stomach settled any, Stanley?" it was inquiring solicitously.

"Eh," came the disgusted reply.

"All that drugstore stuff's no good, for Chrise sakes, Exlax, Feenamint, Milka Magnesia. I'm tellin' ya, Stan—what yew need's a good enema."

Peering over Holland's shoulder around the side of the cubicle, Niles saw a prim pair of midgets, Mr. and Mrs. Katz, the Arkansas Little Folk. They sat in dolls' chairs with dolls' china laid out on a doll's table. Oblivious of their surroundings, they behaved as though enjoying their own privacy, he plainly bored, staring straight ahead, blinking and sighing, she daintily applying a tomato shade of polish to her baby nails, pausing now and then to blow.

"Hot water and soap suds enema, that's what ya really need," Mrs. Katz prescribed in an ocarina voice.

"Shoot a mile, Tennessee," Mr. Katz said. Niles pictured him "assuming the position" with the rubber hose stuck up his rear and Mrs. Katz holding the red rubber bag in one hand while with the other she whipped the soapsuds to a froth.

"Ya shoulda come to the pitchers this afternoon,

Stanley," she said enthusiastically. "I tole ya yew'd of liked it."

"Whadja see?" he cheeped, bird-like.

Gold Diggers of 1935. It was somethin', lemme tell ya. There was this one number, musta been a hunnert girls, all in white dresses and they's all playing on fiddles, ever' one of 'em."

"Christ, a hundred girls dressed in white playing fiddles and there's people starving in Tuleopa."

"Yeah, Stan, but that's what folks want. It's pure excapism, that's all. Who wants t'see people starving in the movies—you can see that on the street any day. That's why folks want to excape, see?"

"Shoot a mile, Tennessee," Stanley replied dolefully.

Close by Holland's side, Niles mingled with the spectators, feeling safe from discovery as the sweating, shirt-sleeved forms of the adults hemmed them in. Bored with the midgets, the group shortly passed along to gawk at a man whose face, grotesque and seamed with livid scar tissue, had no nose, and who rasped pathetically as he puffed a cigarette through a metal lens-like aperture inserted at the base of his throat, releasing the smoke in a cloud through the hole where his nose should have been.

Next there was Bobo, the five-legged pig, an anomaly which failed to produce much interest from Holland, who merely eyed it, coldly, as if he thought it should perform tricks as well. As for Niles, the animal's freakish anatomy caused him to think of Arnie's father, Mr. La Fever, who was with the circus, and something of an anomaly himself, for if he didn't have five limbs he was at least tri-legged.

At the end of the tent the group stopped to stare at a sagging platform where, seated beneath a fringed and beaded lampshade, another attraction presented itself: Zuleika, the Maltese Hermaphrodite—a bizarre and epicene creature whose eyes, dark and wet and slightly popped, were penciled around in some black substance, with a pile of carefully dressed hair curled in black ringlets glossy with brilliantine. The hairless, flaccid body was draped in a sleazy kimono whose coppery sheen glinted like a snake's skin. Gold rings were squashed onto plump fingers which toyed seductively with moist, rouged lips. The half-parted robe revealed one hand closing and opening rhythmically upon a quasi-developed breast, the nipple of which was startlingly large and scarlet-colored. On tiptoe beside Holland, gaping, Niles watched while the creature, with a pleased smile, covered the breast, closed the robe and fastidiously re-tied the sash. He —or was it a she?—changed position slightly and opened the skirt of the robe, teasingly, a little at a time, playing with the onlookers, rolling the eyes heavenwards, displaying finally a dark V of wiry hair wedged between plump, womanish thighs.

It must be a lady, then. Niles looked for confirmation from Holland, and was struck by his scornful expression, the eyebrows fractionally raised, the corners of the mouth lifted in scant contempt.

Thighs spread, and with an arch smile, the creature reached with exquisite fingers to extract from the patch of hair a small white fleshy growth which, like an elastic band, was stretched several times to its utmost length. Then, a supercilious smirk marking her superiority over the curious spectators, she tucked the nub of flesh from sight and, disdainfully closing the robe, crossed her knees, signaling, apparently, an end of the exhibition. When she had arranged her features into a bored mask and reached to extinguish the light, Niles got the impression it was a man—or boy, anyway—but certainly not a woman; in the dark he?—she? lit a cigarette, the flame illuminating for an instant the black eyes which glittered jewel-like, the languidly lowered lids heavy with a greasy film. Inexplicably, Niles felt a sudden wave of pity melting through him; poor, poor freak. He glanced at Holland, whose eyes, narrow, flat, opaque, stared back at the creature in disdain.

Another surge: the crowd swept along close to the entrance, stopping before a rickety oilcloth-covered table. On it sat a large glass laboratory jar, filled with a clear, viscous-looking liquid; in it, hideously floating, its skin white like the underbelly of a frog, limbs, organs, features all formed in detailed miniature, was a male human infant. Strands of hair waving gently in the preservative grew from a skull swollen to more than twice its normal size, the shiny skin stretching taut across it, the astonished eyes wide and milk-glazed like those of a dead fish, rubbery lips gaping as if the thing had drowned or been strangled in the middle of a scream.

The crowd, thrilled by the grisly horror, rubbernecked for a while, pushing and jostling for a closer look. Then, laughing or shivering according to their natures, they gradually filed from the tent. Turning from the repulsive sight, feeling his stomach rise and drop, Niles unconsciously fingered his shirt for the tobacco tin. "Holland—" he began, then blinked, appalled by the look of fascination on the other's face.

"Changeling," Holland whispered hoarsely, tapping the glass.

"What?"

"Little changeling child." His tapping of the jar agitated the liquid and the baby bobbed to and fro, rising and falling; rising again, head back, pale puckered lips breaking the surface as though gasping for breath. "Little baby," he taunted bitterly, "pretty little baby." He turned to Niles. "That's what Torrie's is going to look like, just like that. Won't that be nice?"

Niles was dumbfounded. "No—no, it won't. It'll be beautiful—"

"Will it?" Holland chuckled wickedly. "If you think so, wait and see." And he went away, laughing, into the darkness.

"Hey you!" the barker cried as Niles, hurrying to catch up, appeared at the entrance. Clutching his doll-lamp, he turned and ran in the opposite direction, fumbling for the slit at the rear of the tent. In another moment he had slipped through the canvas, leaving behind only a frayed and gaping hole. Back in the dim light leaking through from the entrance, on the shiny black oilcloth that decked the rickety table, sat the glass laboratory jar, its tiny specimen still bobbing in the solution, the blank marble eyes dead, staring, the mouth pink and toothless, open in its silent scream.

II

In a chair on the veranda, Ada rocked in the soft light coming from inside the house and fingered the coverlet she had been binding with careful stitches. Her hands, the joints red and swollen, were seldom idle; there was always something: beans to snap, fruit to preserve, socks to knit, a scrap quilt, a coverlet to sew; day in, day out, till year's end. And begin again. It was the way she'd been taught. But now it was too dark to work any longer, and she rocked to the strains of music from the parlor while dusk fell about her.

At a sound she lifted her wrinkled lids. Niles crossed the lawn, his shoes making slick, whispering sibilances on the wet grass. Inside, at the top of the stairs, the clock struck ten booming notes.

"I was hoping you'd be up." He blinked at her in the light lying in square patterns about her feet. "Mrs. Rowe didn't take her flag down," he observed, handing her a paper cup of ice cream.

"Poor thing, she is forgetful. Patriotic but forgetful," she said, taking the cup and the small wooden spoon. "Ah, you knew." Eagerly she lifted the cover from the half-melted contents, peeled away the circle of opaque paper on the back and peered at the picture. "Who shall it be? Oh, I *like* Anne Shirley! I'll just put her in my collection, shall I? *Yah* and strawberry, too. My favorite. *Spasiva, douschka.* How was the fair?"

"Carnival," he corrected, and took the time to describe for her the Ferris wheel, the fireworks, the crowd. "And I won this for Torrie. It's a *bood-war* lamp."

"A doll into a lamp, imagine. See that wicked little face."

"And two midgets," he went on, laughing about the impending enema. And Zuleika, the hermaphrodite, and the magician.

"What was he like?"

"A Chink—I mean Chinaman, sort of," he said and told her about Chan Yu's trick. "And he ended up in a paper suit like they wear for funerals."

"Oriental thrift," she replied with a wry twist.

"And I know how he did the trick." He told her how he'd discovered the method by concentrating on the nest of lacquered boxes. "Holland couldn't feel what it was like." Well, she knew about that anyway; it was seldom he and Holland saw things the same.

"And there was a pig," he went on, "a five-legged pig."

"What was that like, I wonder?"

He chortled. "I thought it was like Mr. La Fever." She acknowledged his little joke and he sat on the step while she ate the ice cream. Through the open window came the soft saxophone sounds of a dance orchestra over the Atwater-Kent radio. *Waltz Time,* that would be; Abe Lyman's band. "Do you want to hear *First Nighter* tonight?"

"Is that next?"

"Uh-huh." From his position on the step he could

just see over the sill into the parlor. The curtains were pulled aside to let the breeze in and his eye drifted to Mother and Her Boys, smiling down from over the mantel. That was where Aunt Vee and Uncle George had gotten married, right there in the parlor. He recalled Torrie's tale—no one else in the family ever mentioned it—about how Aunt Vee had come down the stairs in her bridal gown to stand before the wedding guests at the fireplace. And how, halfway through the service, Grandmother Perry had sprung from her chair with a cry to tear the veil from Aunt Vee's head; how she had clawed at the garlanded banister when they led her upstairs; how she had cried out again when they came to take her away.

Finished with her ice cream, Ada laid the Dixie cup and spoon aside, wiping off the cardboard lid on her handkerchief and placing it in her sewing basket. How peaceful it was, sitting there in the quiet night. Partially screened by the branches of the elms, the moon etched into the steel-dark plate of grass fine silvery cross-hatchings. Somewhere a night bird sang. Crickets concertized. Boards answered the creaking chair, a hum along the metal rails announced the streetcar. In the blackness beyond the veranda, out of the patch of electric light, a swarm of fireflies hung suspended, their thoraxes and underbellies emitting a Morse code of phosphorescent dots and dashes, secret messages, Niles thought, for him.

"I saw Mrs. Pennyfeather on the way home. She said she's going to ask you to do the flowers for church Sunday."

"Oh? That will be nice. I must give it some thought. How is Laurenza?"

"She's fine. She asked for everybody." Mrs. Pennyfeather, who had charge of the Congregational choir, under the supervision of Professor Lapineaux, lived with her husband several blocks up the road. Instead of a mayor, Pequot Landing had a town board of selectmen, and Simon Pennyfeather, who was blind, had for many years held the post of First Selectman. He had been Vining's oldest friend and was the executor of his will. Each year there was held a memorial dinner in honor of Granddaddy Perry, and Simon Pennyfeather's jokes always kept the company which gathered in the dining room holding their sides.

"What's wrong," Niles asked. Suddenly Ada was sitting tight-lipped, her hands clutched in her lap.

"Nothing—it's all right." She was fighting the agony in her fingers.

"Does it hurt—have you got the pain again?"

Frightened for her, he raced to get her pills from the bottle over the sink, codeine, to relieve the pain. "Is it gone?" he asked when she had swallowed one with the water he brought her.

"Soon," she told him, and he took the glass back and filled it with cold root beer from the refrigerator, adding several cubes of ice and squeezing in half a lemon to make it tart, just the way she liked it. He returned to her and she sipped the drink, then set the glass down. "*Spasiva,*" she thanked him, catching her breath. He sat again on the step; after a time her face seemed to relax and take on its natural color and she leaned her head back, the chair making *slip-slip* sounds on the raffia runner beneath the rockers. An expression he could not fathom played over her features. With her eyes closed, her head keeping ever so slight time, it was as though the music she listened to was played for her ears alone.

What was she thinking, he wondered, with that tiniest of smiles curling at the corners of her lips? And, as if answering his unspoken question, she made a little face and wrinkled her nose.

"Ach," she said without raising her lids, "Tchaikovsky—with saxophones. Saxophones are the devil's instruments."

That was the Russian in her. Ada Katerina Petrichev. And being Russian, why shouldn't she have her Tchaikovsky pure? It recalled to her her childhood, in the old Russia, that Imperial Russia which existed before the Bolsheviks and the Revolution, the girlhood she loved recounting, he and Holland popped into bed on either side of her, she warming blocks of colored wax with her fingers for them to make little figures, frog, unicorn, angel, and telling them long-ago stories.

Stories of the big estate, the *dacha* outside St. Petersburg where her father worked as the *major domus,* her mother the housekeeper, her two younger sisters chambermaids, and Ada Katerina herself doing all the sewing for Madame, the great lady of the *dacha,* and her little daughter, because, Madame said, how nimble were Ada Katerina's fingers.

Though it was the habit of the servants to be early stirring, Ada Katerina was earlier yet, throwing off the covers of her white iron bed, kneeling on the floor, praying before her icon, then dressing and going abroad to walk solitary along the path between the fields of wild sunflowers, fields spread so wide and far and deep that they seemed unending, stretching away from the path in gentle undulations as far as the eye could see, bobbing and swaying like a sea of gold, on which Ada Katerina had thought a ship might sail away, sail away forever over those waves of flowers, as high as a man's head.

There on the path she felt all the world was yellow, and tranquil. So enormous she could not even begin to imagine how enormous it was. To be alone in that sunflower world was to be at peace, and this was something that belonged to her alone. "Always I would go by myself, for I did not want to talk or chatter like those other magpie girls. And me barefooted—yes, always Ada with her bare feet no matter what *mamuschka* would say, this being in a time when my toes had not corns and bare feet was always such delight for me. I am thinking on these fine mornings how homesick I should be if ever I had to leave my sunflowers, and how contented I was in my heart. And I could see things. That is, one kind of thing in another kind of thing, things that were not really there at all. And I could find faces and figures in almost anything, in everything: in the clouds and in the trees and in the water. On the ceiling, even."

Oh, yes, they had a face too, on *their* ceiling.

"And then, afterward, came the game."

Oooooh, the game.

Stroking her hair with a brush as she leaned back against the pillows of her white iron bed, modestly, "Oh, well, the game is not so hard, you know. Not so special." (Or so she made out, though they knew better.) "A little pretend game is all. There is a trick to it, do you see? Just—well, *thinking,* that was all. Pick

something and look at it. Pretty soon you are looking
and looking and looking at it. And you are thinking
about that one thing, you are thinking so hard, and
sometimes you squeeze up your eyes and you remember the picture of the thing behind your eyelids, and
the sun is making all colored dots behind there, and
then you open your eyes and you can see what that
thing is really like. What it really *is*. Looking into it,
you pass through it."

It's a trick, isn't it?

"*Yas,* I think so, but if a trick, it is a Russian one."
As if that explained it all.

But how? *How?*

"Well, Russians, if you can see it, feel more than
do most people. Deep down. Russians, I suspect,
have a sixth or seventh sense that God didn't give to
most other people. They have a lot more of what do
you call it—" Thinking a moment. "Insight. *Yas.*
That is the word. Insight. They are mystical folk,
Russians, and," she added jokingly, "the drunker
they get, the more mystical they get. Worse than the
Irish, Russians."

But *they* could do it too.

"But of course, you are half Russian. What should
you expect?" Niles

But tell some more. Tell about the little daughter
and the dog, the mad dog that lurked! All excited,
waiting for the familiar tale.

"Well," she would always begin, "that damn dog
was a terror about the place, a big Russian hound
they used on the wolves, and what belonged to the
gamekeeper; named Zoltan, that dog. I am standing
by the thicket near the woods when he goes by,

skulking at the heels of Wasili, who is the
gamekeeper, and I look at it, and I am thinking what
nobody else is thinking, that dog Zoltan is mad."
Tapping her forehead. "Not yet completely, but it is
coming, slowly, you know, and he must be watched.
I say to myself, 'Beware of mad dogs lurking, for
lurking, they shall bite.' Then I think, 'And biting,
shall bite again.' I hear my mind say this to me two,
three times, whenever that Zoltan goes by, and I believe it. Well, one afternoon Madame is in the summer house with the little daughter and some other
ladies, and I am bringing for them *koschnoijca,* tea
and little cakes arranged on a tray, and the gentlemen are away between the stone deer where was the
croquet lawn. The ladies are all talking together and
I am laying out the tea things and I see how the little
daughter is going down the steps and over the grass
to watch the croquet, and behind her at the edge of
the lawn by the wood is that thicket, all dark and
evil-looking with prickly brambles and I am forgetting altogether about the tea things as I am looking
and looking there at that thicket. I am thinking, what
is there about it? And I say to myself, well, a crow is
sure walking on my grave. Now, at once the hair at
the back of my neck is rising, I can feel it, and I am
standing up from my chair with all the lovely tea
things crashing to the floor, and my hand is reaching
out to stop whatever it is I know must happen."

Yes, they say solemnly, knowing what must happen, waiting breathlessly for her to go on. Now there
follows the pale astonished look on the face of Madame, her little cry as Ada Katerina dashes from the
summerhouse, across the lawn to the child, who is

smiling at the croquet players, who do not know anything of what is happening, and Ada snatches up the
child just as the great mad dog Zoltan plunges from
the thicket where it is lurking, its terrible jaws all
white and foamy. It means to eat up the little daughter—"*Ach,* so strong the jaws, so sharp the teeth"—
but instead it gives a fierce bite on Ada's leg, trying to
fell her. But Ada has pulled away, the back of her
dress in the dog's teeth, and, trailing blood, runs to
safety in the summerhouse, where the child is given
into the grateful mother's arms, and then, oh then,
the pain of the doctor treating the terrible bite on
Ada's leg, which to this day still makes her limp
when the weather turns cold, or she is tired or upset.

Madame now took the brave Ada Katerina into
her care, giving her a gift of money and a dress as
well, one from her own wardrobe, and some ribbon
for her hair, and never saying anything about the
broken teacups, which were costly. And how strange,
Madame thinks, that Ada had known about the mad
dog lurking in the thicket; how could she have
known? But, *Beware when mad dogs lurk, for lurking
they shall bite,* was all Ada could reply to her queries,
remembering always to add, *And biting, shall bite
again.* So it became common knowledge in those
parts that Ada Katerina had the Gift, and playfully
they would tease her, Ada Katerina, be for us a bee, a
flower, an owl.

Sometimes in the evenings Madame would call for
her sewing girl, who was now permitted the pleasure
of reading books to her as well, and to come out into
the summerhouse where sat all the ladies and gentlemen, and Ada Katerina, very shy in her new dress

embroidered with flowers, but mysterious looking, too, her hair with ribbons braided in it and hanging about her shoulders like a gypsy's, seated on a stool at the great people's feet, would tell what it was like to be a bee, a flower, an owl.

Ahhh. Yes, Holland and Niles loved that part. But what about Zoltan. You didn't tell what happened to the lurking dog!

"Enough, children, time to go to your own beds."

No, no. *Pajalsta, pajalsta!* And, tugging on their hair, each in turn, she would continue.

"*Ach,* that damn dog. Russians, as you know, are most fond of animals, they can love them with a great love, like you love a person, even though they should do a bad thing. So Wasili the gamekeeper would not destroy the dog, refusing to believe that it was mad at all, and he chained it in the stables. But one night Wasili, who had been out on his horse looking for poachers (so they all thought), came home drunk, they said, for they could hear him singing in the wood. Well, when he got in dat stables dere, de horse became frightened of dat dog Zoltan and he must have t'rown dat Wasili and before you know it dat Zoltan has torn Wasili's t'roat out for him!"

Here Ada would become excited, they could tell, listening, for her English always got worse when she was like that. And sometimes she would shiver at the memory and, laughing, say that a crow was walking on her grave.

Now about Grandpapa! Yes, Grandpapa!

Well, it so fell out that Ada Katerina became in love with the son of the gardener, he who tended Madame's roses, Pavel Vedrenya was his name, and he knew all there was to know about flowers, and when they had enough money together they were married, and he bought their passage to America, and thus the clock that stands at the top of the stairs came to the little house in Baltimore where Ada and Grandpapa lived for many years until he died and where he had a glass house full of plants and flowers to sell. The rest of her family dead, Ada paid for the passage of her sisters as well, Josephine and Fania, who was called Fanuschka, so they might come to America also.

But there were always sunflowers, her beloved *pod-solnechniki,* that Ada would plant to remind her of the fields of St. Petersburg and of the Ada Katerina who had been and who was now Ada Vedrenya, sunflowers in her dooryard, along the fence, beside the garage. And when she came to Pequot Landing she put seeds into the earth behind the carriage-house, where they grew tall and these flowers were favorites of all the others, each with its own sun-face to greet her in the summer morning. *As the Sunflower turns on her god, when he sets, The same look which she turned when he rose.* These lines she had found in a book and copied them out, and the thought seemed to please her. But with the passing of the years the flowers reminded her less of the old country and more of her grandsons, with their twin fringes of bright yellow, like the rays of the flowers, and truly, to her, it seemed their shining faces sent forth rays. And it was only sometimes, like this evening, with the Tchaikovsky music on the radio, that she permitted herself to be reminded of white embroidered dresses and ribbons and the soft evenings in the summerhouse on the big _dacha_ at St. Petersburg.

Slip-slip went the rocker. The music over, Ada opened her eyes to smile wistfully at Niles. "Tchaikovsky with saxophones," she muttered, "it is like salami. _Ach,_ I should not complain—I never hear Tchaikovsky hardly before I come to America."

"Why?"

"In Russia there was no place for us to hear music, except Madame sometimes playing her piano, but she always played French songs, never nothing like Tchaikovsky. And in Russia when I was a girl there was no music for the poor people except what we made for ourselves. _Ach,_ how I _love_ the music!"

"Then the Russians should be happier there today."

"Why is that?"

"Because now they have music for the poor people."

"For the poor people, yas. But I'm not sure they're any happier." And from the sadness in her voice he could tell how much she missed the old Russia.

"You miss the sunflowers," he said, reaching to touch her hand across the space between them. "But we have sunflowers too, not too many, but some," he said, as though apologizing for the paucity of flowers. "And butterflies. You love butterflies."

"Here all the sunflowers have dust on their faces," she said, then fell silent and thought for a time. "Well," she said at last, "I shall have to select some flowers for the church service, no? Some larkspur, I think, and coreopsis; perhaps some baby's breath, if it looks to be good."

Larkspur. Coreopsis. He remembered misty mornings with the sun a white disk behind the mist when they would waken her early and lead her into the still-wet meadow where she would pick buttercups and daisies and wild roses; select others from the flower beds: pansies with faces like oriental lions, violas, petunias; making them into floral processions with petal faces, snapdragon horses drawing carriages of Queen Anne's lace.

"Or perhaps some iris," she thought aloud, "an arrangement either side of the pulpit."

"No—one big bowl, and put it on the table under *her.*"

Her. Ada's smile widened. "Her" was the figure in one of the stained glass windows, the Angel of the Annunciation, arriving with the glad tidings, a beautiful piece of work showing her sweeping to earth on giant luminous wings, one hand clasping a lily. It was Niles who had made up a name for her, "The Angel of the Brighter Day," a kind and loving pretend creature whom he fancied as a guardian spirit.

Ada sat up. "What's that you say? Queen Anne's lace?"

GAME/MENTAL BOND

He had *said* nothing; but, "Sure. There's a ton of it in the meadow. I'll pick you some tomorrow." She had read his mind, even as Holland had. The bond between them was undeniable. It was as if an invisible cord ran from his head to hers, and they could telephone to each other, the one sensing the other's thoughts. He always knew before she spoke what she was going to ask him to do: a book from the library, her needlework, a Dixie cup of ice cream, feed oatmeal to her cat . . . except of course now there was no need for oatmeal; the cat was dead.

"And what else did you see at the fair?" Ada asked.

He thought a moment, then described for her the baby in the bottle.

"*Ach,* such things should not be exhibited for children. It shall make nightmares for you."

"No it won't," he assured her. "But it made Holland mad, and he hit the bottle with his hand and ran away.

"But he was mad anyway."

"*Yas?* What does he have to be mad at?"

"Old Lady Rowe."

She shot him a glance.

"I mean Mrs. Rowe." He was hunched forward, eyes on the blinking swarm of fireflies. "Dot-dit ditdit dit-dot-dit-dit dit dit-dit-dit."

"What's that?"

"Morse code. From the fireflies. Better than our crystal set." His look was hopeful. "Can I do it now?"

"What?"

"The game."

Ach, the game. Tonight she felt weary. Usually, where the family was concerned, nothing was an intrusion on her time, her energies. Fix this, please? Do that, would you? Be this. Play that. Play a game, let's? *The* game, *their* game, the three of them. Here Torrie was an outsider. Alas, she had never been quick to see it; called it "casting the spell," made jokes about gypsies, and Russian superstitions. But the twins were another story. They seemed able to divine the thing, to seize the whole concept of it without difficulty. Yes, Holland's mind occasionally wandered, his concentration obscured by some flibberty-gibbet prank or nonsense that amused him more; but Niles, now—Niles was different. With him it seemed both innate and suitable. Ah, but he was quick! Looking and looking and looking. Then *feeling.* Then *knowing.* And the knowing came as though a light had quite suddenly come on.

Yes, interesting enough, this game, the effects harmless; salutary even. And such fun. *IRONY*

But Niles, she told herself, needed watching; there was a danger lurking. Sometimes it seemed he would actually be hypnotized. And who in the family could ever forget that harrowing experience with the rooster? Chanticleer, they called the bird; wretched creature . . . that damn rooster.

Ever since that baffling Chanticleer occurrence, she had watched closely, cautiously, alert for signs of similar remarkable happenings. But she had witnessed none; only the growing perception of an unusual mind which, in another, less aware, one like Holland's, might be nothing more than the extreme vividness of imagination. But in Niles, nurtured, what might it produce? A genius? A seer? A prophet? Grown a man, what could he not do in the world? It was for this she said her prayers each night.

Was it wrong? Should it be encouraged? No—leave it. Leave it behind; it is a child's game merely and children must grow up. Mustn't they? *Must* they? No —wait, not yet. How she adored indulging Niles, delighting in his whims and fancies, those cat-and-mouse insistences, his alluring make-believe; loved

his guileless face, eyes wonder-widened as his mind
worked. And in time surely he would outgrow it—
the way children outgrow Santa Claus. They must
have their dreams, that is what being children is all
about, isn't it? Childhood was but a few brief summers; winter a whole, cold, lifetime long. No—not
yet, not yet.

"*Can* we?" he coaxed.

How's that? Oh—the game. But the hour was getting late. "It's bedtime, child," she told him. Aw, he
said, Holland was still up. *Pajalsta, pajalsta,* just
once? And his "please" was so earnest, his smile so
disarming, she had not the heart to deny him. With a
deep breath, she nodded her head at the cluster of
fireflies. "Very well, look there. Tell me what those
are like. What do they feel like?" Turning the gold
band on her finger, she waited while he concentrated.

Fireflies. Lightning bugs. What are they like? Tiny
pulses, bright seeds sown in the blackness. They look
so. But what do they *feel* like? Cold green stars, light
years away, their glow produced by layers of special-
ized cells. Miniature neon dots. No—neon is cold.
Hot, rather. Flies of fire, hot sparks burning in the
night wind. Yes, that was it, now he was getting
closer to it. Fire! In the crotches of elm twigs cob-
webs catching moon flames, laddered patterns as if
dusted with golden pollen, burning in the gauzy
night. There! And there! Luminous pinpoints ignit-
ing, now leaping to set the night ablaze, with shadows dancing while ashes swirl upward like black
snow, sucked into the green fire, spiraling death into
the night sky . . . death . . . and horror . . .

He was trembling; goosebumps raised on end the

yellow fuzz along his arms. He rubbed himself, laughing. "Cripes, that's some crow that walked across my grave." He rose from the step. "Well, it's almost time for *First Nighter*. Want to listen? No? Okay. Shall I put your sewing in your room for you?"

She nodded without speaking and he carefully removed her work from her lap to put it in the basket. After he had kissed her, and the screen door clacked at his back as he carried the basket and Torrie's doll-lamp inside, she remained a little longer in her chair, rocking gently, and feeling the warm night grow cold around her, while terror stole across her mind, so quietly, so stealthily, so imperceptibly that, absently fingering her swollen knuckles, she was taken quite unawares. *Terror of what?*

Niles went up to Torrie and Rider's room and presented his sister with the doll-lamp, then returned to the upper hall where he had left Ada's sewing basket sitting by the newel post. He went along the gallery and opened her door. The room had a clean, spare look. Other than a chest of drawers, a straight-backed chair beside a lamp, an iron bedstead painted white like the one she'd slept on in Russia, on the floor a rug she'd hooked herself, in blue and white, the room was quite bare. On one wall hung a single small icon in a gold frame. You could tell a lot about Ada by looking at her room, Niles decided, setting her work basket by the chair. On the bureau was a large picture book, old engravings from the Bible and other world literature, a book whose pages he and Holland knew by heart now. *The Illustrated Doré.*

He lifted the cover and looked at the spidery handwriting inside. *Ada Katerina Vedrenya. Baltimore, Maryland 1894.* A faint aroma arose from the pages: she used it for pressing flowers. He dropped the cover and, softly closing the door behind him, went down the hall and hurried into the back wing to his own room. He didn't want to miss the beginning of *First Nighter.*

The earphones to the crystal set were lying on Holland's bed. He put them on, lay down on the cover, tuned in the set, and listened. The play tonight wasn't very good and he amused himself by watching the face which seemed to form itself out of the center of the waterstain on the ceiling overhead: two eyes, a nose, a mouth. A familiar face. But whose? Whose?

Cripes, what a lousy program. When it was over, he yawned, removed the earphones, and went to open a window to the south. Along the drive, the fir trees, green-black against the sky, appeared a pantheon of bearded gods—Wotan, Fafnir, Thor—their arms stretching, stirring and stretching toward him in the wind. Gold, gold was what they craved—Nibelung gold; Peregrine gold.

From time to time the sky was vividly dyed by fireworks whooshing away down at the green. The pump cast a sentinel shadow onto the drive near the well, bits of gravel glittering, washed white as the waxing hunchback moon climbed the sky. A whistle hooted; a line of smoke appeared beyond the dark treetops as a train wound along the spur of track below the highway. *Too-oo-oot,* as it passed the Rose Rock bottling works at Church Street—a lonely sound, yet, Niles thought, not as lonely as the rattle,

the clatter, the clang of the Shadow Hills trolley.
That was the loneliest sound in the world . . .

And as the hoot of the train died away to the
north, here came the clang of the streetcar from the
south, the Babylon Express, rattling up the track
from Talcotts Ferry. You can set your watch by that
trolley, Father used to say: it's always five minutes
late. Larger and larger it loomed, lights bright,
though bereft of passengers, the solitary Mr. Conduc-
tor lost in thought—wife? home? dinner?—feet
spread wide apart for balance as the car swung along
the rails.

Ding-ding-ding.

There it goes, five minutes late for sure—Niles
checks his watch—the Shadow Hills Express, on the
way out to Babylon. End of the line. He listens to the
bell—*ding-ding-ding*—as the trolley clatters by the
house.

He longed to get on that old Shadow Hills Express
and, sitting on one of the straw-covered seats, ride all
the way out to Babylon, to the end of the line.
Shadow Hills? Oh, it's just a name, Winnie had said
when he asked her about it. Just a . . . a place,
that's all. No, the hills weren't really shadows. Yes,
her folks lived out that way, and Jennie, her sister;
her father worked servicing the trolleys at the car
barn. But was it true, what Holland said? Babylon
was a fabulous place, to hear him tell it. A metropolis
—El Dorado, practically, with a huge palace, grand
flights of stairs, gates of brass, towers, pennants flying from the peaked turrets. Winnie laughed and
shook her head. Bunk. There wa'n't nothin' like *that*
in Babylon. There was just that bleak old red place,

mental unrest

brick, she said, with <u>iron gates and steps leading</u> up, <u>terrible dump—more fort than palace</u>.

Ding-ding-ding—away in the distance now . . .

But Niles wanted to see for himself. Sometimes, when that lonely feeling would come over him, when he would be longing for something—what, he didn't quite know what—suddenly it would come to him that he was feeling homesick for Shadow Hills, a place he had never been to. Funny; <u>how could you feel homesick for a place you had never seen?</u> <u>Babylon—end of the line.</u> And Holland never did any more than shrug and sing his clever little rhyme: *How many miles to Babylon?—Threescore miles and ten. Can I get there by candlelight?—Yes, and back <u>again.</u>* *IRONY*

KNOWS HE HIDES THERE

He had moved to the west window, where he could look out past the barn, the peregrine weathervane motionless in the moonlight, tail to the east, its amber eye seemingly fixed on the river. Thrusting against the water's band of silvery light was the dead sycamore where, summers, you could swing from its trunk and leap into the stream, winters use it as shelter, with old tires burning near its base for warmth while you skated. With a blur Niles remembered it was there that <u>Billy Talcott had drowned</u>, under the ice. That had been over George Washington's Birthday. Niles, bedded with the croup, had gotten up to go to the bathroom. Passing the window, he had looked down at the river. Poor Billy, <u>with his limp</u>, could only hobble around on the ice, but when it gave way under him, he was close enough to the bank so that Holland, poking up the fire, could have rescued him. But, instead, he ran—ran and left Billy thrashing, freezing in the icy water.

Niles turned to see Holland walk in, and go to throw himself down on his bed.

"Did you go to see the fireworks?" Niles asked.

"No." He was staring up at the brown waterstain on the ceiling directly overhead.

"There's a beauty!" Niles exclaimed as a rocket exploded in the distance. No answer. Holland was sulking again. Niles combed his mind for an agreeable subject to ease the tension.

"What's so funny?" Holland wanted to know.

"I was just thinking."

"Yeah?" He looked over.

"I was just thinking about the five-legged pig in the freak show. Remember Mr. La Fever?" He laughed again, the reason being Mr. La Fever, Arnie's father, was not only three-legged, but was a scandal as well —but not because of the extra limb. Mr. La Fever, who worked in the Ringling Brothers sideshow, had some years ago caused a flurry of attention around town by getting a girl pregnant. Their rendezvous, he later confessed, was on the baggage platform of the freight depot across from Fenstermacher's Rose Rock bottling works. The girl, a live-in maid brought up from the Girl's Reformatory at Middlehaven, was brokenhearted when she was returned to confinement, and her tri-legged lover, already married, fled to the circus's winter quarters at Sarasota. The baby was put out for adoption and Pequot Landing hadn't stopped talking yet. Arnie got mad when you joked about his old man.

"Put that away somewhere," Holland growled.

Niles was sitting and, without thinking, rattling the Prince Albert tin. He considered the contents. Peregrine for Perry. The Thing. The Thing was gruesome; of course it was. He tried not to think about it, tried to put it out of his mind. It was all Holland's doing. Holland had decreed it all. Yet Niles was the one who must keep the Secret . . .

Yep, he was getting a Look. "I told you not to carry it around."

Chastened, Niles deliberated over a suitable hiding place.

"Where should I put it? In the compartment?"

Holland shook his head. The whole family knew about the secret compartments Father had built into the matching chests. Even Winnie knew. He took the tin from Niles and went to the wall next to the closet door where, hanging on hooks, was the Chautauqua desk, Ada's present to the twins. There was a blackboard with cubbyholes, and wire coils that held chalk, and a wide scroll of colored chromographs which turned up and down, illustrating Bible stories. Other scrolls in the closet informed not only about nature and paleontology, but biology, astronomy, mythology, and other subjects. Removing one of the spindles, he secreted the tobacco tin behind the picture roll and reset the spindle in position.

Niles shook his head. "That's no good. Mother found the Civil War dollar behind there, remember?"

Holland turned the scroll until *Jesus Delivering the Sermon on the Mount* came into view. "She doesn't come in here any more," he said coolly. Then, something exciting his attention at the window, he gasped and rushed to put out the lamp between the two beds

and hurried back to his place. "Niles!" he exclaimed,
"look!"

"What?"

"C'mere. Look!"

Opposite, in the wing parallel to their own, was
one lighted window, the shade drawn. A man's
shadow was crossing behind it—light, shadow,
pause, light, shadow, pause. Another shadow appeared, smaller, big-bellied; an embrace followed.

"It's Torrie and Rider," Niles heard Holland
breathe. A silence, then: "Come on—let's go watch!"

"Holland!" Niles was shocked.

"Don't worry, little brother, they won't know."
Holland's tone was suave and inviting. "Come on."

Niles felt himself propelled out the door, guided
along the front hall in the path of a flashlight beam,
past the grandfather clock, into the north wing, then
up a pair of steps behind a door, over the landing,
down more steps and into the storeroom. Maniac
shadows leaped about the walls; the trunks squatted
like fat coffins, the dress dummy loomed, big-busted,
narrow-waisted, pins in it glinting. Niles felt his hand
brush a web spun across the wicker cradle; a spider, a
black jewel, dropped to the floor and sidled behind
the rocking horse. He turned, starting nervously at
his own reflection in the mirrored door of the wardrobe. Beyond, through a crack in the far wall, a light
showed. Creeping silently over the floor in the path
of the flashlight, Niles listened to low voices on the
other side of the partition. Through the crack, partly
hidden by a chest of drawers, was Torrie and Rider's
bed, a four-poster, canopied with tasseled netting. On
it Torrie lay, unclothed, a carelessly pulled-down

sheet draped over her feet. On the bedside table, Niles's doll-lamp shed warm light over the delicate contours of her face, her breasts, her swollen belly. Rider turned off the overhead light and stretched out naked beside her, cradling her in his arms. In the lamp-glow he nuzzled her ripe breasts with his mouth, one dark hand gently caressing her stomach, his fingers moving slowly over the mound of her belly.

"Oh," she giggled, "she just kicked, the monster. Feel?"

"Mmm." Rider turned his head sideways between her breasts while her hand traced the curve of his back along his spine. "Hey," he said suddenly, lifting his eyes, "somebody's watching!"

Niles saw Holland start, pull back, flick the flashlight off.

"That face," Rider went on, and Torrie giggled again.

"I think it's sweet," she said, reaching to fluff out the skirt-shade of the fat, impish-looking doll-lamp. "Oops, there she goes again." She took his hand and replaced it on her stomach.

"Well, let's hurry and have this one," he said huskily, "so we can make another."

She raised his head and looked at him, her face languid, suffused with tenderness. "Darling Rider," she said, brushing the backs of her hands along the hollow of his cheeks, "it's going to be a lovely baby. A beautiful baby."

"What makes you so sure?"

"I know. Niles says so. He keeps telling me."

"How does he know?"

"It's that silly game they play."

"What game?"

"I swear they're gypsies." Torrie's voice was muffled behind the wall as she explained about the game, how she and Niles and Holland used to try to be a tree, a bird, a flower; how silly she thought it, how dismayed Ada was with her. There was a summer day when Ada had brought the three of them down behind the carriage-house to see one of her half-dried sunflowers, a giant, over twice their height. Dominated by Ada's will, they had looked, tried to know it. What was it like? Color, texture; how tall, how old? Smell. Hot, cold. Rough, smooth. Their young brains compelled by hers to concentrate, to discover the heart of it, its essence, as Ada called it. *Your mind is wandering* (this to Holland, skylarking about the sunflower patch, doing handstands and cartwheels, an antic gleam in his eye, Don Quixote mad). *Look there, look there.* Leading them a strange way along a strange path to play a strange child's game. The sunflower viewed, noted, memorized.

Then: What does it feel like?

"And do you know what Niles said?" Torrie continued. "He said, 'I feel pretty.' Isn't that marvelous? Then a crow flew by and picked a seed from the face of the flower—and Niles cried, said it hurt. And Holland—"

"What'd he do?" Rider asked.

"He laughed. And Ada shushed him. But I remember her saying this one thing. She said, 'Now do you understand what it is you can *feel?*' See what I mean about gypsies? Honestly! But Niles is just tremendous. He's uncanny sometimes, the predictions he comes out with."

"Did he predict we'd be rich?"

"No, but he said the north meadow'd be onions again, and next year it will—and that was when you were still planning to be a lawyer."

"Pity he couldn't have predicted for Vining or—"

"Hush. Not in front of the baby." They nestled closer and, lying in each other's arms, whispered and laughed and dreamed aloud, Torrie reaching at one point to smooth the skirt of the doll-lamp, Niles's present. And the baby would be beautiful, a girl, as he predicted. They would find the perfect name for such a perfect child. It would be a thanksgiving baby, for it had been conceived Thanksgiving night; out of the storm of grief over her father's death passion had arisen, and though they had planned to wait, it was Torrie's desire that the life lost be replaced. Now, come August, she would give birth. She had hoped it would be a boy—another Vining to take her father's place—but Niles insisted it would be a girl.

A short time later, when Rider had snapped off the doll-lamp, the murmurs became even breathing and they slept.

"Jeeze," Holland hissed, spreading his fingers over the flashlight lens to create weird patterns on the walls. Niles followed him back across the room. When they got to the door Holland whispered sharply, "That's what they were doing!" He gave the cradle a push which set it rocking noiselessly.

"Who?"

"Torrie. Rider. Making that baby. Making it together. Thanksgiving night. I saw them."

"Saw them?" Niles was thunderstruck. *"You watched?"*

"They were on the bed. In the light. He was on top of her—right on top. Moving." The words formed dryly in his throat before he spat them out, describing what he had seen through the crack in the wall. "With the lights on. Damned hermaphrodite. That's what they are—a hermaphrodite. Half-man, half-woman."

"That's what a marriage is."

"Well, I'm telling you this, it won't be a pretty baby like she thinks. Like you think. It'll be ugly and white with pop eyes and a great big head. Like the baby in the bottle!" In his strange humor Holland struck the cradle another blow, rocking it more violently, and his voice was a strangled cry as he threw aside the flashlight and fled the room.

In a moment Niles crossed the floor and picked up the light. Bright moonshine spilled onto the sill where King Cophetua lay, a slain warrior. In the sky stars glittered like snow, brittle and crystalline, turning the summer night into winter spectacle.

Then, standing and looking out, Niles saw a strange sight. The screen door at the head of the outside stairs had quietly opened; a figure appeared: Mother. Pausing uncertainly on the landing, she tripped hurriedly down, one white hand skimming the banister, its enamel paint gleaming in the moonlight. Silently she slipped over the lawn, her lavender wrapper shimmering across the dark grass, like a beautiful spectre, crossing the gravel and into the fir trees, where she made her way between the dark trunks, the pale violet blur almost lost to view, stepping on the thatch of fallen pine needles, until she reached the well, where she stood for a long time, hands hanging limp at her sides, the clover a dark floor around her feet. And as she looked down at the heavy seal over the well mouth, it seemed to Niles that it was as though she were waiting for it to speak.

III

One morning several weeks later, seated in the kitchen, Niles held himself in patience while Aunt Josie performed certain ministrations on his face. Sinister, that was the look; and properly so, just what he'd wanted, precisely the effect Holland had managed: faded, a little decadent, a sort of seedy type, one who, he suspicioned, had a dirty mind; probably did things with little kids; hair parted in the middle, slicked back, patent-leatherish, and, where Aunt Josie had been at pains with the makeup, interesting-looking. A dusting of white practically blotted out his features, with a touch of rouge (roodge, she called it) on the cheeks, a bit of penciling around the eyes, the brows worked up, a reddened mouth, and finally two magnificent curlicue mustaches drawn on.

"Sweetheart, you look just like Mr. Coffee Nerves in the Postum ads," Aunt Josie said as he stepped into Winnie's room to view himself in the mirror.

"Hey—good," Niles called back. "That's really great." He came to stand in the doorway. He had on a top hat and a cape with a red lining, and he leaned sportily on a cane, one foot crossed over the other. "I should have long pants," he said, looking ruefully at his rolled shorts. "And a stiff shirt."

"Soup 'n' fish? I think you look just fine, sweetheart." (Switthot, she said.) "Here, you got a bit too much roodge there." She wet her thumb on her tongue and worked at his cheek. "Okay, Perfesser, I guess you'll pass mustard." She looked at him with her expression of perpetual surprise and winked. "Shall I go along and announce you, Perfesser Rabbitwaters?"

"Well," he said doubtfully, "you go ahead. I'll be out after. There's something else I want to get." He disappeared up the back stairs. RAT?

"Be sure to stop in and show yourself to Zan," she called after him.

The screen door whined as she went along the walk to join the others in the arbor. Built for Granddaddy Perry's wife with his own hands, it stood at the far edge of the lawn next to the vacant lot on the north side of the house, a cool oasis of white posts and trellises, with turf between the flagstones and grapevined shade. The walk was brick, laid down in sand in a herringbone pattern, the corners mossy green and rounded with use, the faces heaved by winter frost. The month was deep into July, the aunts had arrived, and today, gathered around a table in wicker chairs were Aunt Fania and Torrie, with Mrs. Jewett, after an hour of tutoring Niles in arithmetic, and Ada behind an easel, capturing Granddaddy's roses on a watercolor block.

Mrs. Jewett had opened the front of her bouclé knitted dress—rather too warm for the weather—

and was fanning her bosom. "Well," she declared as
Aunt Josie came up, "no matter what anybody says,
carelessness breeds accidents."

"To say nothing of babies." Aunt Josie's deep
laugh rumbled through the arbor like approaching
thunder.

Behind her hob-nailed glass, Aunt Fanny hooted in
spite of herself. She toyed with the bits of fruit floating in the wine punch Winnie had concocted to dissi-
pate the afternoon heat.

"Oops," said Aunt Jo, seating herself. Aunt Josie
was a card. For her, nothing in life was without its
humor, neither Man nor Beast, War nor Peace, Hate
nor Love. Ah, Love especially. Her own spinsterhood
she regarded as a prank life had played on her, a sly
one at that, but what was there to do but laugh? A
trouper from way back, she had for years toured in
vaudeville sketches around the country, but with
talkies in she had found more regular employment
assisting a journalist-photographer in New York,
where she shared with her sister an apartment on
Morningside Heights.

As happens, the aunts looked nothing alike, and
resembled Ada even less. If it were possible to liken
Josie to a favorite chair—comfortable, ample, a bit
lumpy—Fanny was more the auditorium seat: aus-
tere, meager, rigid. Where Josie was merry and
plump, Fanny was all angles and dour; Josie's voice a
gravelly rumble, Fanny's more a bark; in moments of
mirth an abrupt cackle was the best she could manage. But—most important—while Aunt Josie was
fun, told stories, cracked jokes, performed parlor
tricks, played pinochle, did devastating impressions,

Aunt Fanny, alas, remained prim, wore her corset, eschewed cards, knew no jokes worth telling, and abhorred magic.

"Well," she said, picking up Mrs. Jewett's remark, "it seems to me it *was* careless of Mr. Angelini, leaving a hayfork around."

Pausing over her watercolor box, Ada shook her head sympathetically. "He's just a ghost, the poor man. I feel so sorry. It is awful to see him blame himself and suffer so."

"Daresay," Fanny agreed, "but it looks to me like he's been nipping a bit; least he don't seem any too steady on his feet." With a brisk click of dentures she snapped her mouth shut, bobbing her head in time with the piano music that had been drifting across from an open window over at the Rowe house. "Tum-da-da-da-dum," she sang, arranging her skirt and tidily crossing her ankles.

Where Josie was the offhand sort, looking more frequently than not as though she had put on the first thing that came to hand, an old sweater, the odd skirt, Fanny was meticulous in her costume. Today she was wearing an ankle-length dress of écru linen, pale silk gloves, cream-colored hose and comfortable white shoes with punctured patterns which permitted the air to circulate around her feet. On her head was a man's Panama hat with a black band, her face swathed mummy-fashion under the voluminous swirl of white maline she had purchased at the five-and-ten, a precaution against bees and other stinging insects.

"Did you find Russia awfully *changed,* Josephine?" Mrs. Jewett inquired lugubriously.

"Poor," Josie answered. "Rah-sha iss poor."

"I should think so. Those Bolsheviks haven't a sou to their names."

"Rubles, Edith." Josie had spent the month of February in the Soviet Union, assisting her boss on a picture story for the *National Geographic*—a hydro-electric project in the Ukraine. It was the first time she had been back since she was a little girl. "Russia is so poor now," she went on, "the peasants use borscht for blood transfusions." Everyone laughed except Ada, apart from the group and concentrating on her work.

"Did you get to Siberia?" asked Mrs. Jewett.

"No—Siberia's not for the poor folks, dearie. And I'm strictly proletariat." She leaned to snap her garter, rolled in her stocking above a sausage knee. "The aristocracy's all in Siberia."

"Hmp, Roosevelt they should send to Siberia." Sipping, Aunt Fanny adjusted herself in her chair. "Ta-dum-dum-da-da-dah. What *is* that song?"

Torrie rolled her eyes. "Mrs. Rowe and her Turkish Rondo—at least I think that's what it is."

"Oh, Beethoven, of course," said Mrs. Jewett, blowing down her front.

"I think it's Mozart."

"Do you mean to say that old woman still sits and plays the piano?" Aunt Fanny asked. "Does she signal the airplanes any more?"

"Sometimes," Torrie said and Aunt Fanny cackled.

"If she can hear the motor over that racket."

"I should think so." Deciding she was going to learn little of modern Russia on this day, Mrs. Jewett cast about for another subject. "How's Valeria?" she asked brightly, "still in Chicago?"

Torrie nodded. "We think she'll stay a while. She's taken it all very badly."

"Do her good to get away from George for a bit, shouldn't wonder," said Fanny with asperity. Her views on marital bliss—so called—were well known. She regarded her own separate state as a blessing. Although Josie was still a Petrichev, Ada a Vedrenya, Fanny was a Fish—Mrs. Epifania Fish. With Mr. Fish, whose first name had long ago escaped memory, she had embarked on a whirlwind elopement and six months later had secured a mysterious divorce. Now she was more a spinster than Josie, and though she kept the name, there were few who could recall the last time they had heard her mention Mr. Fish.

"And how's George?" Mrs. Jewett wanted to know.

George was fine, Torrie said, leaving out mention of the fact that he had become most irascible and that evenings found him holed up in either the dining room or his bedroom with a bottle of Southern Comfort.

"And Alexandra?" Mrs. Jewett continued, determined to assay by turn the health of the entire family. "Does she still keep to her room?" she asked, unable to see Alexandra's window from her place under the tangle of grapevines. "Can't think how she's stayed cooped up in there for—how long's it been?" She ticked off her manicured nails. "March, April, May, June, July—why that's five months already."

"Four," Torrie corrected her. "She'll be better

when she's a grandmother. She's already helping me
plan the layette and soon as there's formula to fix and
diapers to change—"

"If Winnie'll let her," Aunt Josie said, draining her
glass with a slurp and a smack. "I think Winnie
spiked this stuff with slivovitz. A girl could get a jag
on if she's not careful. Wouldn't think you could get
vinegar from these old grapes, would you? Watch it,
Fanuschka, here it comes again." Her sister had been
flapping a flyswatter at a wasp buzzing around the
fruit overhead, and which was now studiously drawing z's around her glass.

"Eee!" shrieked Fanny, dropping the glass and retreating to a corner of the arbor. "Shoo! Shoo!"

"Shoo, wasp," Torrie said calmly with a wave, and
retrieved the unbroken glass. "It's all right, Fan,"
Josie rumbled, "it's gone. Come sit."

Aunt Fanny's fear of stinging insects stemmed
from an experience she had once had when a bee
stung her and she had almost died, the poisonous
toxin entering her body and invading her whole sys-
tem. Now, visiting in the country, she took elaborate
precautions because, she said, she had a theory (Russian superstition, Ada said) that "stingers," as she
called them, actually *knew* those victims who were
most prone to their danger, hence the veiling and the
flyswatter. Aunt Fan was taking no chances.

"Ooh my," Josie boomed, casting an eye up toward the house, "here comes Winnie with a refill."

At the back-entryway the screen door slammed
and Winnie hove into view bearing another pitcher of
frosty purple liquid. In a second the door whined
again and a figure appeared at the end of the brick

wall, shrouded in black, the white face sinister, macabre, mocking . . .

"Oh my God!" Her veil lifted around her glass, Aunt Fanny turned pale as she stared, making a cross of her thumb and finger and kissing it in the Russian way, and accidentally spilling some wine onto the netting as she did so. "Holland—" *Thinks its him, not from dead*

"Oh for heaven's sakes, Fanuschka," Josie said, "it's not Holland, it's Niles. Look! Watch this, now." The figure approached, the tips of the cape trailing, now and then a flash of red, the silk hat tipped jauntily over one eye. Incredibly, buttoned across the sneakers were a pair of pearl gray spats. Lifting the hat, twirling the cane, bowing, along the herringbone brick came Professor Rabbitwaters.

"The spitting image," Mrs. Jewett said, leaning out of her chair. "Never saw anything—hel-lo Mysterious One," she called coyly.

Without acknowledgment, as though to avoid encounter with the playful Mrs. Jewett, the dark figure cut over the croquet lawn to the horse-chestnut tree and intently studied the bark. He looked up at the branches, thinking of autumn, when the nuts would have completely formed in their prickly jackets and could be knocked down with a stick. Suddenly he stiffened and wheeled as, with a faint crowing, Chanticleer, the old stringy rooster, came haughtily pecking under the tree in search of worms, then, shaking out its tail feathers like a clutch of sabers as it spied the boy, stopped and fixed him with a beady eye. Niles returned the stare, then, head immobile, he backed silently away, cane extended as though to ward off harm, giving the bird a wide berth as he made his way out onto the lawn again, passing Winnie on her way back to the kitchen.

Ada, brush poised in mid-air as she caught the boy's action, observed him thoughtfully while his eyes remained fastened on the rooster. It was the same old story; neither of them had changed, neither boy nor bird. With a pang she thought of how it had gone, that shocking business—the twins must have been ten that year; she had been sitting in almost the same spot under the arbor, shelling limas for succotash; Winnie was in the kitchen shucking corn, Holland and Niles near the well. Head high, pecking, from time to time ruffling out its feathers in the same insolent way, the rooster had circled the pump. Then, eyes riveted on the bird, Niles had slipped quietly behind it, his head duplicating precisely the pecking motions, bent arms jerking, rump sticking out in back, a tailful of feathers seemingly sprouting there. From his throat came the identical half-crowing sound of the bird. A comical sight to be sure. Even from where she sat she could see the beads of perspiration appear on his brow, the fixed, almost obsessed expression on his pale face, the eyes glassy and intense.

Niles, Niles, that's enough, child. No more. Just then Winnie had hollered from the window for Ada to bring the beans; Niles, following the rooster, disappeared behind the barn.

She was at the sink, rinsing off the limas, when she heard the cry: she and Winnie ran out the door to find Holland pointing up at the carriage-house roof, where, on the peak, Chanticleer perched, wings flapping, crowing lustily. Behind him, incredibly, was

Niles, precariously balanced, arms flapping, shrill crowing noises issuing from his throat. Terrified, motioning for the others to be silent, Ada approached.

Niles—enough now, Niles. It is not important now—

Er-rrr-a-rrr-aroo-ooo!

He took no notice; his eyes remained battened on the bird; his head turned jerkily; he pecked, he flapped, he strutted, he crowed, would not, could not cease.

Niles, she said in relief, after Mr. Angelini had brought his ladder and led him down from the roof. *What on earth were you doing?*

I wasn't on earth, he told her excitedly.

But what possessed you?

Breathless, bewildered, eyes luminous with unaccustomed brightness, he tried to explain. *Chanticleer—I was doing the game on Chanticleer.* A fine dew of sweat still lay across his forehead. *Just—you know—to see what it was like to be a rooster. But then, I couldn't stop. I really was Chanticleer. I couldn't help it!*

Couldn't? The word baffled her. *Could you not stop?*

Yes. I think so, if I stopped thinking about Chanticleer. But I didn't—he trailed off, pondering the mystery of it.

What, child?

I didn't want to.

So it had been with the rooster. And still it wasn't over . . .

With a shiver, Ada rinsed out her camel hair brush in a jelly glass and quietly rose. Leaving the arbor, she approached Niles across the lawn. "Child," she said softly, motioning her hands at the rooster, who shook his wattles and pranced away. "Niles?"

"Yes."

"Come along." She took his hand and he went with her toward the arbor.

"Oh Niles is doing ever so much better with his arithmetic problems," exclaimed Mrs. Jewett elaborately so as to be overheard by the boy, and Aunt Josie called, "Niles, sweetheart, are we going to have a show this year?"

"Yes," he said as Ada reseated herself at the easel. He came and parked his rear on the arm of Aunt Josie's chair and she squeezed him tight. "Yes, we are," he said, peering out to the street, hoping for sight of Holland. "With a special trick."

"Oh? Then I must have a new specialty act," she said, nodding so her curls bobbed. Fat and stiff and of an unlikely mixture of reds, these were bent each night into coils; released in the morning, they snapped to life like bedsprings all over her head. "Now, what?" she wondered, "Camille?" She put on a tragic face and coughed loudly. Aunt Fan cackled, but Niles, after consideration, vetoed it. "Something with music and dancing," he said.

Josie racked her brains, then snapped her fingers. "I know! I'll do a Spanish number! With a shawl and a big comb and castanets—Yes?" Brows arched, her mouth a perfect O, she awaited Niles's verdict.

"Yes!" he decreed.

"*Sí sí señor!*" She began snapping fingers at the side of her head, then, irresistibly, got up and, flinging her chintz skirt about, clacking her Enna Jettick shoes on the brick, fandangoed up the walk singing in her whisky tenor:

> *"Lay-dee of Spain, I adore yooooo,*
> *Lay-dee of Spain, I live for yoooo—"*

She leaned to a flower bed and, turning again, a blossom appeared clenched in her teeth. Faster and faster she went, her abandon exposing her rolled stockings till, too dizzy to continue, she reeled out onto the lawn. *"Olé,"* she cried, finishing with a breathless flourish, then called *"Buenos días,* Mr. Angelini," to the handyman, who, coming from the direction of the cider press, lugged in one hand an empty gasoline can, bound for the dump heap in the granary yard.

Ada waved. "Mr. Angelini, when you have time, shall you please bring your ladder and poke down that wasp nest?"

The old Italian stopped in his tracks and, though he stared at the arbor group with a long look, gave no sign of having heard the request. Then he disappeared behind the barn carrying his can. DRUNK?

Aunt Josie knocked a weathered croquet ball aside with her foot and, returning to the arbor, dropped into her chair. "I don't think we'll have a Spanish number after all." She kicked off her shoes and sprawled, testing a curl for spring. "Maybe we'll just do a tableau. I can be Whistler's Mother and sit in a chair. That'd be a sketch. Ooh-a, that's a pun, dears."

While Ada became engrossed again in her work, the other ladies put their heads together and arranged themselves into a tight little symposium for purposes of gossip.

Niles listened to Mrs. Jewett's indignation over the morning headlines. Bruno Hauptmann, she was talking about. Bruno—it sounded like a name for a dog. Well, Bruno Hauptmann was a dog all right. Stole the Lindbergh baby, he had. Put a ladder up against the house and took the baby out the window. Lots of money had been paid by Lucky Lindy to get the baby back, but when he did the baby was no longer alive. Bruno Hauptmann was going to get the Chair.

"And his lawyers are appealing again—think of the poor taxpayers' money going down the drain!" Mrs. Jewett's red mouth was going a mile a minute.

Ding-ding-ding.

The Talcotts Ferry trolley stopped at Church Street, then rolled past the house, wheels clanking, bell ringing. Niles checked his time and made a minor adjustment on his Ingersoll watch. Far off in the distance could be heard the drone of an airplane, banking away from the airfield on its way to New York.

Niles put his watch back on and buckled the strap. Lifting his head, he looked up to the street. Holland was walking along the car tracks. So he'd been off on the trolleys again. He came casually sauntering down the lawn, kicking at the dandelions, squinting at the airplane, which was flying low and casting a giant shadow across Pequot Landing. Soon the roar of the propellers increased in such volume as to drown out entirely the piano music from the Rowe house next door.

In another moment a tiny figure had tripped

Rowe crazy

through the doorway and down the back-porch steps, a little white-haired lady who came out flourishing a red coach blanket around her head. There followed a most entertaining, if singular, performance, attentively witnessed by all eyes in the arbor, and a pair, Niles was quick to notice, outside, where Holland stood hidden by the grape leaves, the Asiatic look on his face.

Rowe

"Hoo-oo," the lady called, blinking and peering up at the sky as she darted across the yard. "Hoo-oo." With her audience half out of their chairs and watching through the grapevines, she continued prancing back and forth in a comical effort to make herself seen by the plane. Trying not to trample the begonias bordering the grass, she scurried in circles around a sundial, clockwise, counter-clockwise, the blanket flapping like the cape of some demented matador.

When the plane had passed directly overhead and disappeared beyond the trees, she stood bewildered for a moment, blanket limp at her side while she caught her breath, then, with a shrug, smoothed back a stray wisp of hair and, the blanket dragging behind, picked her way past her flower beds toward the house, pausing as she went to inspect a planting of portulaca.

"Well, imagine that!" Mrs. Jewett shook her head in wonder and watched the sprightly old lady fold the blanket, tuck it under her arm, and go inside. Presently the piano music resumed.

"It ain't Paderewski, but then I'll bet Paderewski couldn't run the 220 the way she does," Aunt Josie boomed.

220

Mrs. Jewett made certain arrangements to ease her

bosom. "Such an exhibition—really! A woman her age. I thought she had a serious heart condition."

"An amazing woman," replied Aunt Josie.

Which was one word for it. Mrs. Rowe, considered by most people to be rather eccentric, had come to Valley Hill Road as a bride back before the turn of the century. Mr. Rowe had flown with Rickenbacker and, after the armistice, was one of the pioneers of commercial aviation. Thirteen years ago he had been sent by President Harding to South America to investigate the possibilities of continental flying routes. His plane crashed in the jungle and he was never seen again. The news of his death had left his widow in shock, and for several years she had seldom appeared, but after the airfield was constructed south of the city and the planes flew directly over Pequot Landing, coaxed out by the sound of their motors, Alice Rowe had suddenly emerged, waving her blanket as though trying to communicate with her dead husband.

"Does that Mrs. Whoosis still look after her?" Mrs. Jewett said, settled again in her chair finally.

Mrs. Cooney, that would be; Torrie said she had seen her down at the Center a few weeks ago and there had been a little—well, not really an argument, but it seemed that rats had been appearing from Mrs. Rowe's cellar and Mrs. Cooney insisted they came from the Perry barn. "But I told her we haven't had rats over here for years. Not since Ada got her cat and—" She broke off, embarrassed, and while Ada looked down at her painting Aunt Josie began talking rapidly.

"I don't think I've even had a glimpse of old Mrs.

Rowe in—years," she said. "Look out there, Fan."
The wasp had returned and Fanny quickly lowered
her veil, jumping from her chair and retreating again
to the corner of the arbor. Niles laughed at the sight:
Aunt Fania looked like a camp bed, all netted up
against mosquitos.

"Why, will you just look at that," said Mrs. Jewett, pointing to the table where the wasp was hovering over the pitcher. In a moment it had settled on
the lip, then crawled inside where it dropped into the
wine, shortly to be imprisoned by its wet wings on
the darkly shining surface.

"He'll get drunk," Aunt Josie said as it pushed
frantically between pieces of orange and lemon, trying to free itself. Soon it gave up and floated exhausted amidst the fruit.

"Thank goodness." Fanny breathed a sigh of relief.
She undid her netting, still damp from her earlier
accident, draped it over some grape leaves to dry,
and went to stand behind the others, clustered at
Ada's back and chattering blithely as they enviously
watched her add a deeper wash to her roses.

"Oh, Sister," Fan exclaimed, "marvelous depth
you've gotten in your petals. I don't know how you
ever got the hang of flower painting, anyway. Art
certainly don't run in our family. Never had a lesson
in her life," she boasted to Mrs. Jewett.

"Well, I think it's just wonderful. She's an absolute
La Vinci," said Mrs. Jewett, who knew a little about
art. "I can't draw a straight line myself." Off to one
side Niles had taken a long spoon and was fishing the
unfortunate wasp from the pitcher. He poured off the
excess liquid and held the insect cradled in the spoon

out into the sunshine while its wings dried. "There's no such thing in the world as a purely straight line," Josie said. "Then perhaps there's hope for me after all," Mrs. Jewett said, carefully following the tip of Ada's moistened brush with her eye. "What red d'ye call that, I wonder?"

Ada explained that it was the Crimson Lake Niles had brought from the store and Mrs. Jewett said, "I think a red like that shade would suit my coloring," and went on to explain about a *crêpe de chine* dress she wanted dyed for the country club dance. "Oh, and did I tell you? When Joe goes away on his next trip"—Mr. Jewett was a drummer for Sherwin-Williams paints; he often traveled to Providence, to Fall River, to Bangor—"I'm going to have the sunporch redone." Is that so? asked someone, what color? Mrs. Jewett thought parrot green above with a darker color for the dado. There was silence for a spell, then Mrs. Jewett spoke again. "Imagine that poor Alice Rowe being so scared of rats." Honestly, she went on, such a tempest in a teapot, and why didn't she set traps? Torrie replied that Mrs. Cooney had said she was going to buy some pellets to put around for the rats to eat, hoping to get rid of them in that way. By this time the wasp's wings had begun to flutter, and presently it heaved itself up and crawled to the lip of the iced tea spoon.

"Fly away, your house is on fire, your children will burn," Niles heard Holland whisper gleefully as his hand shot out from the sheltering grape leaves.

"Damn you!" Niles said, turning in the direction of Aunt Fan's frightened cry. Her maline net hung drying on the grapevine and, almost as if to confirm her in her theory, the wasp drove straight at her neck.

"Oh! Oh! Oh!" she cried, a volley of sharp, staccato shrieks, while one person screamed and another slapped the wasp from her flesh, and Niles quickly ran to crush it underfoot. Mrs. Jewett had backed against the table, knocking the pitcher to the flagging, where it broke, the fruit lying amidst the turf and glass, the wine leaving a darkening stain on the stonework. Aunt Fan was in an agony of cries and moans and while Mrs. Jewett vainly tried to help her sit down and Aunt Josie tried to draw her up the walk to the house, Ada rushed ahead to get something for the swelling and to tell Winnie to phone for the doctor; Torrie, having gathered up Ada's paraphernalia, quickly followed. Niles during the meantime had been trying helpfully to pick up the pieces of broken glass. Reaching for the last fragments, he found himself staring at a pair of feet; he looked up at Holland's face.

"You bastard," he said, "you dirty rotten bastard." Which was all he could think of to call him; only he wasn't really saying it, only thinking it, seeing the gable-shaped brows lifted slightly as the face peered back at him through the grape leaves, eyebrows lifted in mock innocence (Who? *Me?*), thinking, Oh Holland when are you going to stop, when are you going to *make* it stop!

What was that he was saying?

"—and I want you to take it off," he ordered.

Niles rose with a blank look. "What?"

The costume, he was demanding. Niles must take it off. *He* wasn't Professor Rabbitwaters—Holland was. It was his invention. The One and Only Original Professor Rabbitwaters!

"But—why?"

"Because I said to." Easily; not threatening or anything, just a simple statement. Then, with the old winning smile: "Because Professor Rabbitwaters, bless him, is going to do a trick."

A trick? What sort of trick was that?

"A gr-r-eat trick! Professor Rabbitwaters is going to do the old Hat Trick. But first I need a hat"—relieving him of Granddaddy Perry's silk topper—"and then I'm going to do a command performance!"

"Who for?"

"Who for?" The smile was oh so wide and oh so charming. "Why, for a sweet little old lady, that's who. But second, I need something to pull out of the hat!" And away he went, Holland, out from the arbor and over the lawn, cape flapping, hat on the back of his head, his laughter bright and merry as he skimmed away in the direction of the barn.

IV

The young fry of Pequot Landing often occupied themselves with a pastime, an amusing charade in which Old Lady Rowe played a central role, one which some might think churlish, but one that not only piqued their imaginations but intrigued Old Lady Rowe as well. While it was generally known that her mind was sometimes cloudy, she was in no way stupid, and when the more enterprising children would telephone her in an assortment of cleverly disguised (they thought) voices, she would listen patiently while the little mischiefs tried to pull the wool over her eyes.

"Is this Mrs. Rowe?" (Telephone operator's pinched voice, half-stifled giggles in the background.)

"Yes? Who is this, please?"

"This is the White House calling. One moment, pul-eeze."

"Ha*rum*." (Deep, presidential-sounding tone; more giggles.) "Ah—Mrs. Rowe?"

"Yes? Yes, this is Mrs. Rowe speaking." A twinkle in the voice.

"This is—ha*rum*—the President." The mouthpiece quickly covered; impossible to stop the laughter.

Or, another variation: the operator informs Mrs. Rowe that Hollywood is on the line.

"Hollywood? California? Goodness!" With feigned surprise.

In a low voice, heavily accented: "Meeses Rowe? Thees ees Garrbo."

"Greta Garbo?"

"Yas. Dat's right. Grreta *Garr*-bo."

Thus would begin a lengthy conversation, mirthful on one end, eager, if confused, on the other, with either the President or Miss Garbo, sometimes both, invited to tea. And the parade would arrive, often all the way up Church Street from the Center, for instead of tea Mrs. Rowe always served hot dogs and never seemed to mind the fact that, at the last mo-

ment, the President's schedule had been changed or
Garbo was delayed filming.

She was a gracious hostess, kind and thoughtful
and remarkable in her tolerance of her guests. Nor
were the hot dogs the only attraction: a wastebasket
made from a hollowed-out elephant's foot, a Grecian
wine jug, a Siamese temple dancer's headdress, the
horn of a narwhal, wild animal skins, combs of
mother-of-pearl, jade figures, even a real shrunken
head which her small visitors might handle carefully.

Later that same afternoon, when the doctor had
come to see Aunt Fania and left again, Mrs. Rowe
had gone out to her garage for a bottle of rooting
compound to start a stalk of begonia, shattered in her
dash about the yard. Yes, there was the bottle, right
where she remembered it—her memory wasn't so
bad after all—on the shelf next to the bag of rat pellets; and over there the broken begonia plant. She
picked up the injured stem and was returning to the
house, passing the hen-and-chickens in the rock garden encircling the sundial, when something caught
her eye, a figure just there behind the clump of rho-
dodendrons at the foot of the lawn. Shading her eyes
with her hand, she peered uncertainly at the shrubbery, wondering who it might be. The figure moved
slightly and now she could make out a bizarre face
staring back at her from under an old top hat.

"Oh!" she cried out, astonished to discover who it
was. She stepped quickly back, then drew herself up
before the intruder.

"For pity's sake," she said shortly, "what is it?
What are you doing in there—in my rhodies?"

"Nothing."

"Come out then, sir, where I can have a look at you. And be careful of my portulaca."

Cautiously he stepped over a flowered border and stood on the lawn, head lowered, looking at her from under dark slanting brows.

"Well, have you come to call me more names?" she demanded starchily.

"No'm." A cane slipped from his hand to the grass.

"What then? What are you doing in my garden? What do you want? Are you up to further mischief?" She pointed to the open garage door and the shelf beside the ball of twine. "Don't you know that stuff's poison? That's why I have put it out of harm's way."

"Yes'm."

"Then you march right along home. Boys who use such words are never welcome at my house."

He turned and started away.

"And pick up your cane, for heaven's sake. Don't leave it around this place, I've enough clutter."

He retrieved the stick and started off, an almost tragic figure, mournful-faced under the tall black hat, the hem of his cape trailing on the ground. He seemed to be encountering difficulty with something or other moving inside his pink shirt.

"Just a moment." She seemed uncertain. "Now— see here, Holland—" she took a step toward him. "Perhaps—perhaps if you said you were sorry—per- haps if you could apologize, you wouldn't have to go."

"Yes'm."

"Yes, what?"

"I'm sorry."

"Are you, dear?" Her tone entreated his contrition. "Are you truly?"

"Yes. I'm sorry I called you names. It wasn't very nice of me." He shook his head most gravely. "Not nice at all."

She beamed at him as he came back and reached up to kiss her. "Well, gracious me," she said, taken aback. "Why—I don't know what to say. Nobody's kissed me in—what is it, do I have something there?" He had reached to wipe a smudge which had appeared on her cheek. "Now, we'll just pretend that other business never happened. We'll say no more about it, shall we?" She seemed so relieved to have it over and done with. "You're Watson Perry's grandson," she said, marveling. "We went to school together, your grandfather and I, did you know that?" She bent to him, spry and tiny and white-haired. "You boys have grown so. Why, I can remember the last time I saw your brother. He came to tea one day, with some of the other children. I think it was he that came." Pressing the broken piece of begonia between thumb and finger, she sounded not quite sure. "Or perhaps it was the little Talcott boy—"

"He's dead, Mrs. Rowe."

"Oh mercy, you don't mean it! Why, he couldn't have been more than nine or ten, could he?"

"No'm." He explained about how Billy Talcott fell through the ice on Washington's Birthday. She clucked and drew him along. "We mustn't speak of such things. You have a sister too, don't you? She'll be quite grown up by now."

"She's nineteen, Mrs. Rowe."

"Nineteen?"

"Yes. Torrie's married."

"Married? That little child? Who did she marry?"

"Rider Gannon. You know the Gannons—they live in the big brick house down on the green."

"Gannon, Gannon." She tried to place the name. "Not Charlotte and Everett Gannon's boy? Why, wasn't he killed?"

"That was Harvey, Rider's older brother. He was killed in France."

"Oh? Yes—that's what I meant. Oh, that was Harvey, was it? Now I remember. It seems to me Gannon's in the fire department, isn't he? I saw him go by in the truck just the other day. I was putting up my flag for Memorial Day. There was a fire up at the old Wooldridge place on Packard Lane, they said."

Smiling, he shook his head and pushed the hair out of his eyes. "No, that's Al Gammond that drives the firetruck." The Wooldridge house had burned to the ground a year ago Fourth of July.

"Oh," she said, musing a moment, her face clouding briefly as some unspoken wisp of thought played hide-and-seek across the meadows of her memory. She brightened again. "Well, have you come to visit me, Holland?"

"If you want." One hand was busy fiddling with something under the folds of his cape.

"Isn't that nice. You should be off with your friends, not spending time with an old lady like me. But as long as you're here, would you care to come in and have tea with me?" She inclined her head formally, awaiting his answer.

"Sure, I'll come. I was hoping you'd ask me."

"Why bless your heart. And *look* at us, will you.

Goodness, I've never seen anything so fascinating." Truly, she seemed to find his appearance astonishing and was unable to take her eyes off him. "What are you all got up for, a play?"

"We're going to have a show in the barn. I'm Professor Rabbitwaters, the magician."

"A magician!" She clapped her hands enthusiastically. "How grand."

He gave her an odd look. "Yes. Would you like me to do a trick for you?"

"Well, wouldn't that be nice!" she said. "Come along then. If you don't mind, we'll just go in through the kitchen. Company usually comes in by the front door, but we mustn't stand on ceremony." She laughed gaily and, opening the back-porch screen door, followed him inside.

"I'm afraid I don't *have* any frankfurters today, but there's lemonade and ice cream, and I *think* some cake . . ." Stepping toward the kitchen she started and gave a cry of surprise. "Oh, there's *another* one!" She pointed to a shadowy corner where a trap had been sprung by a large gray rat, its neck flattened under the heavy clamp. "Holland—" she said, "would you—" She gestured at the dead thing. "I simply can't bring myself to go near one. Mrs. Cooney always took care of such things."

He pulled out the trap, released the rat, and held it up by the tail. The coat of gray hair was stiff and matted, the eyes shut tight, the pink mouth forced open, exposing rows of tiny white teeth. "What should I do with it?"

"Take one of those paper bags, dear, then drop it in the garbage, would you?" White-lipped, biting the

back of her hand, she watched him deposit the dead
animal in a sack and roll up the top, pulling back in
terror as he passed her and went to the garbage can
at the garage door. Seeing that the rat was safely out
of sight and the garbage lid replaced, she waited for
him to join her and together they went through into
the kitchen.

"Some more lemonade, dear?" Mrs. Rowe asked,
holding out the pitcher for him.

"Yes, thank you," he said politely. They were sitting in the parlor before the empty fireplace. Case-
ment curtains obscured the view from the street, but
the afternoon sun shed a diffused light through the
side windows, between heavy velvet portières pulled
back over ornate glass ticbacks. Opposite them an
enormous mirror with twining leaves and fruit and
cupids duplicated the room in all its particulars,
making it appear that there were four people, two
white-haired smiling ladies and their guests, two serious young men in opera clothes, taking tea together
—tea for the ladies and lemonade and cake for the
young men. Lamps of colored crystal dripped flashing prisms which tinkled faintly. Dried flower clus-
ters and bright birds were everywhere imprisoned under transparent domes. A bowl of wax fruit collected
dust. Beside a marble mantel stood a glass case, its
shelves cluttered with a provocative collection of me-
mentos and curios.

"Well," said Mrs. Rowe, "isn't this nice." She had
brought out her best cup and saucer, from which she
sipped as she rocked in her chair. "An unexpected
surprise, which is the best kind! And just such an

afternoon. I must confess, I was longing for company
—I miss Mary Cooney so. I always enjoy having visitors, though they do seem to come more rarely. I
particularly like seeing children, like yourself, Holland. I have always thought that having the young
around keeps me young myself."

"It's nice to be here," he offered agreeably. He
could see what she said was true: her face had about
it a certain little-girl quality. In a second his gaze had
drifted again to the glass case, which had captured
his interest. His eyes searching the shelves, he
mechanically reached into a pocket, removed the
harmonica, and began a song.

Nyang-gang-ga-dang-dang ding-ding ga-dang-
dang-dang—

"Why, aren't you clever," said Mrs. Rowe. "I used
to play the cello years ago; what is that ditty?"

"Oh, it's just—nothing—a nursery rhyme." He
sang a few lines to her:

> *"How many miles to Babylon? Threescore*
> *miles and ten—*
> *Can I get there by candlelight? Yes, and back*
> *again."*

She clapped appreciatively. "I see you're interested
in my curio collection. That belonged to my husband"—pointing out a silver sword—"he brought it
from Toledo; in Spain, you know. All the best sword
steel comes from Toledo. You may take it out if you
care to. I know how young boys enjoy things like
that."

He got up and, laying the harmonica on one of the
glass shelves, removed the sword from the case, in-

spected it, then took up an ivory comb and held it to the light.

"That came from Peking, China," she explained. "See how fragile it is. And that glass ball is from Prague, in Czechoslovakia. Aren't you warm with that cape? Why don't you just slip it off—that's better. My, spats and all, I declare. Such a pretty shirt. I love pink, it's so—Are you quite comfortable, Holland?" He seemed to have a problem keeping himself still, as though something inside his shirt were tickling him. "Do you need to use the facilities?"

A blush stole over his face. "No'm—I'm fine," he said, still fiddling at his side. "Say," he continued, as though the thought had just struck him, "would you like to see me do my trick now?" Though the blush had faded, his expression was alight with expectation.

"A trick? Ah, you want to sing for your supper, is that it?"

"No, not *sing*. Do a trick. I want to do a *trick* for you." He looked at her anxiously.

"Why, that would be very nice." She sat forward in her chair as he slid into his cape again and made a circuit of the room, lifting in turn each of the portières from their glass tiebacks and letting them fall across the windows.

"Oh my," she said with the slightest trepidation as the room grew dim, "is that necessary?"

"It's a better light for the trick," he said matter-of-factly, and returned to take up a position before her.

"Oh, very mysterious, is it? All magicians are *misterioso,* aren't they? Would this be a card trick?"

"Oh no. Card tricks are for kids. This is a grown-up trick." Turning his back to her, he made certain arrangements which, though she failed to grasp their import, did not fail to pique her curiosity. At length he faced her again. Her eyes bright with anticipation, her hands folded comfortably in her lap, she observed as he removed his silk hat and held it in front of him, tipping it upside down and tapping it in the tradition of all magicians, to prove its bonafide emptiness. "Professor Rabbitwaters," he announced dramatically, "will now pull something from his hat!"

"Heavens," she said, leaning forward still further from her chair, "something from his hat! Will it be a rabbit?"

"Not exactly," he said cryptically, a naughty grin on his red mouth, and though she laughed, a tinkling crescendo ending in a little grace note of disbelief, he made no other reply but went straightaway about his business, performing abracadabra and hocus-pocus, using his eyes strangely to divert her attention from his hands, moving adroitly beneath the cape, and then, his grin ever-widening, answering her eager smile, he stepped briskly forward one more step and, without further ado, performèd his trick.

V

Hot. Getting hotter.

By day and by night, summer bloomed, blazed. The horse-chestnut tree became a darker green, its leaves broadening, glistening with a leathery, waxy sheen, its branches sprouting small prickly balls. The lawns, however, sprouted only dandelions, crabgrass, and witchweed. Awnings were useful. While certain people returned, sorrowfully, to the city, others arrived to enjoy the blandishments of the country. Some loved the weather, some endured it, some suffered from it. My, wasn't it muggy, sticky, damp, humid? And in an age before air conditioning, too.

But complain about the weather as you might, you couldn't do anything about it. So saith Mr. Crofut, the mailman, blowing his whistle every half-block along the Valley Hill Road to announce his coming. "T'ain't the heat, it's the humidity." That was another of Mr. Crofut's sagacious, oft-repeated observations. And folks all over Pequot Landing were feeling it.

Mr. Pretty, the vegetable man, wiped his red face with a bandana and rang his cowbell from the cab of his truck and waved at Mr. Klepper the seafood man, who shouted "Fish!" at the top of his lungs and wished he had more ice. Mr. Swate, the Congregational church sexton, rake in one hand, a watering can in the other, paused at his labors over a grave and cursed the thermometer, softly, not to shame those underfoot. Mrs. Jewett, her husband being in Providence or Fall River or Bangor, was having the sunporch painted, and her house smelled of turpentine; she retreated to her hammock under the backyard beeches and put a newspaper over her head. Rose Halligan, whose day off from the Ten Cent Store it was, boarded the Center Street trolley uptown to take in an air-cooled double feature. Mr. Pennyfeather, being taken for a walk by Mrs. Pennyfeather, he in seersucker, she in a pongee dress and a barrette to keep her hair out of her face, strolled along the sidewalk and said hello to Mrs. Joacum, digging worms from her front grass. Mr. Angelini pushed the lawnmower—*cleckcleckcleckcleck*—around a square of lawn behind the Perry house while—*snip . . . snip . . . snip*—in the rose garden beside the carriage-house, Niles was clipping Granddaddy's Emperor roses.

Snip.

The steel nippers of the rose shears were shining and sharp; they parted a stem neatly and Niles made a deft catch before the flower hit the ground. But today his mind was elsewhere. On magicking, to be precise. There was this trick—*snip*—the one he had envisioned for the show in the barn. A difficult one to bring off, particularly with Aunt Josie being gone, and he mulled over in his mind how this feat might best be accomplished. *Snip.*

Carrying a sizable bouquet, he went to replace the red-handled rose shears on their nail next to Father's hip boots hanging on the wall of the tool shed. All of Mr. Angelini's tools had blue-crayoned outlines around them, indicating their proper spaces.

At a sound, he looked through the door to the breezeway, where he saw the hired man, standing back in the shadows, regarding him silently.

"Hi, Mr. Angelini."

Under the battered straw hat, there was a strange look in the dark, red-rimmed eyes. Then, tentatively, the man raised his arm in salute and let it fall to his side.

"It's all right, Mr. Angelini," Niles said, stepping

across the threshold with his flowers, reaching to touch the old man's sleeve. "It wasn't your fault. It'll be all right." He waited while Mr. Angelini, who said only, " 'Scusa me," heaved a sack of fertilizer into a wheelbarrow and stumbled away.

Wonderful odors wafted forth from the kitchen: Winnie was baking one of her marble cakes.

"Wipe yore feet!" Her familiar chant ended in a rising inflection warning of dire consequences.

"I did," Niles hastened to assure her, the screen door clattering behind him as he stepped over a basketful of root beer bottles and left a trail of grass cuttings across the linoleum to the sink. At her ironing board, Winnie shook a woeful head. For how many years had she tried to train Perry kids not to track up her floor? Fall, leaves; winter, snow; spring, mud; summer, half the lawn, natcherly.

"Where you been?" she asked amiably, over the bleat of her radio program.

"Oh, around," he informed her.

Enormously edified, she watched him lay the roses on the drainboard, pull out a cabinet drawer, and step up on it to reach a high cupboard. "What're you doin'—yore grandmother's good vase! If you put them roses onto the piano, put a saucer under. Honest."

"They're not for the piano, they're for Mother." Dragging a chair to the sink, he busied himself with the faucet.

"Niles, what're you doin' there?"

"Washing off the bugs."

"Bugs?"

"There's lots of June bugs this year and—"

She rolled her eyes heavenwards. "Oh God, in my sink."

"When's lunch?"

"When's it ever?"

"Noon."

"All right, sir. 'S'not eleven, yet."

"What's to eat?"

"Croquettes."

"Cro-*quettes?* Wow!"

She marveled at the amount of water he managed to spatter over the vicinity. "What's for supper?"

"How can you be thinkin' about supper when you ain't had yore lunch yet?"

"Just asking."

"What's today?"

"Friday."

"Then what's for supper?"

"Oh. Fish. Shad?"

"Shad's 'bout gone by."

"Swordfish?"

" 'S'early fer swordfish, lest you want salted. Tonight's haddock—if Sam Klepper ever gets here."

"Fish—ick."

"If anybody's around to eat it, that is."

"Why?"

" 'Cause it's Friday, that's why—yore uncle's got American Legion, I got Jennie to visit, you got choir practice, and yore mother's got no appetite, so that leaves Missus to eat the haddock."

"It's okay—a full stomach makes me burp. And if I burp I can't sing so good and Professor Lapineaux makes cracks." He had gone to produce a box of Sunshine biscuits from the drawer of the Hoosier

cabinet, and was munching. Winnie carefully folded
a shirt and, to keep it from harm's way, put it on top
of the refrigerator, where a Gothic-shaped radio sat,
at all hours rivaling the Atwater-Kent in the parlor,
the larger one most regularly broadcasting *Amos 'n'
Andy* weekdays at seven on the Red Network, the
smaller competing with *Easy Aces* on the Blue.

"Fish is good for the brain, they say," Winnie
pointed out as she deftly maneuvered the nose of her
iron around the buttons on a pair of pants. "Not that
you need more, if you'd use what God had the grace
to give you. Ni-YULS! Get that monster out of my
kitchen!"

With the most angelic of faces, he picked up the
chameleon he had placed on a carton in the open
Hoosier, hoping to see it turn blue or yellow. He
dropped it down his front and got back on the chair
to stick the roses one by one in the vase.

"Niles, angel, why'd you use that chair?" It was a
Hitchcock arrowback, and an antique.

"To stand on," he told her, as if she couldn't see. *STILL*

"Who'd of guessed. But you're more than tall *KID*
enough to reach the faucets without—" She appealed *IN HIS
HEAD*
to her God. "Lord, how them kids treat the things in
this house—I swear the Salem rocker's going to fall
apart, the way it's treated."

"Did Buffalo Bill really sit in that rocker?"

"Beats me. I ain't *that* old."

Old or not, she had been there in her kitchen domain since before he and Holland were born; Winnie,
her homely face continually flushed from heat or ex-
ertion, always puffing, her coiled braids casting a
constant trail of pins as she lumbered about, fluffing,

dusting, plumping, wiping, buffing, paring, mending, washing, cooking.

"What're you *doing?*" she demanded as, pushing his rear end out, he pranced about on the wooden chair seat in time with the music.

"It's a dance step. Torrie taught it to me. See—?"

"Quit!" A sergeant's order. Her perspiring face waled like corduroy with ribs of consternation, she turned off the radio and whisked him from the chair with a sturdy arm. "Yore sister didn't teach you no dancing on no antique chairs." With little time for talking, Winnie chose rather to holler, as though communicating with the deaf or foreign-tongued. Setting him down, she pinned her braids more securely and blew out her cheeks exasperatedly as Ada came in from the front hall, a bundle of bedding in her arms.

"I've stripped all the beds but Alexandra's, when you have time," she said, handing the bundle to Winnie, who chucked it into the back-entryway. Just then an oven timer went off, and Niles, in his deepest *Amos 'n' Andy* voice said, "Buzz me, Miz Blue."

"Oh God, I fergot my cake—I hope it ain't burned." Winnie grabbed up a potholder and went to the oven, the linoleum quaking beneath her tread. She opened the door of the range, flapped at the hot maw with her apron to shoo the heat, removed two cake tins, and placed them on a damp towel on the porcelain-topped table. She snatched at a slip-strap as she produced an additional pan of cupcakes, and turned the gas off. "Lord, it's hot. Think I might just run a couple of these extras over to Mrs. Rowe's when they cool."

"I don't imagine she's eating too good, with Mrs. Cooney gone," Ada said, counting rubber canning rings from the drawer of the Hoosier.

Winnie unplugged her iron, lugged the board out to the back-entryway, then returned, puffing, to bear away the laundry, tripping over the basket of filled root beer bottles as she dashed out to catch the fish man.

"Niles, child," Ada said, "that root beer will never ferment if it don't get out in the sun."

"With this heat, it'll cook in no time. How come you always like a lot of lemon in your root beer?"

"Because I do not care for the taste of root beer."

"Try sarsaparilla, why don't you?"

"Here all the sarsaparilla is too much bubbles. They hurt my nose. I don't think sarsaparilla is good for people."

"Holland likes it."

"We all have our likes," she said, her look rather severe. "And shall you please get your bicycle out of the way before your uncle drives in and runs over it."

Niles sighed. Why was he always the one to catch it? "That's not my bike, it's Holland's. Mine's got a flat. And anyway, Uncle George's got Legion, so he won't be driving in. But I'll move it," he said, catching her warning look. "Ada? Did Buffalo Bill really sit in the Salem rocker?"

"Why yes, he did. It is a most historic chair."

"Why did he come here?"

"He was here with his Wild West show. Up at Charter Oak Park. Before you boys were born."

"Yes, but what was he doing *here?*"

"In the house? Why, he was a friend of Granddaddy Perry's, I believe. They had the same dentist, which was how they became acquainted. It became a tradition for the two men to get together. Your Granddaddy was a great believer in tradition. He had many famous friends. Mark Twain and Buffalo Bill and Mrs. Stowe." Yes, certainly, the lady writer. Why, she exclaimed, you never would have known Daddy Perry was the Onion King. A farmer? Nonsense; he loved wearing spats, and in the summer he always had a bachelor button in his lapel. Oh, the pride in his roses. Pride and tradition, that was Daddy Perry. Was that why he gave the money to the town? Niles wanted to know. Well, he gave the money because he had a generous spirit. And after Grandmother went away—well, never mind that. But the Memorial Dinner was given every year in his name because he thought about other people as well as his own family. Not a public demonstration, by any means, but a private ritual, honoring the generosity of one kind man.

"And that's why we get to drink the toast too," he said, " 'cause we're his grandsons, Holland and me, and we believe in tradition too," and went out through the swinging door bearing away the silver vase filled with roses for Mother, with Ada calling after, reminding him to lay out the root beer bottles in the sun.

"Darling, they're beautiful," Alexandra said when he had carried the roses to her room. Chin in hand, she was sitting in the chintz-covered chair with the copy of *Anthony Adverse* on her lap. "Twelve hundred pages—it's awfully long. Almost Gargantuan. But I've so been looking forward to reading it."

It pleased him when she said that; she looked forward to so little any more. Mother would enjoy her book, and that was good, he thought, putting the roses on her dressing table and turning the vase to advantage. It seemed to him her mind was elsewhere today; she was more restive, her face looked strained under the bright spots of color on her cheeks, and the eyes more melancholy, with faint circles beneath; when she dropped her lids he saw that their edges had a bluish cast.

"It's twelve hundred and twenty-four pages. But you're a fast reader. Miss Shedd says once you start, you won't put it down." He took the book from her and, seated on the dressing table stool, read a page or two aloud. "What is it?" he asked, pausing to look up at the moth-pale smile that crossed her face.

"I was just thinking how things change. When you were younger I used to read to you boys. Every month, when *Good Housekeeping* came, Martin Johnson's story about Africa—Martin and—what was his wife's name?"

"Osa." He closed the book on his thumb.

"Osa, yes. You both thought that was such a funny name for a lady hunter. And there was Tom the Water Baby—"

Niles giggled. "And Wampus Tommy."

"Wampus Tommy? I don't remember him."

"Ada used to read it to us. He was a cat."

"Cat?" She frowned at the thought and lightly put her fingertips to her eyes. "I remember Piggy Look-a-doo. He got roasted with an apple in his mouth, poor greedy thing. One of Holland's favorites, wasn't it?"

"No—that's the changeling, remember? In the fairytale book?"

"The changeling? Oh, what a horrid story! How could that be anybody's favorite?" She prowled from her chair to a window, where she lifted the curtain and gazed down at the arbor, one hand raised to her breast as though feeling for her heartbeat. "Poor Aunt Fanuschka, it's sad that she came all the way up here only to get stung by a bee."

"Wasp—it was a wasp," Niles said, picking up the photograph of the poverty party, smiling at Father in his dress and rubber hip boots.

"Yes dear, a wasp. And of all people, with all the pains she took." It was pitiful. As soon as they had gotten Aunt Fania into the house, Dr. Brainard had been called, but all his shots and pills were unavailing, her whole body swelled up, her hearing had been affected; finally she was removed to Harkness Pavilion in New York, where Aunt Josie, who had to get back to the photography studio, could be near her.

With a sigh, Alexandra sat again; she reached across Niles to take up the hairbrush, toyed with it, put it down.

"Here, play with these." He picked up the three sliced pieces of tan-colored bean he had bought for her and laid them gently in her hand, where they proceeded to dance around. "They'll jump more if you warm them," he explained. "Each one's got a little worm inside—a moth larva. That's what makes them move." He closed her fist over the jumping beans and squeezed it tight.

"Goodness, is that how it's done? Where do you learn all these things? Certainly they don't teach you about jumping beans in school."

"It's not a bean, it's a seed. It tells all about them on one of the Chautauqua rolls." *Reminder*

Abruptly her head lifted.

"Mother—what is it?"

She was looking at him so peculiarly. "Chautauqua," she mused; a brief flicker of her lids, and her expression altered, quick as a flash. He cleared his throat in the uncomfortable silence. What was it? Something unspoken hung in the air. He was waiting for something . . .

"Are you okay?"

"Yes. Surely, dear. Ada's Chautauqua—it's a mine of information, isn't it? I'd forgotten."

She drummed her nails on the crocheted runner on the dressing table. She opened her mouth, closed it, compressed her lips. Her smile seemed to him exhausted. "Darling," she said brightly, "hadn't you better be outdoors, playing? I'm not sure you should be reading that book anyway."

"What did Mrs. Stowe write?"

"Harriet Beecher Stowe? Why, *Uncle Tom's Cabin*. You remember that. Liza crossing the ice, and Simon Legree?"

"Yes."

"I recall once when we were sitting right here— you and I and Holland—we were reading that book and you looked at me very innocently and said, 'Mother, what did you do in the Civil War?' "

Her look was sad and wistful and he laughed, trying to instill in her some of his own mirth; but she only laid her head back and closed her eyes.

"Mother?"

"Yes dear?"

"Are you all right?"

"Yes dear."

"Want me to read some more to you?"

"No dear." But she caught him before he could start away, and pressed his hand. He scrutinized her face, saw the fluttering hand, feverish, indecisive, somehow poignant. It was something about the tobacco tin, he felt sure. Yes, that was it; Holland's secret. No, she didn't really want to ask; not really. Prince Albert, wasn't it? Very lightly, hardly mentioning the matter. The kind Father smoked? Oh, she was foolish, her eyes were playing tricks. He knew what she must be thinking. *Oh Mother, Mother darling . . .* how he wished he could help. *We help by understanding. That is the only help there is.* Yes; he understood.

She had the jumping beans between her palms and was rubbing them briskly together, rubbing her thought away. "I'm silly—you've got a silly mother, and there you have it. When you go down, dear, tell Victoria to be sure to take her tonic. She's sitting in the arbor. Dear Victoria, you are doing a terrible thing to me, making me a grandmother. Perhaps it will be twins—they do run in families, they say."

Niles shook his head. "No, it's going to be just one and it'll be a girl."

"Wizard," she said, taking a playful tone. In the distance a bell sounded.

"Here comes Mr. Pretty," Niles said. "Did he really used to be the iceman?"

"Before you were born, when we had an icebox."

"Now we have a Kelvinator."

"So does half the town; which is why Mr. Pretty is now the vegetable man."

"That reminds me—I have a new joke for you."

"Do you, dear?"

"Yes." He giggled in anticipation; a ritual. "Ready?"

She put on a proper listening face. "Yes, darling, I'm ready."

"Do you know the one about the mouse in the refrigerator?"

"No, I don't think so."

"Well, it seems there was this lady who went to her refrigerator and when she opened the door she found a mouse lying on top of the butterplate. So she said to the mouse, 'What are you doing in my refrigerator?' And the mouse said, 'Isn't this a Westinghouse?' And the lady said yes and the mouse said, 'Well, I'm westing.' "

"Oh Niles." She took his hand and squeezed it again, as if that slight pressure could, of itself, elicit the response she sought. He saw her face beginning to crumple. In a moment, he knew, she would try to laugh it off, as always, would try to keep from crying, from causing the least scene, the least distress.

Oh Mother, Mother—come with me. Come into the parlor and play the piano. You and me, while Holland's gone. Duets. "I Hear as in a Dream" from *The Pearl Fishers,* or "Country Gardens." Mother, seated at the keyboard, elegant, slipping the flashing rings from her fingers, nails clicking like scarlet beetles on the keys. No; it was out of the question; she was frightened. He gave her back her hands. They wilted into her lap as if possessing no life of their own.

He kissed her and bid her goodbye, closing the door part way when he went out. In a while she got up and opened the scarf drawer; the bottle she brought out was empty. Hearing a step, she replaced it and quickly resumed her chair. Winnie came in with an armload of fresh ironing.

"Here's clean sheets and pillowcases for you, Mrs. Alex," she said, perspiring from climbing the stairs. "I'll be back to change yore bed."

"Thank you, Winnie," she said, helping her sort the linen from a pile of fresh laundry. "Honestly, this shirt of Holland's is practically a rag by now. Look how the sleeves are frayed. Can't you make a dust-cloth of it? People will think we're poorer than we are."

"Oh, I wouldn't do that, Mrs. Alex," Winnie protested. "I wouldn't dare do nothing with it."

"All right, Winnie. I suppose. Thank you."

"I got to get down and see to some vegetables. I heard P. C.'s cowbell. Anything special you'd care for?"

"Winnie, will you be going to the Center today?"

"Ah no, m'am. You know what the doctor said." She pulled away and made a considerable business of laying the shirts across her arm.

"Winnie!" Alexandra cried gaily. "Look at yourself in that apron! Why, it's ancient. And look at how the rickrack is worn. You see, people will say we are absolutely *poverty* stricken!" She dug around in her pin dish for a five dollar bill. "Now you take this and stop by Miss Josceline-Marie's this afternoon and see if you can't find a pretty cotton print for a new apron. I'll cut it for you and Ada can put it on the machine. No, I insist. A little present from me to you. And Winnie, while you're down there, just stop next door for me—please? Use the change from the apron. That's all right, you go along now. Perhaps we could have corn-on-the-cob for dinner, if P. C. has any nice Golden Bantam. Just leave those things on the bed, I'll put them away for you. No, no trouble. I haven't been in the boys' room in—why, it must be ages. I think I'd like to have a look."

She was left then, alone, staring at the pieces of tan seed leaping in her warm hand, erratically and to no purpose, activated by no apparent force; and the warmer her hand grew, the more insane became their movement, insistently, aggravatingly nonsensical, like the answer to the question that kept jumping in her mind. *Role of Niles in Holland's death, etc*

VI

"Mornin', Niles," the vegetable man called as the boy came through the back-entryway, lugging an apple basket filled with quart bottles, their dark amber liquid and bright brass caps winking in the sun. Thursday, when Ada took the streetcar up to the city for Russian Orthodox services, was always root beer night (Rose Rock provided George with sarsaparilla and ginger ale, but no root beer, everybody's favorite) and each morning for the next week the capped bottles had to be distributed on the grass to ferment.

"Hi, Mr. Pretty," Niles called back as he quickly laid out the bottles in spiral formation and slung the empty basket back to the door, almost hitting Winnie's portly figure as she emerged.

"Ya missed me, kiddo," she said, then turned to greet the beaming Mr. Pretty. "Mornin', P. C. How's for some Golden Bantam t'day?"

Mr. Pretty polished up a cucumber on the bib on his overalls. "Sorry, Winnie," he said, munching. "Jerry had to go up to Hazardville with a load of turnip. Corn won't get picked until this afternoon. I can come back if ya like."

Winnie looked dubious. "Mrs. Alex asked special. What else ya got?"

"Swiss chard's nice t'day."

Niles sauntered over, making a face. "Swiss chard —ick. Tastes like dandelion greens."

"Let me have about a peck, P. C. And you'd better come back with the corn, I guess. Mrs. Alex don't ask for things often."

"Say, dandelion greens," P. C. said, "that reminds me, I been wonderin', yore neighbor-lady, Miz Rowe —she gone away or somethin'?"

"That's what I was wonderin' myself. I made some cupcakes and I was goin' to take some over and I says to Missus, I haven't seen Mrs. Rowe for a week or more. You haven't either?"

"Not hide nor hair. Usually Miz Cooney boils her up a mess of tripe Fridays and I bring her some dandelion greens. I knocked and rang, but I couldn't raise a soul."

"You knew she'd left, Mrs. Cooney?"

Mr. Pretty was measuring out the greens under Niles's baleful stare. "Yep. She come out to say good-bye to me before she went. Reckon how Miz Rowe misses her. I don't think Miz Rowe's such a good housekeeper. You can't *believe* the smell over there."

"Smell?"

Mr. Pretty's eyes were huge. "You'd swear some-thin' up and died."

"Maybe there wa'n't nobody to put her garbage out."

P. C. scratched doubtfully. "Here, here's a couple cukes for ya. On the house." He added cucumbers to the mass of Swiss chard he had cradled in her arms. "How's yore sister?" he inquired solicitously.

"Oh—'bout the same, P. C., thanks for asking. She don't complain." Jennie Koslowsky had rheumatic fever and every Friday Winnie used her night off to take the streetcar out Babylon way to visit her. "Niles, angel, fish in my purse for P. C., wouldja?" Niles ran to take from her apron pocket the worn change purse he and Holland had given her four birthdays ago. "You can pay for the corn now."

"How much, Mr. Pretty?"

"Well, lessee. How many corn, Winnie—dozen and a half ears? Sixteen times five is eighty and a quarter for the Swiss chard ought to do it, no charge for cukes, that's eighty and twenty-five is a dollar five. Have some parsley, too, it's on the house."

"No, that's your mother's five dollars," Winnie told Niles, "give P. C. the dollar bill and find him a nickel, angel." She marched inside, her plump brown arms garnished like Sunday roasts with the Swiss chard, cucumbers, and parsley. "S'long, P. C., much obliged. Wipe yore feet!" she loudly cautioned as Niles popped in after her. In a moment he reappeared, running to the vegetable man with a frosty pop bottle from the refrigerator. "Here, Mr. Pretty, have a root beer—it's on the house."

"Why, thanks, Niles." As the boy uncapped it with the opener on his jackknife, Mr. Pretty squeezed himself back into the cab of his truck. "I'll return the bottle when I come back later," he shouted with a cheery bob of his red face, amid a salvo of backfires, his truck chugging, rattling, swaying from side to side as he circled the pump and coaxed it up the drive, awning flapping, scales banging, and, swinging wildly at the rear bumper, the red kerosene lantern he used as a taillight.

Niles went to move apart several bottles that were touching and might possibly explode in the sun. He kicked aimlessly at the dandelions in the grass, swung his arms loosely in their sockets, shrugged. Took a stick and whacked awhile at the baby horse chestnuts. Traced his finger on the fading rings of the target Father had painted on the trunk. Threw the stick as far as he could. Got bored. Looked around for something else to do.

Phew, it was hot. He ambled over to the pump, pushed the handle, took a drink. He wiped the bitter copper taste from his mouth and hung the cup in its accustomed place. Then he filled the pool under the spout, put his hand over the drain, and watched

where the water formed a face for him—not a perfect
one, but near enough.

"Niles."

Ada was calling through the screen door. She
pointed at the bike, still in the drive.

"Okay."

He rolled it under the tree and leaned the saddle
against the trunk. Holland's *Reddy Racer,* red, black,
and chrome, with a kickstand, a wire basket, a rack
behind, and instead of a bell, a klaxon. He pressed
the heel of his hand on the plunger: *Hahroogahr!* it
sounded.

Where had Holland gotten to now? Where, for
that matter, was everybody? Anybody? Torrie wasn't
in the arbor, as Mother said; he could hear her over
the way, laughing with Mrs. Joacum. Mr. Angelini?
The mower had been abandoned in the middle of the
lawn, but of the hired man, not a trace. The heavy air
was saturated with the sour odor of grass cuttings. A
katydid sang in the elm out front. Winnie had her
radio on again. Mr. Crofut's whistle sounded.

July was a pain. And more than a week of it left.
Just plain boring. If you didn't go to the seashore or
to camp, you were bored. Holland didn't want to go
to camp, and with Father dead and Mother the way
she was, who, Niles wondered, would take them to
the seashore? Meanwhile, suffer. T'ain't the heat, it's
the humidity. Well, there was one refuge sure to be
cool—the icehouse.

He trotted across the drive and under the breezeway. He ran through the granary yard and past the
dump heap, where Mr. Angelini had stuck his empty
gasoline can. It lay on top of the pile, radiating heat.

Taking the slope past the wagon room in a series of bounds, Niles dashed into the buttery meadow, arms flung from his sides in imitation of airplane wings, palms skimming the tops of the grass, golden skin flashing below his shorts. Avoiding the road, he cut through the grass, leaping and whooping and hollering around the blackberry bushes, over the patches of devil's paintbrush, the clumps of briars, the long whips of wild roses, down to the river.

The icehouse was fronted by big doors, warped and wide enough for a wagon. Leaning against one, he let his weight swing it inward. The interior was cool and dim; sun through the ruined roof sketched in beams, rafters, scaffolding; through the giant hole in the platform flooring, where the blocks of ice used to be hauled up, the river was a lake of murky green. Cattails clustered at the bank, sausages skewered on slender wands. Removing his sneakers, Niles waded kneedeep into the water. A flat bug skittered across its surface, spidery legs tracing intricate geometric patterns behind. Slippery gray mud at the bottom oozed between his toes; he gripped for balance as he edged along a narrow shelf and reached out to break the stalks of the rushes.

With a goodly harvest, almost more than he could manage, he footed his way back along the mud shelf to the loading platform. He dropped the cattails in a heap and lay on his belly beside them, head hanging over the platform edge, eyes staring meditatively down at the water. It was pleasant there in the shadows. It smelled of coolness, like a fern garden; like the well once had before they sealed it up. From upside down, one piling, gloved with green algae and slime, and larger than the rest, seemed to rear back as though resisting the gray mud that mired it. He squinted, looked hard, saw: primordial ooze, spawning strange beings down below, a race of quasi-lunged, half-legged creatures dragging themselves along the bottom; a world sunless, gloomy, nocturnal, where sunken logs lay, sodden and heavy, poor dead drowned things, and with them, hidden in the murk, savage bloated creatures, mouths wide as shovels, thick lips nuzzling threads of water-whitened ganglia, picking clean of flesh skeletons through whose empty eye-sockets coldly glowing eels wound like night trains, while overhead, through the ruined roof, pterodactyls soared the vacant sky.

He drifted, dreamed; and dreamed some more.

Just past the icehouse, where the sycamore trunk tilted out over the water, was a clear deep pool, perfect for swimming. At the tip of the tree a small platform of planks had been nailed as a crude diving structure; girdling its middle was a frayed rope used for climbing onto the platform.

Toes curled around the sawed wooden edges, the sun hot on his naked skin, Niles stood poised for a moment, then dived. The water felt deliciously cool as his body sliced through it. He stayed under and opened his eyes. A shoal of silvery minnows darted by, clumps of weeds danced, pebbles gleamed whitely. Blowing air from his lungs, he left a trail of bubbles as he gradually sank to the bottom. He bent his knees, pushed off, and with a rush shot to the surface, exploding halfway out of the water.

His feet touched bottom and he stood, arms

akimbo, looking over at the bank. Something moved behind the bushes.

He whistled a few bars of a tune:

> *How many miles to Babylon? Threescore
> miles and ten—*

And smiled when, out of the bushes, came the answer:

> *Can I get there by candlelight? Yes, and back
> again.*

Holland stepped around the shrubbery and stood at the water's edge, a broad smile on his face.

"Hi!"

"Hi!"

"Where've you been?"

"No place."

"You been down to the train tracks?"

"Nope."

"Didja go up to Knobb Street?"

"Nope."

"Packard Lane?"

Holland shook his head and Niles, out of guesses, sighed. He knew where he'd been all right: Babylon, end of the line. "C'mon in," he called to his twin, standing at the bank. Holland shucked off his clothes and in a moment was leaping at him in the water. Niles threw himself backward out of his path, submerged, then surfaced, his wet hair whipping a fan of sparkling drops about his shoulders. Then he arched casually into the shallows and swam across to the small sandbar just breaking the river's surface. Holland threw himself after and flopped down beside him. Panting, Niles gave himself up to the caress of the sun, the cool smoothness of the stones beneath his back, the bright dancing spots beneath his eyelids.

"Hot," he heard Holland murmur. Niles opened his eyes. Against the sky his twin's face looked saturnine, satanic almost, as he shot Niles one of his oblique looks and then, with a lazy half-smile of contentment, closed his own eyes.

There's that secret smile again. What was it, this thing that amused Holland so, this past week or more? What is it? Say. Tell me. No, you won't—you never do, have, will. It wasn't fair. They had come from the same cell, had lived nine months curled around one another. They should have already learned each other's secrets. And he had given his up, all of them. Is that the way it was supposed to be with twins? The Gemini, Castor and Pollux? I already told you all my secrets—all of them. But you keep yours, you hide them. Miserly, sly, secretive Holland, angry half the time, indifferent the rest; twins are supposed to be together, aren't they? *Aren't* they?

He felt overcome; the old, sad feeling, that longing for—what? He could not tell. Fugitive tremors ran through his body, along his limbs, vague yearnings assailed him; again the Shadow Hills came to mind. He tried to picture them. Nothing. His brain groped; what was it? Something he had forgotten? Never learned? Was it a taste, a smell, a place? Babylon—end of the line?

What *was* at the end of the line?

Flinging an arm across his eyes, he slid off the sandbar and floated, while beneath his eyelids an im-

Is he aware of where mad people go?

age hovered: a figure lying there in the coffin in the
parlor, the bottom part closed, the rest hinged back.
Father . . . Father . . . He idled in the water.
"What d'you suppose it's like to be dead?"

"Jeeze, if you're dead, you're dead. That's all. It's
like nothing. They put you in a box, paint your face
up to look like you're alive, but only asleep. Then
they shovel out a hole and lay you in it and that's
all."

"But if you're dead, you've got to go someplace—
heaven or hell or *some* place."

Holland hooted. "Who believes that stuff anyway?
It's just grown-ups' talk for Sunday school."

"But you've got to go somewhere, don't you?"
Niles thought some more. He lay back in the water,
watching first the sky—clouds scarcely more than a
ruffle, like lace on a petticoat under the wide blue
skirt—then dropping his eyes to his twin's face.
"What's the last thing you'd like to see before you
die?"

"Hm?"

"The last thing. If there was one very last thing
you could wish to see before you died, what would
you pick? Like—a sunset? A person? The ocean?
What?"

Holland sniggered. "Listen, if I was dying, I'd be
too busy doing just that to be looking at sunsets. And
so would you."

Floating vertically, his feet lightly touching the
sandy bottom, Niles turned and looked across the
water to some cows ruminating in the meadow below
the Avalon ridge. "I'd wish to see her," he said.

"A cow?" Holland had a fit.

angel of Brighter Day

Niles shook his head and smiled. No, he meant the Angel of the Brighter Day, he explained, his tone serious. The Angel was the last thing he would wish to see. He conjured her up, her hair hanging about her shoulders, shining white wings gently beating, and her smiling as she offered him the lily . . . bearing him away to Paradise . . .

"How d'you know she wouldn't take you to hell?"

"Angels don't go to hell. Only bad people do."

"The devil was an angel once, and he went to hell."

"Lucifer? He went to hell because he was evil." Niles was treading water, his head partially submerged; under a darkened fringe of wet hair on his forehead his eyes shone bright across the glistening water. "You know what that is, don't you?" he asked mildly.

Vil

"What? Evil? Evil is bad, that's all."

"And an evil person is someone who does bad things."

"I guess. I never stopped to think about it." Holland obviously preferred another subject. "I've been thinking about the show."

"What about it?" Niles swam back to the sandbar.

"If we're going to do the trick, we've got to get some light down in the apple cellar. Those cattails are too dry now to use matches. We'll have to get a lantern, hang it somewhere; it'll give enough light."

"Where'll we get a lantern?"

Holland thought for a time, but didn't reply. Then he said, "Have you thought any more about the trick?"

"Yes."

"And?"

Niles knew what he was getting at. "Well—" he began lamely.

"It won't work, will it?"

"Yes it will. The only problem is to make the cabinet—"

Holland chuckled. "Niles Alexander, you've forgotten something."

Had he? What? He was sure he'd figured it all out, Chan Yu's disappearing trick. He couldn't think—

"You forgot. How can the two of us get in the cabinet?"

Ohh. Dumb stupid Niles. Well, he hadn't planned on two. He'd assumed, naturally, since he'd been the one to figure out Chan Yu's trick that he'd be the one to perform it. But no; Holland had other ideas, was shaking his head again.

"You're forgetting something else, too—it *still* won't work."

"Won't? Why won't it?"

"Because of the Slave Door. Remember? No? C'm'on. Put your clothes on. I'll show you."

It was called the Slave Door because, years ago, before the Civil War, when Connecticut had been the first to go abolitionist, Great-Grandfather Perry had passed runaway slaves through it: men and women, children even, sequestered in safety until they could be sent on their way via the underground railway to freedom in Canada. Holland leaned against the wall opposite and said, "Now. Look at me, Niles Alexander. What else have you forgotten?"

Niles didn't know.

"Think. Suppose we build the platform over the trapdoor, say we drop down into the apple cellar. Say it works fine up to that point. Then what?"

"Then we jump off the mattresses, change costume, go out the door, run upstairs and appear in the audience."

"What do we do?" Holland was forcing him to think.

"We run—out—the—" He deflated audibly. There it was, staring him in the face. He was looking right at it. The padlock. Because of Uncle George's orders, a stout padlock and chain secured the hasp and staple, rendering the Slave Door useless. And the key was in Uncle George's pocket. Without it, there was no other way out.

Holland flashed a triumphant smile. "All right now," he said, like an officer taking command of a sinking vessel, "come along," and he ran back up the stairs. He raised the trapdoor and looked down into the cellar. "Listen, I can do it," he said eagerly. "I know how to work the whole thing. You leave it to me."

Niles looked down. All that snow. Snow in July, for the Winter Kingdom of the Akaluks. The shredded cattails lay in soiled drifts, sinking into corners, forming a downy carpet underfoot, bits flurrying upward, swirling snowflakes carried by the air currents. Against the cellar's whitewashed walls the banks of pale stuff made it seem as if a snowstorm had blown in through the trap.

"How? How will we make it work?" His voice was disappointed. "Holland—?"

"Hmm?"

"It isn't going to be any fun, is it?"

"What—the show? Sure it will. I toldja—I've got it all figured out. I know where we can get the lantern. All we need is a Chinese mustache, and a hammer and a saw to build the cabinet."

"Where will we get the lantern?"

"Well," said Holland with a wicked roll of his eyes, "wait and see."

And, yes, Niles guessed, not wanting at all to go through with the show, yes, he'd have to wait and see . . .

VII

Here's July in Connecticut. Here's the whole of Pequot Landing, stupefied in its post-prandial torpor. And here's the sort of mischief a boy can get into on such an afternoon while folks are trying to beat the heat. Here's *Reddy Racer,* black and chrome and red, kickstand, wire basket, and klaxon—*hahroogahr!*— whizzing along Valley Hill Road. Come on along, up to the corner of Fiske Street. Here's Mrs. Jewett cloistered under her beech trees, hammock, newspaper . . . A nifty idea would be to sneak into the house and, using the brush and paint left behind by the painter, write something on the fresh walls with the ceiling color, something nasty, something dirty, something *fun.*

So long, Mrs. Jewett!

Hahroogahr!

Further north, up to Packard Lane; happen upon Mr. Pretty's vegetable truck, parked behind the Pilgrim Drugstore while P. C. downs a lemon phosphate. *Reddy Racer* makes a quick stop—then off and away. P. C., kiss your lantern goodbye. *Haw haw.*

Hahroogarh!

East on Packard Lane to the Thomas Hooker Highway, then south, wheels whizzing, spokes twinkling. There goes Professor Lapineaux in his Hupmobile—*Bonjour, Professeur! Au 'voir, Professor Rabbitwaters Lapineaux.* At Church Street, east across the railroad tracks, take the time to lob a rock at a window in the freight depot when the clerk is out on the loading ramp. Crash! "Hey you, you damn kid—!"

Hahroogarh!

Have a look behind the Congregational Church, where the sexton is laboring in the cemetery. Mr. Swate lifts his sunhat and wipes his brow again. He blinks, can't believe his eyes. "Hey—you! Fer God's sakes, kid, *not on the grave!* Sweet Jesus! Hey—hey you, come back here, you little sacrilegious—" He chases, gives up; takes a closer look at the flowers on the grave; cannot believe his eyes.

Hahroogarh!

Down the drive, out through the wrought-iron cemetery gates, past the church, the green in front, just as the Center Street trolley stops to let off a passenger.

Look out!

"Honest ta Pete, ya think ya own the world, kid? Lookit what ya did ta my stocking!"

"————on you, Roundheels, keep your eyes open."

Hahroogahr!

In spite of the abundance of signs admonishing "Handle at Own Risk," when it came to mouthed peashooters, smudged comic books, or pocketed notions, the proprietress of the Miss Josceline-Marie Gift and Novelty Shoppe was Argus-eyed. From a stool strategically placed behind her cash register near the door, the lady was able to survey her domain while doing a brisk cash-and-carry business, incidentally blotting up whatever gossip chanced to be spilled across her counter.

This afternoon she was having a busy time of it, in spite of the humidity. Such a commotion. Customers coming and going, every which way, quick as a wink —she scarcely had time to powder her nose. Several folks were browsing in the back when a cluster of bells announced further trade. Patting a sea of Jo-Curled waves drying under a net, Miss Josceline-Marie contrived a little face with which to greet her customer.

"Afternoon, Rose. Ohm'gosh, ent that a cute *blouse.*" Miss Josceline-Marie had a face which was round and flat, like a dish, and which seemed to have little pockets in its cheeks, like a chipmunk, where she stored things. She was an enthusiastic lady; you could tell she meant practically every word she spoke.

"Honest ta Pete!" her customer exclaimed, limping in on her high heels and dabbing with a wet thumb at a stocking run. "The kids today!"

" 'S'matter?"

Rose Halligan brandished her thumb over her shoulder. "Why, I was gettin' offa the streetcar just now and some kid darn near run me down on his bike. Look what he done to my stocking. So I says to him, watch where yer goin' and he says ta me, oh, what *he says* ta me—"

"Whadde say?"

Though Miss Josceline-Marie would have been shocked to hear, Rose did not care to enlighten her further. "Got any Belle Sharmeers in?"

"Hosiery, table two, just help yourself m'dear." At no pains to disturb herself, Miss Josceline-Marie pointed out the stocking selection.

"Got Sahara?"

"Just look, m'dear, but don't mess 'em all up!" she shrilled querulously as Rose rummaged.

"Honest honey, it's like a needle in a haystack here. You must be all outta Sahara."

"Take Sand, then. Practically the same—Sand, Sahara," said the other lady, making a plausible connection.

"Welp, they'll just have to do. I'm in a herry." She wobbled to the counter and put her nose in her pocketbook, looking for money, while Miss Josceline-Marie silently remarked how the roots of her customer's hair betrayed the sincerity of its color.

"Got a marvelous new thing in," she said, making change. "Helena Rubinstein's just come out with a new type touch-up for blondes. You might like to give it a try. Not working today?"

"No, my day off. I ben ta the pitchers."

Miss Josceline-Marie's look plainly said Poor You.

"Well, you sure missed all the excitement, didn't you?"

"What excitement? Where?"

"Up on the Hill. Awful thing—can't imagine it—must have been just dreadful—the poor creature—Harold Foley'll have his work cut out for him—"

Rose was trying to get any one of several words in edgewise. "Who—? What—? When—?"

"—just the most ghastly thing this town's seen in a spell, let me tell you. Sixty, seventy-five, one dollar." Miss Josceline-Marie moistened her fingertip with the end of her tongue to slip out a paper bag and said, *sotto voce,* "Listen, m'love, you want to hear something'll freeze your blood in your very veins?"

"Sure." Rose dug Chiclets from her bag.

"Oh, Winnie," Miss Josceline-Marie caroled to the back of the store.

Winnie, who had been selecting apron fabric from the remnant table, approached the counter. "Winnie, this is Rose, Rose Halligan. Tell her what you told me about—you know—*next door.*"

Without preamble Winnie recounted what she had already told Miss Josceline-Marie, how this morning Mr. Pretty the vegetable man had noticed the smell over at Mrs. Rowe's, how, later this afternoon, his route finished, he had returned and tried to look in the back windows, then the front, then the side where there was a space between the closed portières . . . how he had come rushing across and used the telephone, how Winnie and Ada had gone back with him, and—

"—and there she was," Miss Josceline-Marie inter-

Rowe

rupted at this crucial point, "in the parlor. Terrible
way to die."

Rose turned to the horse's mouth. "Whaddja see?"

"She was sittin' right there in her rocking chair—"
Winnie said.

"Her favorite," Miss Josceline-Marie put in.

"—she'd had a heart attack."

"Dead as a doornail. Must of been a week or
more."

"Eek," said Rose, chewing. "Go on."

"Well—"

"Face all purple, mouth wide open, body stiff as
taffy," said Miss Josceline-Marie, troubling to paint a
little picture for Rose. "And the smell. Why, a body
could *die* of it—well, you know what I mean."

Winnie agreed. She and Ada had gotten the windows open while waiting for the constable, who put a
sheet over Mrs. Rowe and called Mr. Foley.

"And she looked natural as life, didn't she, Winnie?" Miss Josceline-Marie plowed on, "setting there
with spider webs spun right across her lap."

"Spiders!" Rose eeked again.

"Spiders," confirmed Winnie.

"Spiders," came Miss Josceline-Marie's echo, her
round cheeks wobbling with indignation.

"Ooh, I'm getting the creepy-crawlies," Rose said,
rubbing away goosepimples.

"It's too too grisly to speak of," Miss Josceline-
Marie said. "Now, please, let's talk about something
pleasant. Oh Winnie, were you wanting that end of
cotton?" Applying a measuring tape to it and squinting to see. "Two and a half yards, m'dear, not

enough for a dress, I'm afraid. An apron? Oh, plenty
for that! 'Bye, Rose."

Practically gasping, Rose, who had spied Esther
from the Maison de Beauté, lurched out the door to
share her exciting news and, while Miss Josceline-
Marie bagged Winnie's remnant of print, back in the
corner at the magazine rack, a little face, gray eyes
bright under the gable-shaped brows, a purloined
Chinese mustache tucked in one pocket, remained
quiet as a mouse.

It was gone.

Discovering that the *Sermon on the Mount* had
given place to the *Marriage Feast at Cana,* Niles removed the Chautauqua scroll spindle and searched
behind it. The Prince Albert tin was gone! He looked
everywhere, on top of things, under things, behind
things. Went on, tearing both beds apart and remak-
ing them, ransacking the drawers, feeling behind
books. Under the beds, only dust kittens. In the
chests, nothing. Yes—hold it—hidden there in the
secret compartment in Holland's chest—*wait a minute!* The glasses—the thick-lensed, steel-rimmed
glasses of Russell—*the missing glasses!*

He went to the window to catch his breath. Funny
things were happening. Ada, cleaning up over at the
Rowe house all afternoon since Mr. Pretty's unhappy
discovery, had returned in a highly agitated state—
naturally enough—except that there was more to it
than that, more than the mere, sad fact of Mrs.
Rowe's death. What had happened over there to distress Ada so? Why did she keep scooping the kitchen

with looks, biting her lip in puzzlement, trying to fit pieces together?

It was very strange.

And then, after Ada had gone back to the Rowe house to see to some other things, Winnie, leaving for her sister's, dropped her bombshell. Mother, she said, had mentioned earlier something about having a look around the boys' room. Cripes! Niles had fled, raced up the back stairs and . . .

. . . *it was gone!*

Worried, he looked out over the barn to the meadow, letting his eye ramble the night. Though the air was still warm, he felt chilled, and his forehead, the back of his neck were damp. Outside, no breeze stirred. Skeins of mist lay along the river. Across the water lights danced in the blur, milky globes of unlikely brilliance, slowly floating up through the blackness like bubbles. Leaning against the horse-chestnut tree, Holland's bike sparkled in the moonlight. Along the drive Fafner and Thor were rigidly unstirring, aloof. There was no movement at all—except . . .

Apprehensively Niles drew his chest closer to the sill, eyes straining to see. Caught a slight movement, just there, under the trees, a figure sprawled out upon the thatch of needles by the well . . . the movement of a tightly closed fist, beating at the cement slab.

Now, suddenly, he knew where the tobacco tin was.

"Mother?"

She was half-prostrate, hair across her face, looking up over her shoulder at him as though he were an intruder, her fingers madly scrabbling at the slab of cement.

"Mother!" Alarmed, he ran forward. He took her hands and drew her to her feet. She whimpered and he could see blood on her fingers where she had injured them. Snatching her hand from his, she knelt and groped for something lying beside the well.

"Mother, come away," he begged and, like a child, she let herself be led out onto the drive. "Mother, what is it?"

She shook her head, remained mute, hid her hand in the folds of her dressing gown, the hem whispering over the grass as he brought her across the lawn to the foot of the outside stairway. Her free hand flitted distractedly to her mouth, as though holding captive unspeakable words. She weaved, seemed about to collapse. Reaching to steady her, he caught the familiar odor. She shrank back against the bottom railing post, her body trembling, bending as though unable to support the unsupportable.

"Please, Mother." He waited for her to go up; again her hand flew to her face and he saw that she had broken a nail near the quick. She started up then, her gown trailing along step by step as she mounted the stairs, and, following, he saw her hand leave a trail of dark spots along the railing.

When she reached the top landing she faltered uncertainly and hiccuped once, leaning against the post while he stepped past her and opened the screen door.

"Niles." Still her words choked in her throat, her expression that of some dumb creature caught in a trap whose jaws have sprung upon some vital part of the body. "Niles." Again she stopped, and the long, silent pause spread apart the moment like doors closing off a room, dividing it into separate chambers. Still mute, she took her hand from the folds of her gown and opened her fist; in the palm lay the gold ring, Peregrine for Perry.

"Oh," he said softly, reaching for it. "You found the tobacco can. I knew you had." A slight movement: she was holding the tin in her other hand. When she spoke it was with immense difficulty.

"Niles, what are you doing with that ring?"

"It's Father's."

"I know that. And your father gave it to Holland. What are you doing with it?"

"Where's the packet that was with it, Mother?" *The Thing; she has opened, has seen it . . . Holland . . .*

She drew in a sharp, short breath, as if a deeper one would cause her some injury inside, deep in the delicate workings of her anatomy. She swallowed, shook her head; again the words were unutterable. In a while she said, "Tell me, Niles—what are you doing with that ring?" Barely a whisper.

His answer only agitated her further. She gripped the post tighter, squeezing more blood from her wounded finger, turning the knuckles ivory in the moonlight.

"How? How can it be yours?" She was impatient to understand: the weighted gesture of her body, the frantically entreating eyes attested to her need to fathom facts her mind could not comprehend.

Unwillingly he spoke. "Holland gave it to me."

The words seemed to strike her in the face, each a separate blow. She averted her head.

He looked at her earnestly. "He did, Mother, honest. I didn't steal it."

"But it was decided—Holland—Holland was to keep it. Ada said it was decided."

"Yes, I know. But then afterward, he said he wanted me to have it. He told me I could have it. He made me take it—honest he did." Somehow he *had* to make her believe the truth.

"When? When did Holland make you take it?"

"In March. He gave it to me in March."

"March." Silently she mouthed the word, examining it, trying to find some kernel of rationality there, something acceptable to her mind. "When in March?"

"After our birthdays."

"Your birthdays. How long after?"

"Two days."

Then horror swept across her face, of the sort that closes and seals off all the corridors of the mind. "Where, Niles? In the name of heaven, say," she implored. "Where was Holland when he gave you the ring?"

"Here."

"In this house?"

"Yes. Downstairs." He slid the ring on. It felt like ice. His finger pulsed hotly. Then he asked for the packet, the blue tissue paper packet. She stared lifelessly. He awaited her answer, letting his breath out a little at a time. A minute passed. She did a little thing with her mouth, whimpered slightly, but no word was spoken. Below, the staircase stretched away into the void.

Finally: "Where is it, Mother?" he repeated gently.

Her hand grasped her throat as if its manipulation would allow her to speak without choking, would somehow articulate her desolation. "Did he give you that too?"

"Yes," he said dully. How could he explain it, to her satisfaction, that grim piece of anatomy? "Where is it, Mother?"

She fumbled the lid of the tobacco tin and spilled The Thing out into her palm, the tissue paper blooming brightly in the moonlight, a blue moon-rose. Then, a sudden rush of breath; the packet dropping, the tobacco tin, her hands moving out and away from her, pale wings fluttering toward him like birds. He stepped forward to catch, to cage them. Meeting, her body lifted, hung there an instant, suspended, like the marionette in the storeroom, dangling on strings. The hem of her robe describing a graceful figure around her ankles as she spun, a pale lilac swirl, she seemed all at once to crumple, as though those strings controlling her movements had suddenly slackened, permitting her a ridiculous little step, dancing forward on the landing, then back against the white-painted post, then falling sideways, away from him altogether. "Oh," she murmured briefly, her tone surprised, apologetic almost, to discover herself falling. And, standing there, petrified, arms rigidly outstretched, watching her fall, even before the darkness blotted out her white face and she lay in a broken tangle at the bottom of the stairs, he felt that in some way, in that instant, all her questions had finally been answered.

VIII

Dusting the ash of her Melachrino cigarette from the front of her flowered smock, Miss Josceline-Marie directed her attention to the young paying customer coming from the rear of the shop. "Well," she sang out to the sweet face, "did we find something today?"

"Yes." Carefully Niles held up a figure with a wide ruff, shoes whose ends curled, a pompom on the hat, a label saying Venetian glass.

"Oh, he's lovely, Sig-nor Palacchi is"—Pagliaccio, she meant; it was a clown—"ent he lovely? Sweet. Did we see Mrs. Palacchi too? Make a lovely pair."

"No, just the one today," he said, refusing the bait. Her face fell a mile. "And I'll take this too," he said, laying on the counter a small tin music-box painted with flowers and cherubs and hanging on a loop of ribbon. "Could you wrap the clown as a gift, please?"

"As a gift?" She made a little bud of her mouth. "I don't usually do gift wrap; do it for you, have to do it for them all, don't I?"

Winnie, who had been browsing at a nearby counter, stepped up.

"That's all right, Niles, I'll do a wrap for you when we get home." She turned to Miss Josceline-Marie and explained, "It's got to look like a special present."

The bud mouth burst prettily into bloom. "Shoot,

why I guess I can wrap a tiny little clown. For Niles Perry I certainly can. A special present, you say? Would I be being nosy Parker to ask who it's for? A little girlfriend, perhaps?" She clutched under her stand for a box and some gift wrap.

"No, it's for someone else." Embarrassed by the inquisition, Niles went back to the newspaper rack to read the latest headline about Bruno Hauptmann, the Lindbergh baby kidnapper.

"Now who do you suppose Sig-nor Palacchi could be a special present for?" Miss Josceline-Marie wondered, shrouding the glass figure in tissue, tucking it in a box, and scissoring out the smallest smidgen of paper possible from a roll of silver gift wrap. "His *mother?*" she twittered, keeping her voice low. "But whatever will she do with it, for heaven's sake? Fell eighteen steps, they say; why, must of seemed a mile. And sitting in a wheelchair, can't even talk? Practically a vegetable, they say. But she hadn't been right for a long time, had she?" She made a lovely bow on top of the box. "What with Vining dying the terrible way he did, and then—"

"She can move her hands some," Winnie said, bridling. "She puts on her own makeup, and she can even roll her chair around a bit."

"Oh, then she writes notes, does she, to tell you what she wants?"

"No. You ask her a question and she can blink her eyes—"

"Why, just think of that! But the poor thing, in her chair, what does she do with her time, I wonder?"

"Niles reads aloud to her—"

"Why, if he isn't the best thing!" Miss Josceline-

Marie clapped her little hands. "And Victoria with her baby. Miracle she didn't lose it altogether. Brought on by the accident, of course. Shock, I suppose. But they say them incubator babies grow up healthy, don't they?" She smiled her satisfaction with the results of being kept in an oxygen tent for two weeks. "Are they going to continue living in the house, Torrie and Rider?"

"Yes. Torrie's bringing the baby home this afternoon." She tossed a look across the street where Ada was marketing. "Missus wants to keep everything as much the way it used to be as we can. Mrs. Valeria's back last Wednesday, too."

Miss Josceline-Marie tsked and blew a stream of smoke in Winnie's face. "Well, I don't know if that's such a good idear, is it? That place seems to meet misfortune at every turn. I hope Mrs. Perry appreciates the pains I took," the proprietress said, handing the silver box to Winnie. In a moment Niles returned again with a magazine.

"What's that, m'dear, a ten-center or a quarter? Oh, Doc Savage, is it? My, ent that some cover— positively lurid. Now look there, ent that a lovely-looking gift?"

Niles thanked her and took it from Winnie, juggling box, magazine, and music box to pay for the purchases.

"I'll just run next door for a sec," Winnie told Niles, "then you meet me at the market to pick up Ada's order." She went out; Niles collected his change, gathered his things up, and hurried after her, colliding in the doorway with another customer who, bent on looking at something in the window, failed to see him. Niles's things scattered in all directions, and he busied himself picking them up.

"Hot enough for you, Rose?" Miss Josceline-Marie called a greeting through the open door.

"For the love a Pete!" exclaimed Rose Halligan angrily, teetering, "why can't you be more careful, kid!" She grabbed at a shoe and lurched toward Miss Josceline-Marie's stand. "Say, who *is* he, anyway?"

"That? That's Niles Perry."

"Well, there's twice he's knocked me down, damn near."

Miss Josceline-Marie was surprised. "Knocked you down? When?"

"Why, just now is once, and then the other day when I got off the streetcar from the thertur he hit me with his bike. You remember—he's the one ran my stocking and called me a dirty name."

"Tut, dear, you don't mean *that* one. That's *Niles.*" She trilled a little laugh. "Why, if I didn't know better, I'd think you were talking about Holland."

"Holland? Who's Holland?"

"Holland—Niles's twin brother."

"You mean there's another?"

"Takes two t'make twins, don't it?" She tittered. "A holy terror, Holland. Only it couldn't of been him."

"Why not?"

"Holland Perry? Simple," she went on, elaborating her statement, her round cheeks quivering, her bud mouth opening and closing, pink and eager to offer her logic, and then, astonished, drawing back with an alarmed cry as, in a furious crash back through the open door again, Niles flung himself upon her, his packages spilling helter-skelter, shouting *Lies! Lies! Damn you, it's not true, it's not!* while Rose Halligan teetered and lurched, hands flying at him, trying to stop his hands, and Ada appearing just at that moment from the market, she too trying to seize him, his hands hammering, reaching up over Miss Josceline-Marie's plump bosom, trying to shut the hateful little bud mouth, and she, all ruffled dignity, refusing to countenance such outrage when he had breathlessly backed off, saying she could not, could *not* understand such a thing and Rose saying, "But what was it, for Pete's sakes, all you said was—" and Ada breaking in to apologize, chagrined, hurrying after the boy as he fled the place.

She caught up with him outside the church, where, through the open doors, organ music sounded. He stood, red-faced and furious, looking up at the Angel of the Brighter Day, her brilliant colors now obscured, seen from outside in, and refusing to acknowledge Ada when she approached.

"Child, child, what a thing to do! What could have possessed you to act in such a manner?"

"It's a lie," he said stolidly, meeting her eyes at last with a defiant look.

"*Nyet,* it is not a lie and you know it. Come, child, you shall admit it."

"No!"

"You shall! This must not continue!" And then, all at once, stern and forbidding, she was dragging him along the walk, through the wrought-iron gates and into the cemetery, hurrying him along beside her, her soft features hardened and set.

Grassy lawns sloped away in every direction where

eleven generations of Pequot Landing people lay buried under leafy trees. Beyond, a field, green with tall corn, a scarecrow's face askew above the rows. She pulled him past the blossom-decked monuments, over the markers, ancient and new, large and small, ornate and plain, of red sandstone and polished granite, identifying their various owners, Talcotts and Standishes and Welleses, until she had brought him relentlessly to a large oak tree, where, sequestered in its deep green shade, like a dark cave, the sun bright and golden without, lay the family plot. Blinded by his tears, he peered vacantly at the sides of the gravestones, where dying flowers sat in chipped green containers. The noontime air was torpid, the scent of bloom sour, nearby a faucet dripped on stone, somewhere in the branches a locust chirred. Overhead the summer sky was bright blue, the perfect, translucent blue of a Dutch china plate, glazed with an awful clarity, stunning to the eye, but brittle like the shell of an egg; if he stared too long at it, it would crack, shatter to bits, a deadly blue hail falling about him.

"Now, child," she told him, "you shall say it."

"What? Say *what?*" he demanded, bewildered, shaking his head in wonder at the very thought of whatever strange thing she was willing him to say.

"Say the truth, child," she said, her voice patient and tender and sad. "Say the truth. Out loud, so we shall both hear it, the two of us together."

He felt a chill. He ducked his chin, butted his forehead against the material of her dress, felt his eyelashes brushing its softness. She took his chin in her hand and forced his head around. "Read, child," she instructed, and with a submissive sigh he repeated the words chiseled on a grave marker:

VINING SEYMOUR PERRY

Born August 21, 1888   Died November 16, 1934

In Loving Memory

He bent and pulled a blade of grass, cupped it, and began to whistle on it.

"Go on," he heard her urging. She was holding him in front of her, gripping his shoulders, directing his look past the brown marker to one of newly polished granite. "Look there. *There,* child." Uncomprehendingly he blinked up at her, trying to see her face above him. Vibrating against the sky, repeating exactly the shape of her head, was a white outline, not, he thought, unlike the halo around the Angel of the Brighter Day. "There!" she repeated, her voice choked and hushed as she pointed.

Across the blue shell of sky, curved like a bowl, a network of fine lines appeared, like the roadways on a map, the veins in a leaf. He studied it; alas, too long. The lines multiplied, one upon another; the shell cracked, splintered into a million jagged fragments; they showered around him, sharp, painfully sharp and tinkling like blue rain. The grass felt prickly as he threw himself down, knocking aside the withered flowers—daisies and coreopsis and sunflowers that Ada had used to decorate the grave—dug only in March of this year—his trembling fingers spreading over the cold stone with the panicky touch of the newly blind, groping their way Braille-like across the freshly carved lettering that formed the terrible inscription:

HOLLAND WILLIAM PERRY

Born March 1922   Died March 1935

THREE

Now that was an event, wasn't it?

Poor Holland.

You can see how it is. Very simple, really. Holland is dead. Dead as a doornail, to repeat Miss Josceline-Marie's unfortunate simile, used <u>an hour ago</u> in Niles's hearing. It's true. Make no mistake about it. Do not be further deluded. Holland is gone. Trying to hang Ada's cat in the well, <u>he killed himself also.</u> Such are the ironies of life. Killed himself in the well by the cloverpatch, back in March, on his birthday. This is why the mother stays in the room and drinks, <u>because she cannot face the loss</u>, and this is why, bereft, forlorn, all alone, <u>unwilling that Holland should be dead, Niles has re-created his twin, has</u> conjured him up, so to speak, has resurrected him.

Witness this astonishing reverence, this passion for a corpse; the boy is in thrall to a cadaver, obsessed by a ghoulish inamorato; not a ghost, not a vision, but a living breathing thing of flesh and blood; Holland, *he himself.* Such are the properties of the game. <u>Be a tree, be a flower, be a bird—be *Holland.*</u> With this— creature—he acts out his little pageants of blissful agony, the happy, subtle tyrannies, <u>loving his twin, yet supplanting him, idolizing him, yet tearing him from his place;</u> it is not enough to be Holland's twin, <u>he must become Holland himself.</u> Peregrine for Perry. He who wears the ring . . .

You can see how it is. It is summer. School's out.
Niles solitary. Remember, I pointed out that he has
no friends, or, having them, does not seek their company. Did you ever hear of a schoolboy without com-
panions? Seldom, I think. But there is Niles, finding
faces—as Ada has taught him—faces in the clouds,
one face, *his* face, the face of him—the other. In
clouds or in the pool pump or on the ceiling, it's all
the same. He is there—the other. In the cracked and
yellow plaster with the ripply brown watermark. You
will understand. I do the same thing here, lying on
this bed, with my watermark on my ceiling. See? The
two eyes, the nose, the mouth that curls slightly at
the corners? What is it Miss DeGroot calls it? I still
can't remember. I must be sure to ask her when she
comes. I don't think it was an island after all, I think
it must be a country. Oh, that reminds me—it seems
to me her first name is Selva. Selva DeGroot. Odd
name, isn't it?

In any case, there is Niles, whiling away the summer, playing Ada's game—on dead Holland. And
how else does he pass his time? Remember Russell
Perry? And Mrs. Rowe, who lived next door? Well,
no matter. Whose fault is it, you ask, these tragic
circumstances, the bizarre transference of the boy to
his dead twin. No one's, you may say. It just happened. I would disagree. As far as I'm concerned, the
fault is Ada's.

I have been thinking about her a lot. I do not like
her. Oh, I suppose she is worthwhile enough, taken
all in all. Though not without sentiment, she is not
guilty of sentimentality, that most lugubrious of pit-
falls. An interesting enough type, she is, I suppose, a

kind of peasant-aristocrat; and the Russian mind is sometimes strange. She has a certain humor in her thinking, in her dealings with the boy. She is not self-indulgent. She has restraint. She does her work, keeps her house, tends her flowers (ah, the sunflowers!), accepts her tragedies, tries to keep the family together. There is marrow yet in those poor old bones; they do not break easily. She is seemingly unconquerable, yet—and she does not know this—she has been conquered. The old woman has indulged the child too far, indulged him in his mad fancy; and madness, surely, it is; where else was it they took the other grandmother, Isobel Perry, if not to the asylum? And Ada knew there was insanity in the family. You will see in time how bitterly she comes to regret this (nodding and smiling, all compassion, watching Niles looking into the water in the pump pool—and for what?), this failing to take into account the all-too-obvious fact, and in time the realization will break her heart, knowing that it was she who first planted the seeds of the tragedy. And while you may suffer with her, the foolish woman, I shall not. The poor benighted creature, all the time unwitting, not in the least mindful of the lengths to which it has gone . . . the macabre lengths . . .

Well, not entirely unwitting. If Niles is afraid Holland may go away, *she* is afraid he has come back . . .

I

Now see Niles in the parlor, standing behind the keyboard of the piano. The buzzing is in his head, the annoying buzzing sound that is always there when he hears people say Holland is dead. Dead, or buried, or gone away. It isn't true, of course, he tells himself, but it does make him anxious. (It is for this reason that he went today to the cemetery and peed on the flowers on Holland's grave—it doesn't help much, but it does cause the buzzing to go away. Except when he hears the twanging of the harmonica in his ear. That buzzes too.)

There, on the gleaming piano top, lies the packet of blue tissue paper, the paper all unfolded, its contents open to view, Niles staring, with Holland's spellbinder look on his face, fascinated, almost hypnotized by the finger. The finger: hard, dried, slightly crooked, the nail carefully manicured. If someone comes, he will snatch it from sight; but in the meantime the child is rapt in his grisly souvenir.

Now, coming from outdoors, from the bright sunshine, he finds the parlor gloomier than usual, the air fustier, the atmosphere more dense. Where once the room held a gaiety and vividness most particular to it, now the dark woods, the worn plum-colored plush of the davenport, the damask curtains all lend it a somber, ponderous air. The reds in the rugs are tired, worn to the color of—what? A cooked, sunbleached lobster claw, he thinks. The Atwater-Kent radio has been silent—silent, that is, until Aunt Vee's return from Chicago three days ago—and most of the trifles that bring a room alive, that give it its character, have been put away; their accumulation of dust only makes more work for Winnie.

Grandmother Perry's silver vase sits in a saucer on the piano, filled with blown dahlias, their ivory-colored blossoms flatly mirrored in the polished wood. His fingers strike a chord and Niles observes how the vibrations of the instrument cause the petals to drop, with them a fine mist of yellow pollen sifting down. He sits, fingering the treble notes of a duet from the sheet of music before him, watching the soft curling petals slipping silently here and there around the stiffened finger, its desiccated flesh absorbing all his thought.

The finger . . . the well-remembered blue-black dot where Russell stabbed the knuckle with a pencil . . . Holland's gift. The buzzing has stopped; replaced by a cry. Hear? A fierce miaow! *Miao-o-o-ow!* A cat somewhere, somewhere there, locked inside his head. Cat; here kitty kitty kitty . . . that day last March, he was playing in the driveway, then the cat was yowling, crying, *screaming.* Ada's cat, Pilakea, as Holland comes dragging the animal along by a rope around its neck. Then the struggle, only a blur, the cat swinging in the noose, the fall, afterward the dull impact below; he had dashed to the well, had clambered onto the curb, craned his neck over the edge, looked down into the blackness, the stones

rough, cold, mossy green; fingers gripping in pain
and horror until someone came to tear him away,
blood pounding in his ears, streaming through his
brain. He felt dizzy, wanted to vomit, to fling himself
after. *Help! Rescue!* Gladly would have blinded his
eyes rather than let them see what lay at the bottom
of the well—hurt, who knew how badly? *Help!*
Down there on the stones, the shallow water lapping
at the tangle of rope and cat and broken child. *Help
him! Someone help him!* The grotesquely twisted
body, and the redness and the black. In seconds all
the blood vessels in his head seemed to have broken;
had ruptured and exploded in his brain, had come
pouring into his throat, strangling him. There was
Holland—in the well—hurt—*Holland has hurt himself!* He stuffed his fist in his mouth to stop the
screams. He was still screaming when they led him
away. Afterward, when he stopped, finally, he didn't
talk any more, not for days, didn't say anything to
anyone, or eat, or move, scarcely, or see or hear.

He was gone, then, departed to some other country
in some unfamiliar landscape where everything was
fuzzy and people spoke in distant echoes (where,
mercifully, the picture of the well was obliterated),
where people with pale frightened faces came to
gather around and peer down at him, strange faces:
an unknown man with a silver phone and black rubber tubes from his ears; another face, worried yet
determined; far-off voices conferring.

  *"Traumatic experience . . . shock . . . he'll come
out of it."* *"Oh God, please."* *"Missus, Mr. Foley's*

downstairs in the parlor . . . says the ring won't come off the finger . . ."

Hearing, he stirs in alarm, a groan from his lips. No . . . no . . .

"How's dat—de ring?" Another voice, in surprise. "What do you mean, the ring? What ring?" . . . "His father's gold ring with the bird on it. He must of been wearing it. But his finger's all swole up and it won't come off, Mr. Foley says. What should he do?" A pause; then: "Dat damn ring! Melt it down . . . throw it away . . . anything . . . nothing but sorrow. No, wait—tell him to leave it where it is . . . leave it on the child's finger; better it should be buried too . . . safe under the earth . . . what more harm can it do, sealed up in the casket . . . let it be buried."

Wait! No! The ring? Peregrine for Perry? That was to go? No! Yes, said they, yes, making horrid faces: here they all came, fie-ing their fingers at him like imps, like elf-changelings, shame, shame; selfish boy, let it be an end then, an end to the ring. Oh for shame, to want the ring so! Thou shalt not covet . . . let it be buried, certainly. Let it go . . . let it go . . .

No! No-o-o-o!

The glint of silver; a quick jab, peace. He sleeps. Unquiet, dreamful sleep, fearful unhappy dreams: everywhere night; you can see—a desolate, forbidding landscape—but still night, earth and sky one darkness. And from the deep center of this darkness rushes the peregrine falcon—not that golden bird on the weathervane, but another, alive, crying out, its wings swiftly beating. And the dark wings become

white ones, the bird becomes another creature, becomes—an angel! The Angel of the Brighter Day! See
how her white robes sway, the wings rhythmically
lifting and falling, the face ever so kind and lovely,
the mouth smiling. See how her arm stretches, the
hand beckons . . . beckons . . .

And now *he* comes, The Other—all bathed in a
golden light, and Falcon Peregrine perching, wicked-
eyed, upon his shoulder. He raises his hand, *that*
hand, and on *that* finger he wears the ring. Now,
behind him, the Angel enfolds him into the soft curtain of her wings and before Niles's very eyes they
seem to float away together, Angel, child, bird—*and
ring*.

No, wait—don't go! Stay!

But he cannot stay them. Back, back they go, together into the deep darkness. A whisper—*Goodbye*
. . . fading . . . fading. And he is left with the
memory of a face, the familiar face, smiling, mocking; whose . . . ?

It is later.

He is awake.

Standing in a room; another room; dark and still,
the curtains closed, the air stuffy; *this* room. A coffin.
Shiny cords and tassels; sprays of gladioli, already
slightly withered; Mother and Her Boys, smiling
. . . the Sheffield candelabra shedding gloomy light.

He reaches out a hand. Lifts the lid. Sees a face;
that face. It is no dream. But why so silent, so cold,
so unmoving? The candles illumine the pallor beneath the skin, the flesh cool and smooth; whoever
could discern the claw marks now, the cleft bone, the
flesh so bruised?

"Holland?" No reply. Yet he *is* there—*it is not a dream.* For a long time he stands staring at the face on the pillow, the satin pillow. A vigil.

Still the face sleeps.

Forever, it seems.

With patience the wait continues. He is looking, and looking, and looking. He gazes down at the closed eyelids; after a time the room begins to contract in upon him; the stillness gathers itself into one great hush, static and precise; the air is thinner; he has trouble breathing; feels faint; the floor threatens to tilt. *Holland?* Odd, a moment ago his mouth had seemed so expressionless, or, rather, a too-firm articulation, like that of a poorly made statue. Now its corners appear to have turned slightly up in an ambiguous smile. He bends nearer. Upon his own, those lips feel stiff, rubbery, unnatural. In his nostrils a peculiar odor, medicinal, like formaldehyde: he thinks of biology class.

He leans closer, never once taking his gaze from the brown lashes so serenely curved against the pale cheek. *Holland?*

He draws a breath; voices his thought: "Open your eyes." A plea, willed with might and main. No; they remain closed. With a finger he lifts one eyelid, then the other. The gray irises shine silver in the light. "There, that's better." It was, too, somewhat better; ah, the bright shining eyes.

"Better." It seems he hears the word repeated, altogether clear and distinct, and, a second after, the echo. *Better—better-better-better* . . .

Startled, he puts his hand to his mouth, not daring to move, to break the spell. He concentrates . . .

"Holland—"

Holland. Hollandhollandholland . . .

Again his own intake of breath.

"How is it?"

Is it? comes the response, *is it—isit—isitisit* . . . ?

It is well. He can make out the pulse of a little vein throbbing there, just under the left eye.

"Are you comfortable?"

Yes; quite comfortable. Niles breathes again; a satisfactory answer. He looks comfortable enough, head agreeably angled on the pillow, shoulders tilted slightly. "Good," he says and then Holland says, "Good," and after a while they smile at each other. In a moment he hears Holland's whisper sounding quite plainly in the hushed room.

"Come closer, little brother." Eyes gleaming in the candlelight, the odor stronger, the heavy, persistent frog-smell.

"Yes?"

"Niles Alexander." And the ardor in his voice touches his brother's heart.

"Yes," he says breathlessly.

"Come closer. Closer still. That's better."

"Yes."

Holland gives him a long deep look and it says all that Niles desires it should. "You're here, then. I'm glad."

"Are you sore, Holland? Does it hurt?"

"Sure it hurts, what didja *think?*"

Speaks of other things, inconsequential things. Niles waiting for them to get around to The Thing, the most important Thing.

Finally he hears Holland say there is something he

has for him; something special he wants him to have (for action above and beyond the call of duty), and Niles, hoping he would say this, is surprised by the surprise in his own voice. Really? Yes. Can he guess what? *Welll.* Niles doesn't know, but he is hoping. He can't see it (hidden as it is, one hand folded over the other) but he can imagine it, resting there, there where it has been left; he covets it—Midas gold, Peregrine for Perry.

What's that? A present? "Yes, a present, you fool. Behold, a gift!" Still, he feels obliged to protest: "Ada says you're supposed to keep it—Mother wants you to, too." "Jeeze, Niles, I told you—I want *you* to have it." A halfhearted demurring: "I shouldn't . . ." ". . . head of the family," Holland counters. "He who wears the ring, so on and so forth." Sort of crafty, wily, very Achilles-like. Well, if that's the way he wants it . . . And so, the pact, a bargain sealed to the satisfaction of both. Holland: (chuckling) "It's okay, I won't tell. If I don't, and you don't, nobody'll know." See? Crafty.

Okay?

Okay.

And that was the Secret, of course.

Niles is pleased.

"So take it." Now Holland's voice sounds curiously flat and impersonal.

He considers. Could he? Should he? Why does his head feel so feverish, so light? He is sweating. His hand trembles as he lifts the one cold hand from the other. Pries the fingers open. Ah, there it is, flashing on the fourth finger.

The finger. The one with the bluish-black dot where Russell stabbed it with the pencil.

Gingerly he touches it with a forefinger. The heavy seal winks, throws light into his eye. Ah—he longs for it. He pauses, uncertain; at last he lifts the cold hand and tries to turn the ring; it refuses to budge. He *wants* it.

Take it.

Now it slides as far as the bruised knuckle, where it sticks.

"It won't come off." He sounds disappointed.

Take it! Impatient to be rid of it.

He turns it again, gently forcing the gold against the joint; but the red and swollen flesh refuses to surrender the ring. "I can't. It won't—"

It will. Will—will-willwill. Take it! Do you want it or not? Nobody's here—now's your chance!

With his spit Niles wets the knuckle; the ring is stubborn, will not come off.

Take it! Angrily.

"How? How can I? I'm trying, but it won't come off!"

Shall I tell you?

He nods eagerly, bends his ear to the proposal.

"No!" he gasps, horrified. He straightens up; turns away; will hear no more; the suggestion is disgusting.

Look at me, Niles Alexander. Most coaxing. *Look at me.* Slowly he turns his head back and looks. "Now. Go get them, Niles. Yes. Do it now, Niles Alexander." The voice honey-smooth, faintly mocking. "Do it." He can feel the gray eyes holding his, unfaltering, sure, irresistible.

What can he do but give in? Leaving the room,

going down the hall and out through the kitchen,
passing the frozen vegetable garden blanketed with
frost rime and winter leaves, the garbage pails sparkling in the moonlight, beneath the falcon weathervane up on the cupola, he enters the barn. And when
he returns he does as he has been bidden. Holland
smiles when it is done and seems pleased.

Niles closes the lid, secures the little latch, and
goes away again, feeling quite certain he has replaced
Mr. Angelini's red-handled rose shears on their
proper nail in the tool shed.

Peregrine for Perry.

He was screaming, shaking his fist at the bird, hideous, hateful bird . . . he felt cold . . . hot and
cold . . . people were crying . . . he was being
carried . . .

When he awoke, he was in his own bed.

And across the night table, in *his* own bed, was
Holland.

By April he was well again. The forsythia
bloomed, and the pussy willow, then the laurel, the
lilac. By May, when the orchard was in bloom, it had
become quite natural to see Holland in all manner of
places, upstairs, downstairs—though not in my
lady's chamber (Mother was crying; wouldn't come
out)—at school; in the barn, the pigeon loft, and, best
of all, the apple cellar.

Niles was content . . .

At the sound of a knob turning, Niles's thoughts
evaporated. Ada came in, closing the parlor door behind her. He started, then froze; dreaming away, he'd

forgotten what lay on the piano, the finger in the blue tissue paper; with difficulty he kept himself from reaching for it, that blue paper rose beside the vase, half covered with dahlia petals. Forcing himself to look at her, he waited for her to speak, hoping she would leave quickly, not daring to move, to drop his eyes to the telltale finger.

ADA

She stood in the center of the rug and looked at him, a queer, puzzled expression on her face, her heart clearly agitated, her usually serene mouth working, doubt faintly flitting across her brow, hovering, disappearing, reappearing; her head, usually quiet, moving in a series of little nods, watching as he once more struck the keys, hard, trying desperately to camouflage, to bury the finger under the last of the dahlia petals, fingertips against ivory keys, keys against hammers, hammers against strings, vibrating; still the blue tissue paper showed, the blue rose amid the pale petals.

"Niles, can you stop that pounding for a moment, please?"

"Yes."

"Niles, I have been asking myself something. Do you know what it is?"

"No." Questions questions questions. And the Look.

"How do you suppose Mrs. Rowe died?"

He thought about it. "She had a heart attack—you said."

"I did, didn't I? But what brought it on, I am thinking?"

"I don't know."

"And something else comes to mind. After Mr.

Foley took Mrs. Rowe away—you knew Mr. Foley had done that—?"

"Yes." He held his breath; she remained where she was, had not noticed the finger lying on top of the piano.

"After Mrs. Rowe was gone, I stayed to try to put things in order. And do you know—?"

"What?"

"I believe Mrs. Rowe had a guest. A guest, for tea. She had brought out her good cup and saucer. And—"

Waiting.

"—I also found this, lying on a shelf in Mrs. Rowe's curio cabinet." She opened her hand. In it lay the harmonica.

"Oh," he said, surprised, and reaching to pocket it hastily, "Holland missed it. I'll give it to him."

She gave him another worried look. "Was Holland over at Mrs. Rowe's that day?"

"I don't know. Perhaps. He goes everywhere."

Her eyes had narrowed, giving this reply special consideration. "He does, doesn't he."

Niles shifted on the bench. "I'll ask him."

"Will you?"

"Yes."

"And you will be sure to tell me what he says?"

"Yes." He struck the keyboard again to break the tension, hoping she would go away. Still she had not seen what lay among the petals. The sharps and flats from the piano seemed briefly to instill a forced life into the room; for a moment he thought he could smell his father's pipe tobacco, could hear the crisp snap of his evening paper, the rustle of Mother's dress, Holland's mischievous laughter as together they wrestled on the davenport. He looked up at the painting over the mantel. A sphinx-like trio, the three figures with their faintly smiling mouths guarding their secret: Mother and Her Boys . . .

"Yes," he repeated emphatically. He played a little more of the melody, a few bars only, then stifled a sound in his throat. She was looking directly at the fallen petals. Had she seen it? He could not tell; she made no sign, remained where she stood, looking, thinking, analyzing . . .

The door opened again.

"Oh!" White-faced and irresolute, Aunt Valeria paused on the threshold. "—Niles. I was—I was looking for you." She laughed. "I thought for a moment—that song, do you remember Ressell used to play it? Isn't that the one? Schubert's *Serenade?*"

"No, Aunt Vee," he said, "it's the 'Berceuse' from *Jocelyn.*"

She looked blank and Ada turned with a forced smile. "It's a lullaby," she explained, with a lift of a shoulder that questioned, not only his choice of selection, but why a lullaby should be played so *fortissimo.* She had come right up to the bow of the piano and was peering down at the broken flowers, the fallen petals not quite covering the betraying bit of blue tissue.

Yet she had not discovered it.

With brow wrinkled, Aunt Vee said, "Niles—I wonder—would you mind just taking your mother's tray up and trying to feed her. You're so good at it, and honestly I'm so nervous today, I just seem to upset her more. Winnie's canning tomatoes and"—

she glanced at his grandmother, her expression saying Poor Ada, seems so distrait, can't imagine what the trouble is, don't like to bother her. "Would you mind, dear?"

"Sure, Aunt Vee, I will. In just a minute." He studied the keys. Would they never go? What? What was it Ada was saying?

"—certainly these flowers have seen their day; what a mess they've made." Niles, fingers of ice curved about the keyboard, did not blink. From where he sat he could see clearly in the dark surface of the piano the reflection of bright blue crinkled paper. She had cupped a hand at the edge of the piano top and was about to sweep the litter into it, packet and all, when, outside, tires spun on the gravel; doors slammed, footsteps sounded along the veranda, voices traveling ahead.

"There's Torrie," Ada said, wheeling, leaving the debris where it lay, hurrying from the room.

"Yes, here's the baby," said Aunt Vee gaily, floating away across the rug. "I could have sworn I heard Schubert . . ."

"See what's for lunch!" Niles said just as gaily, carrying the tray into the room, a book tucked under his elbow. He kicked the door shut and set the tray on the dressing table. He pulled an electric fan nearer, tilting it up to the ceiling to circulate the air; the blades whirred like the wings of some giant insect, the hum of the motor rising in a flapping crescendo as the machine turned in a 180-degree arc. Somewhere a small clock ticked with tooth-and-tongue disapproval. As he rolled the wheelchair from the corner the wire wheels protested the disturbance. He stared down at the ruin that was his mother.

Through eyes dark and dead like the empty windows of an abandoned house, she returned his look, vacantly, almost inanely. Her skin had the shiny blue-white pallor of the invalid. Her reddened mouth hung slack like a wound; two rouged spots on her cheeks were like those on the painted face of a toy soldier. A trickle escaped her lips to run down her chin, dribbling onto the front of her robe where it left a damp stain.

"Mother?" he said softly, and with a cloth gently wiped her mouth, then bent to kiss her. He shook and plumped the pillow and replaced it behind her back. He went into the bathroom, rinsed out the cloth under the tap, returned, and patted it around her neck. When he had smoothed her hair and further adjusted the pillow, he drew up the stool and took the tray in his hands.

"Mother, wouldn't you like some of this lunch? Winnie's got cold soup for you"—he looked the tray over—"and chicken salad. Looks pretty good. And tapioca for dessert. With peaches—Holland's favorite," he added, trying to make it sound appetizing. He reached for the soup and a spoon, holding the bowl in front of her. "Don't you want to try a little?" he urged.

Her face was a mask as she blinked twice, a woeful signal, "no." "Please, Mother," he attempted again, "have just a little. So Winnie won't think you don't like her cooking." Filling the spoon, he held it to her mouth and waited. She looked at him, then emptied it with a loud sucking noise. "There. That's good."

Another spoonful. Her eyes, crookedly outlined in black, were watering. It pained him to think of the prodigious effort required each morning to make up her face. She looked like an apparition. "Another?" Little by little he coaxed her to finish the soup, wiping her mouth with a napkin after each spoonful. "Now, how about some chicken salad," he suggested, picking up the plate. She closed her eyelids twice, slowly, almost painfully. "All right, Mother." He sighed and returned the plate to the tray and covered it with the napkin. "That's good; you ate a little anyway. I wish it wasn't so hot. It's not the heat, it's the humidity, that's what Mr. Crofut always says." He laughed at the cliché and continued. "Holland and I are going swimming this afternoon, so we'll have a chance to cool off. The river's dropping. Shall I bring you some sherbet later, when the ice cream man comes by? I'll be sure to listen for his whistle . . . Mother?"   torment

Still she stared, the dead eyes fixed on some spot just to the left of his head. He leaned, trying to ensnare her vision, to produce some flicker of recognition, but she seemed to be looking right past him as if he weren't there at all. The atmosphere in the room was unutterably silent, a vacuum in which nothing stirred, as though the life had been drained from it, as for an exhibition to be privately viewed, an authentic reconstruction of some particular time and place that had even at that precise moment passed, an almost-real, life-like room with its almost-real, life-like figure, but one of wax, imprisoned forever in a wheelchair.

"I took *Anthony Adverse* back. I'm sorry. I know

how much you wanted to read it. But Miss Shedd says she can't let you renew, there's so many others waiting for it. Perhaps later. But I've brought you something else I thought I could read to you, if you like." Another trickle from her mouth. He put the book down again and wiped it. "Oh, cripes, what's the matter with me, I almost forgot. I bought something for you." He quickly turned away, then turned back holding closed fists behind him. "A surprise. Go ahead—pick one. Which? Left or right? Ah *ha,* the right? No. Try again. Left?" She blinked once and he produced the silver box. "It's for you. I picked it out myself. Want to open it?" He placed it in her hands; she fumbled at the ribbon, fingers trembling as they pulled the bow and parted the wrapping. The cover stuck and he knelt before her to help; he lifted it off, watching closely as she opened the tissue paper and looked at the glass piece. "It's a clown, Mother. His name's Sig-nor Palacchi. And he has a wife—" She stared dully, and when he had further removed the tissue, he discovered that the figure was neatly cracked at the waist and lay in two sections in the box. "Oh gee, it broke. I guess I dropped it. Well," he said, picking out the pieces and putting them into the waste basket, "I can get Mrs. Palacchi some time—if she's still there. You'll have to wait, though, until I save my allowance again. Gosh, I couldn't even afford to get the Chinese mustache Holland wanted." He prattled on, saying how Holland had crooked it, and Holland was going to have the show anyway. "I told him it wouldn't be any fun with Aunt Josie gone, but he's insisting. One problem, though, about how to get out of the apple cellar, but he's got that worked

out. *And I know how.* But it keeps him out of trouble,
anyway. We're going to send the money this time to
the newspaper Camp Fund, so some more unfortunate child can go to camp. Oh—and the best news.
We have a new baby," he continued with a smile.
"Torrie's baby has come home from the hospital. It
can be out of the incubator now, and she's so beautiful, so strong and healthy. It was a girl, just like I
said—you were right, I *am* a wizard. Perhaps they'll
bring the baby to see you. Do you know what they've
decided to name it? Another empress. I told Torrie,
since you were named after the Empress of All the
Russias, and Aunt Josie after the Empress of the
French, and herself after the Empress of India, the
baby should be Eugenia, after Eugénie, the Second
Empress of the French. And that's what she and
Rider decided on. Isn't that neat?" He chuckled appreciatively, then broke off to see tears running down
her face, long, grotesque streaks of black, her shoulders pitifully shaking, mouth pulled askew in silent
anguish.

"Mother, Mother, don't—please. Please don't cry.
It'll be all right." Her lids blinked twice. "Yes, yes it
will, it *will,* Mother. I promise." He leaned to her,
laid his head against her knee, patted her gown, trying to communicate to her some measure of childlike
reassurance.

When she had quieted, he made himself more comfortable on the stool and again took up the book, his
place all marked where he intended to begin. He held
the book up for a moment so she could see the title:
Fairy Tales of Long Ago. Another chuckle. "Like you
said, Mother, once you used to read to us, now it's

the other way around. Well," he said, a little preamble, and commenced. *CHANGLING*

"Once upon a time there were some elves who
dwelled in a wood, and happening upon a cottage one
day, they spied a cradle beside a fire. The mother was
nowhere to be seen, so they stole into the cottage and
what did they behold in the cradle but a beautiful-
looking child. Now the elves were bad and mischievous creatures and they loved nothing so much as
doing harm to others. So they took the child from its
mother and left in its place a changeling with a big
head and staring eyes, an ugly creature of impish
countenance like themselves who did nothing but eat
and drink—"

An unexpected breeze swept through the window,
fluttering the curtain, dropping it, and scurrying to
expire in the far corner of the room. Niles sat very
still. The only noises to be heard were his own slight,
even breathing, the thrum of a beetle at the screen,
the disapproving clock pendulum, the fan's erratic
buzz, and the queer-sounding, inarticulate sobs that
spilled finally from his mother's throat as, holding
the book so she might enjoy the illustration, he felt
her tears dripping like hot wax upon his hand.

Poor Mother, her makeup was running. He felt so
sorry for her; she was so pathetic, sitting there in the
wheelchair, twisting her hands in her lap, shuddering. She didn't care for this story. She would rather
have *Anthony Adverse*. But *Anthony Adverse*, he had
discovered, was dull; *he* didn't like it at all. She
would have to take what he cared to read, not what
she wanted to hear. Poor, pathetic, nosy Mother. Curiosity killed the cat, as Holland would say. Poking

around in the Chautauqua desk, looking for some old tobacco tin.

What else could Holland have done—what else could *anybody* have done—except to reach out and push her down the stairs?

Leno Angelini was sure drunk—in the bag, as Uncle George would say. Standing in the passageway beyond the apple cellar, a tool in one hand, silent and unobserved, Niles watched through a partly opened door of the cold-cellar, where the jars of jellies and pickles were stored. Mr. Angelini was helping himself to the wine at the bottom of a small keg sitting on a stone shelf. By the light of a candle he bent over the spigot, holding the copper cup from the pump and waiting while it filled. Well, why not? It was practically Leno's wine—he had trod it out from the grapes in the arbor just as he used to do in the old country, Niles himself and Holland helping the past couple of years. But look at the way he was drinking it, almost losing his balance, head tilted back, red wine dribbling over his chin; no wonder he was in the bag. Now he was making funny sounds in his throat as he emptied the cup and returned to the keg, wiggling the spigot and waiting for the wine to run. When it failed, he cursed and struck the cask with the heel of his hand. The cask tottered a moment, then tumbled to the floor and rolled hollowly back and forth on the stones. "All gone, *finito*," he mumbled, shaking his head and grabbing another keg from a corner. Uncle George would sure be raising hell if he found Leno had opened a new keg. Now that was strange—Mr. Angelini was crying. Cripes!

Striking his chest; and hard, too, that big fist doubled
up like a hammer head, pounding himself on the
chest as though to punish himself for something. _guilt over pitch fork_
Now what? He had picked up the bungstarter, the
heavy-headed wooden mallet used to knock the bung
out—cripes, now he was slamming the mallet down
on the top of the keg, big heavy blows. Mr. Angelini
was mad, or hurt, or both. That must be the Latin
temperament Ada spoke about sometimes. Wow, he
was really letting that old keg top have it, wham,
bam! And muttering; no good trying to figure out
what, Niles decided, since he couldn't speak Italian.
Holding his breath, he wedged his eye closer to the
crack as Mr. Angelini stepped back, his features wild
and contorted, lifted the mallet over his head with
both hands and struck at the top of the keg. It
smashed the thin wooden membrane, the pieces
splintering in all directions as the bungstarter
plunged into the wine, splashing the red liquid into
Mr. Angelini's blank and surprised face.

Niles pushed the door open and stepped into the
room. "Come away, Mr. Angelini," he said, trying to
take the old man's arm. "Come away." But Mr. Angelini only stared uncomprehendingly amid a spate of
piteous broken Italian.

"What? What are you saying?" the boy asked.

"Da wine, she's-a go sour," Mr. Angelini explained with a mournful look at the mutilated cask.
"She's-a da last from last year, now she's-a go bad." _Bad wine_
His arms were crossed over his stomach as if to keep
his pain from spilling out like the wine, his head
shaking in some bewildered, speechless denial, his
eyes hollow, staring as though at a ghost.

"Come, Mr. Angelini, come out of here."

"No!" Wrenching himself away, he yanked a piece of canvas tarpaulin onto the floor and knelt. "Leno fix, *subito. Questo vino è male.*" With mighty yanks he tore a square from the canvas and flung it over the open top of the cask. Taking a length of cord he made several turns around the keg and secured the canvas. "There, that's-a good, eh boy? She's-a no go bad, this-a wine." He started as he glanced down at Niles's hand. "Boy, what you got there?" he demanded with a scowl.

"It's your saw," Niles answered, holding up his hand.

"What you gonna do wit' dat dere saw?"

"Nothing, Mr. Angelini. It's all done."

"All done? Den you hang dat saw back in dat shed, eh? Like-a Leno tell you."

"Yes, sir, I will." Taking Mr. Angelini's hand, he pulled him to the door. Upstairs, Niles returned the saw to a nail on the tool shed wall.

"No no no," Mr. Angelini was shaking his head. "No, boy, the hacksaw, she's-a go *here.*" Setting down the copper cup, he moved the tool to the appropriate spot, just above the rubber hip boots Father had worn to the poverty party. Leno chuckled. "You fadder—he's-a funny man, eh? He's-a dress up in you' mudder' dress for da party—dat's-a funny man." He chuckled again, then his smile faded as he gave Niles a long look. "Boy?" he said softly.

"Yes?" Thinking how, with his mournful gaze he had that Tribal Elder Look, waiting as though to offer up a judgment.

Mr. Angelini opened his mouth to speak, then

closed it, muttering, *"Niente, niente,"* and with a
long look at the tool shed wall he went out under the
breezeway and disappeared around the corner.

Niles picked up the copper cup and went to return
it to the pump. He hung it up, pumped enough water
to fill the pool under the spout, then crouched over it,
put the flat of his hand on the drain to stop it, and
waited for the water to become still. He remained
motionless for a time, staring back at the face in the
water. Then, abruptly, he yanked his hand away. As
the water disappeared he stood, flinging the wet
drops from his hand onto the gravel. Glancing up at
the stairway landing, he saw Ada by the post, watching him. How long had she been there? He didn't
know, and could read nothing in the little hopeful
smile she gave to him. Then she went in.

Back under the breezeway again, Niles took out
the harmonica and played a few bars on it.

> *How many miles to Babylon? Threescore
> miles and ten—*

Repeated the phrase.

> *Can I get there by candlelight? Yes, and back
> again.*

Pretty soon, little by little, in the shadows, almost
as though he were the Cheshire Cat, appeared Holland: first the smile, then the shock of hair, then the
bright pink that was a shirt, then the rest of him.

The ritual:

"Where've you been?"

As it usually did, Holland's crooked grin widened.
"No place," he answered evenly.

"Been down to the train tracks?"

"Nope."

And: Packard Lane? Nope. Talcotts Ferry? Nope. To *Babylon?* The catechism ended with a shrug from Holland. "Just around," he said, the usual formula.

Niles offered the harmonica. "This is yours. Ada found it over at Mrs. Rowe's house." Where Niles thought to see guilt, Holland's face was quite expressionless.

"I'm to ask you—"

"What?"

"Ask you—"

Holland was waiting.

"Nothing."

"You're crazy." ← *true enough*

Niles saw him returning his look with a level gaze, a half-smile playing about his mouth. As they stopped beside the door of the tool shed Niles whispered something behind his hand.

"Who suspects?"

Ah ha, Niles thought, *that* would get a rise out of him. "Sh. Ada."

"Does she?" Today Holland's face seemed blurred. Why was that?

"Yes. She almost saw—this." He had reached into his shirt for the tobacco tin and was spilling the blue packet into his palm.

"Angel—if you'd take that shirt off and let me wash it—" That was Winnie, leaving Torrie and the baby in the arbor, on her way back to the kitchen. And to Ada, inside: "Seems like you can't *get* Niles to wear another shirt 'ceptin' that old rag of Holland's."

Holland was whispering angrily about the tobacco tin. "Jeeze! Put that away! You want somebody to see it?"

As expected. "I know," Niles reassured him. "Don't worry." Coolly he stepped into the tool shed and after a few moments returned, empty-handed. "I won't tell."   *hides can in tool shed*

"Won't tell what?"

"You know." He could be as cryptic as Holland, if he wanted. Wait till Holland looked for Russell's glasses.

"I hung the lantern in the apple cellar," Holland was saying by way of conversation.

"What lantern?" Niles whispered.

"The lantern from Mr. Pretty's truck."

"You mean you *crooked* it?" Niles was shocked; turned his back on him; saw Torrie in the arbor, holding her baby. Torrie, sitting in a chair beside the bassinet, the baby cradled in her arms—pretty Torrie, Torrie with her red hair and brown button eyes, fondling her baby, cooing to it, pulling the string on the music box Niles had bought—"Rockabye Baby On the Treetop"—and the little baby hand, reaching for it, pretty Eugenia, he was sure she must be the prettiest baby that ever was born, just look at them: Madonna and Child.

"—and she's got the littlest fingers you ever saw," he pointed out to Holland. "Just like a doll's."

Holland's nod was wicked. "Like that doll-lamp you won at the carnival."

"No. Bigger. And each finger's got a nail on it."

"Niles, you're crazy. That's the way babies are born." And then he was gone. Amidst his laughter, just like that, he was gone, and there was nothing Niles could do then to bring him back. He stood there by the pump, digging his toe at the gravel, and wishing and wishing, but Holland was gone.

And Niles felt afraid.

He didn't know why, or what it was that made him feel that way, but, returning to the granary yard to lob rocks at the empty Richfield gasoline can atop the dump heap, he saw before him not the target at all, but, instead, Holland's face, and the look on it before he'd gone away: the Asiatic Look.

II

About a month later, just before school opened, the weather turned mean, one last oven blast of summer before the frost which would drop the mercury and turn the trees gold.

One afternoon shortly after Labor Day George Perry had come home early from his golf game. He dumped his clubs in the kitchen, and before supper he and a group of cronies from the American Legion drove merrily off in the Reo to Springfield, a distance of almost a hundred miles, to see the night races at Agawam Raceway. It being Friday, Winnie was to visit her sister and left in plenty of time to make the long trolley trek to Babylon.

At suppertime Ada went out to call Niles. Receiving no reply, she went looking for him in the barn. She stood on the threshing floor, certain she could

hear laughter somewhere, the twanging of a harmonica playing a nonsense rhyme. It was coming from
below, in the apple cellar. She heaved the door up
and looked down. Red shadows dyed the whitewashed walls; on the floor lay dark drifts of snow,
wine-colored in the light from the kerosene lamp
hanging from a hook in the beam under her feet.

"Child, what are you doing down there?"

"Nothing. Playing, is all." He had a book on his
lap, a large volume belonging to her; she wondered
how he could make out the pictures. "Come up,
please. You know nobody is given to play down
there, don't you? That is why your uncle had Mr.
Angelini put that lock on the Slave Door. Why shall
you disobey? Just look at you, what is that stuff all
over the floor? Cattails, you say? Why, you have got
it all over your clothing. Now brush yourself, Winnie
will have a fit. I say it is no wonder it is all over the
house, that fluff." She stopped and lifted the lamp,
blew it out, replaced it on its hook.

Her crossness made him wonder if the heat hadn't
gotten to her. Or perhaps she was ill—he couldn't
tell. She seemed in some sort of pain.

"Have you a toothache?" he asked as they came
through the breezeway, but, "Hush," was all he got
for an answer. Then she became cranky again, her
eye spotting what lay in the middle of the drive.

"Why, Leno must have lost his wits to leave this
here," she said, pointing to a new five-gallon Richfield can.

"It's for the cider press," Niles explained.

"But *here.* If your Uncle George comes home tonight in his usual condition, he'll be sure to hit it."

Did Niles/H put it there?

Grabbing the bail handle, she dragged the can from the gravel to a patch of weeds at the corner where the breezeway attached to the carriage-house. "Shoo! Shoo!" she cried at Chanticleer the rooster. She flapped her skirts at the bird, scratching in the weeds, and hastily pulled Niles up the drive. "Now there's the phone again," she muttered, striding ahead of him through the back-entryway.

Niles let the door slam, pausing a moment to survey the sky. Ada always insisted a mackerel sky meant rain, an old New England notion she'd picked up. The sky was clear, but it was going to rain, Niles was certain. The sun was getting ready to set, and high above the fields of Avalon across the river hung the thinnest slice of moon, the quintessential new moon: it looked like Ada's pin, a perfect crescent, visible up there in the early evening sky, only it was silver instead of gold. The sun and the moon appearing together—a rare sight. Making it both day and night, both a beginning and an ending, at one and the same time. Church bells tolled in the distance. Aloft on the cupola the weathervane was pointing due north, the gilded peregrine casting his amber eye and signaling brightly in the waning sunlight some cryptic message for all to see. An omen of some sort. But who was there to read it?

Meanwhile the sun dropped more swiftly, like a ball of blood.

Aunt Valeria was sitting in the kitchen, listlessly waving a palmetto fan.

"Who rang?" Ada asked her.

"Mrs. Brainard, looking for the doctor. Wondered if he had stopped in to see Zan. I told her no. Mrs. La

Fever wants him, her boy's down with something."
She got up, took a napkin from the drawer, and laid
it beside a plate on a tray. "I know we should be
using paper napkins," she said as she carried the food
out, "but it's so hot, and poor Zan—" She left with
the tray.

Niles put his book down on a spare chair and went
to wash his hands, covertly watching Ada, who stood
in a peculiar attitude, hands clasped at her breast.
Her face was tired, the bright eyes clouded. Her
hands shook, and the little nervous nodding of the
head had become more pronounced. Worry seemed
to have etched firmer lines into her forehead, the
creases around her lids were deeper, he thought, and
above her cheeks were dark marks he hadn't noticed
before. He wasn't sure, but he suspected she was not
sleeping well. Her spirit was troubled, he decided.

She smiled wanly as he stood on tiptoe to reach the
faucet handles. "You're growing up, *douschka.*"

"Huh?"

"You don't use a chair any more to wash."

"Winnie told me not to. She said I'm too big."

"That's what I meant."

"Why, it's as hot as Chicago, I do believe," Aunt
Vee said, coming in again. The evening continued
sweltering and the room was oppressively sticky. A
fan caused a screw of flypaper, black with flies, to
sway; otherwise nothing moved. Niles moved his
book so his aunt could sit down, and she began picking at the plate of cold salmon and watercress salad
Ada had fixed for her.

Near the table stood the bassinet; in it lay Torrie's
baby, the little Eugenia, diaper-clad and uncovered

because of the heat. Carefully wiping his hands on his napkin, Niles leaned over and offered his finger to be played with, then tickled the pink stomach. He gave a delighted laugh at the gurgling smile and pulled the string of his music box, hanging at the baby's head.

"Ressell was the happiest child you ever saw," Valeria offered. "Never a peep, not even when he got hungry. For heaven's sake, Niles, all that *sugar!*"

He had broken slices of dried beef into his bowl of crackers and now was covering the whole with a heaping tablespoon of sugar. "That's the way Father used to do," he asserted, reaching for the milk pitcher.

"You'll get diabetes, sure," Aunt Vee said. "Isn't the thermometer ever going to drop?" she fretted, fumbling her fork to her mouth.

"It's going to rain tonight, then it'll cool down," Niles announced.

"No," Aunt Vee said positively, "the weatherman predicted it's going to last through Saturday. It's just—"

"Tonight," Niles insisted. "You'll see."

Her expression inquired, What can you do with the boy? "Say, isn't this Friday?" she said suddenly. "Aren't you going to church?"

"No choir practice tonight—the Pennyfeathers went to Cape Cod."

"Lucky Pennyfeathers," said Aunt Vee, fanning.

Niles nodded with a discouraged sigh. It seemed everyone had gone away, with the exception of themselves. Torrie and Rider, down at Indian Neck, where Rider's mother and father, staying at an inn on the Sound, had invited the young couple for a long weekend. The inn did not appreciate infants, so the baby had been turned over to Ada and Aunt Vee to mind.

"Well," said the latter dolefully, "I suppose we won't be having the Memorial Dinner this year."

"Why shouldn't there be the dinner?" Ada asked.

Aunt Valeria looked surprised. "Why, what with—one thing and another, I supposed—"

"We shall have the dinner as planned," Ada replied. "It is a tradition in the family and we shall not let our personal troubles interfere."

"But do we want all those people in the house? With poor Zan—"

"Zan will not even know they are here. It is not a public demonstration, you know; it is a private ritual. For Granddaddy Perry. Besides, a party takes one's mind off less pleasant things."

"Very well," Valeria said, mollified. "Is your jaw bothering you?" she asked, concerned, as Ada probed her face.

"I have a bit of the toothache tonight." She winced, rising to salvage the leftovers.

"Oil of cloves is what you must have for toothache. I'll bet the druggist has some. I remember once when Ressell was seven—that was the year we went to Wisconsin—he had this awful toothache. We were off on the lake, not a dentist in miles, but I remembered I'd put some oil of cloves in along with the medical things. Just the ticket. And do you know, Ressell never had another one, not in his whole life. Five after," she observed as the seven o'clock trolley rattled by—*ding-ding-ding*—toward Packard Lane.

"Late again," Ada said.

Niles smiled. "Which is its wont."

"Honestly, you and your big words," Aunt Vee giggled. "Just like Holland used to be."

The fan's buzzing seemed louder in the quiet room. Nobody said anything for a time, then Niles spoke again. "What *is* at the end of the line, I wonder?"

"What do you mean, child?"

"The Shadow Hills Express. What's at the end of the line, out there in Babylon?"

The women exchanged a look and Aunt Vee sprang suddenly to life. "Five after? Why, *Amos 'n' Andy* is on! Niles dear, be an angel and put Uncle George's golf sticks away in the hall closet, will you?"

Ada was putting dishes under waxed paper into the refrigerator. She scraped the remainder into the garbage, and got out the Oxydol from under the sink. Then she washed her hands and, drying them on her apron, started out.

"What—?" Niles was out of his chair.

"I must have my laudanum. Stay with the baby."

Niles played the music box again, and while the melody continued he hitched his chair closer to the bassinet, laid the big book across his lap and opened the cover. It was bound in faded velvet, the corners frayed and eaten away.

"Now, baby, do you want to look at the picture book with your uncle?" he said lightly, leafing to the opening pages. He paused at the frontispiece, his brown hands flattening the pages and bringing the book close to the baby's head. "See? Selected from the Doré Bible, Milton, Dante's *Inferno,* Dante's

Pur—" he stumbled over the word—"*Purgatorio,* I guess that is. I think that means hell, where bad people go, so on and so forth." He stopped at an engraving of a dark figure with batlike wings, hurtling through space toward a cloud-ridden sphere. "Satan approaching the confines of the earth," he read, and thumbed some more. "Satan is the devil, and he's very *bad,*" he pointed out. "He's the baddest of everybody. He likes to do evil." The next picture was one of a wild-haired, all-but-naked man poling a bark on the water. "This is Charon, the ferryman of hell, baby; he crosses the river, see? And the river's called Acheron, the river of sorrow, and it flows on forever and ever, everlastingly." He leafed some more: pictures of devils rioting in conclave, demons dancing, serpents coiling and uncoiling, dragons, beasts, humans in turmoil, suffering hellish agonies. These he described with relish, passing over serene and lovely pictures of Paradise between whose pages Ada had pressed leaves, oak, maple, sassafras, a flower or two, a rose, some sunflower petals.

He was gazing at a page, a long, silent stare, his eyes riveted to the engraving, lost in its design. The baby made a sound. "Yes," Niles said, coming alert, "this is a good one." He described in detail the awesome Biblical scene depicting *Babylon Fallen:* a nightmare creation, with immense piles of ruined masonry, towering monoliths topped by stone elephants, monstrous sphinxes, scavenging birds, the teeth of howling wolves gleaming in the moonlight. Then he read to the baby the lines from the Book of Revelation: " 'And he cried mightily with a strong voice, saying, Babylon the great is fallen, and is become the habitation of devils, and the hold of every foul spirit, and a cage of every unclean and hateful bird.' Oh baby, hush, there, don't cry, little baby," he crooned softly to the crying child, putting the book aside and tickling the baby's chin.

"You look like a baboon, grinning that way," Holland said. He had appeared suddenly, a wide smirk on his face. "What're you smiling at, anyway?"

"Because I'm an uncle. That's what uncles are supposed to do, rock and tickle and smile. You're an uncle too."

"Like hell."

"Don't swear in front of the baby. Torrie's your sister, her baby's your niece, that makes you an uncle."

Holland sniffed. "What d'you all pay so much attention to it for? What a fuss you make. Look at that stupid little face, how can you stand looking at it? How can anybody? Little baby, little changeling baby." Niles saw him reach and pinch the baby's tender flesh between his fingers. With a squall of pain the infant began crying anew as a red mark appeared.

"Cripes, Holland!" Niles swore in a whisper, pulling the diaper over the mark, trying to quiet the child.

In a moment Ada hurried in with Alexandra's tray. "What is it? What is wrong?" she said in alarm. "I thought I heard Eugenia crying." She looked, to find Niles soothing and lulling the little bundle in his arms while he paced the floor, the music box playing "Rockabye Baby."

"It's all right, she was just hot, that's all. Yes,

baby, that's all it was, wasn't it? The sweet baby," he said, jouncing it lightly the way Winnie did.

Ada set the tray down. "Your mother wouldn't eat a bite. I don't know how we will ever get food into her. Doctor says she'll lose what little strength she has left." She touched her hand gingerly to her face again.

"Did the laudanum help?" he asked, returning the baby carefully to the bassinet.

She shook her head, exploring with the end of her tongue the sensitive tooth that was distressing her.

"I'm sorry," he said.

Later, when he had helped her with the dishes, he picked up the Doré book and cradled it in his arms.

"Where are you going?" she asked.

"Well," he replied with an engaging smile, starting for the door, "I thought I'd go up to Mother's room and show some pictures to her before it gets too dark." *what pictures will he show?*

A warm wind was blowing up across the meadow from the river and the grandfather clock striking nine when Niles came down the hallway after returning the book to Ada's room. He met her climbing the front stairs, carrying the bassinet. "Wait." He ran to help her, taking one end while she shifted hands and together they went along the corridor, the baby between them.

"Did your mother enjoy the reading?"

Yes, he assured her, Mother did. More or less. "Except she's sort of nervous again," he hastened to add. "Can't seem to stop crying."

In Torrie and Rider's bedroom the wicker cradle

hung suspended on its stand between the two windows. An ample square of white netting fell around it from the ceiling to screen out mosquitos. Torrie had tied silk bows along the rim and the inside was a downy nest, cushioned with a soft pad, over it a sheet, and the coverlet Ada had sewn. Niles held the baby carefully as, lovingly, he laid it in the cradle on its stomach, the way Torrie had shown him.

"It's too hot for that," he said as Ada drew the sheet over the baby, who immediately tried to kick it off. He bent and lifted it back, folding it neatly at the foot of the cradle. "There, that's better."

"She'll be all right now until it gets cooler; she don't need a cover, you're right." Rearranging some things on the bureau, Ada inspected her open mouth in the mirror, prodding the malignant tooth with a finger, a grimace on her face.

"Does it still hurt?" She nodded, and he said, "I think you should take one of your pain pills. The ones Dr. Brainard gave you."

She hesitated. "I do not like to take those pills, they make me dizzy sometimes."

"Then you must lie down. I'll get you some root beer and bring the pill."

Oh, the child was so thoughtful. She fanned her face with her hand. "I think for once you are wrong. I do not believe it will rain tonight." She reached to draw the netting around the cradle.

"Yes. It's going to. Here, I can do that—you go along."

"Don't forget to turn off the lights."

Standing beside the cradle, he rocked it a moment, smiling down at the baby—the little angel face—and

humming to it. Suddenly remembering the music box
still looped on the bassinet, he changed it to the head
of the cradle. He started it and, as the tinkling melody began, the infant stirred. *Rockabye baby, on the
treetop* . . . Niles put his finger out; she clasped it
contentedly and closed her eyes. Little peaceful per-
sonage. He watched it hovering on the verge of sleep,
leaned close to brush the soft pink flesh with his nose,
kiss the red mark on her tummy.

Oh-so-gently removing his finger from the little
hand, he enclosed the cradle with the netting and, the
music box running down, rewound it. *When the wind
blows, the cradle will rock* . . . He switched off the
light. A fretful cry stopped him in the doorway; he
turned back. On the bureau sat the doll-lamp he had
won for Torrie at the carnival. He switched it on: the
bulb under the skirt shed a soft circle of peach-
colored light over the cradle, melting away into the
darkness beyond, the little imp-face grinning out into
the dark.

Satisfied, he started to go, then paused, suddenly
tense, like an animal which, sensing danger, strains
to hear. There was nothing. Only his imagination
again. That and the wind outside, and from downstairs the muffled sounds of Aunt Valeria's radio. He
stepped to the window. Overhead the sky was still
clear, star-strewn; clouds were moving in from the
west; the wind felt hot and damp against his face.
Still he hesitated, listening. He looked over at the
crack where he and Holland had watched from the
other side of the wall in the storeroom. No light
showed there. Yet he had the distinct sensation . . .
uncanny . . . a sense of something impending. Silly;

it was only the gathering storm. He tiptoed to the center of the room, then halted, just on the periphery of lamplight falling onto the cradle. Holland . . . ? Where was he? With an uneasy sigh, he left the room.

Passing the hall closet by the grandfather clock, he suddenly remembered Aunt Vee's asking him to put Uncle George's golf clubs away. Ever helpful, he ran down to the kitchen, carried the golf bag upstairs, and put it in its place in the closet. Phew, it was hot in there. Smelled funny too. Hanging on a hook was a leather coat, one Father had worn in the war; it gave off a pungent, leathery odor as he leaned the golf bag in the corner and tried to close the closet door. Cripes, it still wouldn't shut; he pushed at it several times, then gave up, standing at the top of the stairs and looking down the Oriental carpet into the lower hall where a faint light showed. Outside, the wind continued to roil up around the house; inside, an uncommon number of noises: curtains flapped like annoyed white hands at the windows, somewhere crystal tinkled, a pane of glass vibrated, beams snapped behind the plaster. The closet door rattled as though some presence inside wished to escape. *Tock*-tick, said the grandfather clock, *tock*-tick.

It was as if the house itself were breathing, exerting some effort of its own, struggling to maintain a curious lifelike equilibrium, as a spoon balances on the rim of a glass. Suspense had magnetized the air. Poised at the head of the stairs, pinprickly with anticipation, Niles waited with the brooding house for the storm bunching blackly across the river. Then he decided he would go and tune in the cat's whisker on his crystal set.

But not before he had gotten Ada her pill.

It held off till shortly before eleven. The first-appearing lightning was no more than a snap. Clouds like blue-black ink had spilled out of the west, spreading before the hot wind, now doing violence to the orchard. It hurled apples to the ground like bombs, cracked limbs, scattered leaves in a panic, bowed the long grass as it swept up through thc meadow past the barn, shook the tops of the firs, rattled the horse-chestnut tree in a frenzy, punished the grapes in the arbor.

Another flash. Lying in bed, staring at the water-stain directly overhead, making a face of it, Niles adjusted his earphones. More flashes. Removing the phones he went to the south window and looked out over the drive. The sky went silver, he counted fast: 1-2-3-4-5. With five, thunder. The sound of a shingle splitting, ending with an enormous crack, followed by a low booming roll. Now a lurid light washed the black shapes outside; they glowed eerily. Niles shut his eyes, waiting for the clap to follow. Before it died, the rain came: long shafts like arrows arching down the sky, stinging wet and cold in his face. He leaned on the window sash and slammed it down. Hair drenched, knuckling water from his eyes, he hurried to close the others. As the last window hit the sill he peered through the rain slanting at the squares of glass: in Torrie's room he glimpsed a light glowing from two open windows, their shutters cracking frantically against the house. He could feel the hair on his arms start to lift. In the tumult, faintly he heard the twang of the harmonica: *Nyang-nayang-a-dang* . . . *How many miles to Babylon?—Threescore miles and ten* . . .

He flung open the door and dashed along the corridor. At the head of the stairs he stopped dead. Below, the front door swung wide, banging rhythmically with metallic shocks against the radiator. In the parlor the Atwater-Kent blared. Gusts of wind spilled wet leaves across the floor, cartwheeling along on thin edges, sliding into corners, flying partway up the stairs.

Niles spun, rushed down the hall into the north wing, along the passageway, through the door. Thunder cracked around the chimneys, over the eaves, rain shot through the open windows. Puddles glistened on the floor under the sills, trembling as a shutter slammed against the clapboards. A current of damp air streamed steadily through the room, carrying the lace curtains inward, flapping them wetly against the casements. It rang the tassels on the bedtester like cotton bells and flourished the mosquito netting, wafting gauzy billows above the wind-tossed cradle. From inside came a light: grotesque, eerie, unnatural. He approached. The wicker basket rapped hollowly at the wall. The netting brushed across his eyes. He grabbed at it, brushed the fabric away to stare down at the place where the little doll-lamp lay, with its fat brown face and its impish leer, the bulb under its skirt-shade casting a dim, peach-colored light over the coverlet Ada had made, and up onto the sides of the forlorn and empty cradle.

III

One thing he could tell: she was following him, you bet. Had been right along, wouldn't let him out of her sight. Grim-faced and pained and fearful, he thought. A puzzled fear, like she didn't quite know what to do about it. Though he could have told her, if only she'd asked. But she didn't—like she was afraid of the answer. So she just dogged him, limping a little, watching, watching . . .

Well, he had a trick or two up his sleeve. Ducked quick as a wink into a shop doorway. Bells jingled.

"Well m'dear, see who we have here. Hello, Niles," said Miss Josceline-Marie, determined to be forgiving of the boy, in spite of her justly righteous indignation.

"We're all praying, Niles," said another lady.

"We certainly are," said a third, fervently.

"Hello," he said softly and, giving them the benefit of his eyes, went to read the magazines at the rack. Behind his back, he could tell, significant looks were being exchanged.

"There you are, m'dear," Miss Josceline-Marie loudly proclaimed to Mrs. Fenstermacher—he had certainly recognized *her*—"Lovely cards, ent they? Don't get too much of a call for *Yom Kippurs* in these parts." She was craning her neck as far as her fat neck permitted to peer across the green to the church. "Funeral still going, ayuh. Sad, when they die so young, ent it? Such a tragedy."

"Whose funeral?" one of the ladies asked.

"Why, it's the La Fever boy—meningitis. Went like that." Miss Josceline-Marie snapped her fingers.

"Oh my, you don't say? Anna La Fever's boy. Sorrow upon sorrow, isn't it?" The voice was lowered, though not sufficiently that Niles couldn't overhear. "What with the *disappearance.*" An appropriate emphasis.

"Ayuh. Though if you ask me, I haven't heard of any month-old babies just getting up and *disappearing* of their own accord. I'd say it's purely a case of kidnapping. The Lindbergh thing all over again. You'd of thought that Hauptmann person would've taught some folks a lesson."

Niles flipped a page. They were speaking about Holland and the baby.

"Well," Mrs. Fenstermacher said, "I talked with Mrs. Blessing after church Sunday and she said Constable Blessing says—"

"Pooh, Mr. Blessing. Mr. Blessing's a codger, dear. No kind of a constable for a growing town like this. Should of retired by now. Won't solve this affair, be assured. What it wants is suspects, and suspects is what they haven't got. Over a week and nary a clue. Mark me, nobody'll see that child alive again. See you got out your coat, Ruth."

Niles stole a glance at the third lady, inspecting a piece of china. "Well, it's got so nippy over the weekend."

"Don't drop that, m'dear, it's Copenhagen."

"Lord," the lady went on, "I feel so sorry for those

folks." Niles looked away before she caught him. "Ethel Landis says her children absolutely cross the street when they go by the house. You'd think the place was haunted, the way some're carrying on. And all them reporters hanging about."

"I thought they'd all been pulled off the story," Miss Josceline-Marie whispered in a surprised tone. The ladies drew their heads together over the cash register.

"Noo," said the lady, "that man from the *Courant*'s still around, and I saw the one wears the mackintosh, the one came up from New York."

"Well, if they come around here, I could give them a story," Miss Josceline-Marie said, trying unsuccessfully to keep her voice down. "Up to and including some things most people don't even know about."

"Such as?"

"Such *as*, Winnie stopping in so often at the—" The look she tossed in the direction of Sweeney's Liquor Store next door was freighted with innuendo.

"Goodness," Mrs. Fenstermacher said, "that's no news. Everybody knows George and Valeria enjoy their liquor."

"All the Perrys enjoy their liquor," said the third lady.

"That's it exactly. Everyone knows George only drinks bourbon. Valeria too. But I got it out of Harry Sweeney that it wasn't any bourbon Winnie was picking up practically every time you blinked. It was rye. And I guess we know who's partial to rye in that house." ZAN

"*Was*," Mrs. Fenstermacher said knowingly.

The bells jingled again and Rose Halligan from the

Five and Ten came traipsing in on her high heels.
" 'Day, Rose," the proprietress greeted her.
"C'm'ere, m'dear. Listen, didn't Harry next door
come right out and tell me that was Fleischman's rye
the Perrys' maid was getting?"

"Welp, yes—" Rose began.

"There. What'd I tell you. The place is awash with
spirits."

"Not *any more* it isn't," Mrs. Fenstermacher could
not contain herself. "Or hadn't you heard?"

No, they hadn't. Well, Fred—Fenstermacher, that
was—had gotten it straight from George on his way
to the Rose Rock bottling works this morning. Took
her away in a closed car, *you know where. No!* No,
not *there,* to a nursing home. Miss Josceline-Marie
thought that was only right, and said so. But why, at
long last?

Mrs. Fenstermacher wasn't sure. "She got violent,
I heard. Fred said George said she just went completely out of control and got violent."

"And—?"

"And that's all George said. That's enough, isn't
it? My heavens, Alexandra Perry—*violent?*"

"Pooh, if they took folks away for getting violent,
they'd have to take away half the town."

"Well, at least they've gotten her away before the
dinner," Mrs. Fenstermacher said.

"What dinner?" asked Rose.

"You don't mean to *say!*" Miss Josceline-Marie
was astounded. "Do you mean to stand there and tell
me George Perry is going to hold the *dinner?*"

"*What* dinner?" Rose insisted.

"The Perrys have this memorial thing every year

for the Board of Selectmen," Miss Josceline-Marie explained.

"Memorial thing?" Rose looked blank.

"In memory of old Mr. Perry," put in Mrs. Fenstermacher; Fred Fenstermacher was one of the town selectmen.

"Granddaddy Perry, that'd be. His will provided that every year money was to be given to the Town Fund for Children."

"Fred says none of the Board wants to go but—"

"But?"

"But—" Mrs. Fenstermacher was flummoxed. "But it's been decided."

"Well, if you ask me, that dinner's no more than an excuse for them gentlemen to get drunk." She took four or five steps down the aisle and called over to the magazine rack. "Niles, was there something particular you are looking for?"

"No'm. Just looking."

"We don't like our young people thumbing the magazines, please," she said. He replaced his comic book and started for the door. "Don't you *want* that?" she cried after him.

"That's okay—thanks."

"Well—!" The jingling bells cut off the rest of her sentence and Niles stood on the street looking right and left for the black-coated figure. No, she didn't seem to be around. Over in front of the church was a line of cars. Music sounded from inside. He crossed the green and approached. Two of Mr. Foley's assistants, flowers in their buttonholes, were murmuring to each other in the vestibule. When their backs were turned Niles slipped in through the open door and hid in a far pew. Around him, shadows. Before him, the rigid backs of mourners. A woman weeping. In the pulpit, droning, Mr. Tuthill . . . blasted buds, blighted hopes, Everlasting Life. Casket, candles, flowers, the familiar appurtenances. A rendition from the organ loft by Professor Lapineaux.

Niles turned slightly, his face catching the rainbow of light streaming through the stained glass window where he beheld in all her glory the Angel of the Brighter Day: her wings so white, so lofty, her raiment pristine and flowing, her countenance radiant, peaceful, serene, her figure bending, one graceful hand offering him the lily.

For a while he dreamed in the shadows, his attention now on the Angel, now on the funeral proceedings. When those concerned had left to bear the casket to the cemetery, Niles remained cloistered in the pew, listening as the Professor's organ continued—practicing selections for Sunday, Niles suspected—and he went on gazing at the Angel. *Rock of Ages, cleft for meee.* One of Ada's favorites. It always gave him a feeling of hope. But not today. Hope? What hope was there? The baby was gone.

And *where was* it?

It had been raining still when the search for the missing Eugenia first began. Then, the wind driving the storm away to the east, Mr. Blessing had come in answer to the frantic summons; he in turn roused deputies who strode about scouring the house, the passages, the storage spaces, the closets, any place where the child might have been hidden; spread outside, their flashlight beams crisscrossing the lawn, shining behind shrubs, down the drive to the pump, into the arbor, the barn, everywhere. Though in those early hours of the disappearance no one had yet mentioned the dread word "kidnapped." But Niles knew. Certainly he did, knew exactly what had happened.

With his own flashlight he had crept along the hall, through the back passages, into the storeroom next to Torrie and Rider's room. Holland would be there, Niles was certain. *Only he wasn't.* Down the back stairs, out to the kitchen. The hayloft, the cupola, the cold-cellar, the apple cellar: no Holland. The trapdoor was closed, and when he pulled it up he found the room dark and solitary and empty; the cattail snow lay undisturbed, the kerosene lamp hung cold and unlighted on the nail above the ladder.

Down the road to the icehouse, along the river-bank to the landing, back up through the wet meadow to the house, bare legs stinging from the grass. Deputies in the hall revealed their bafflement. In the parlor, on the davenport, Ada sat, her face bewildered as she stared at Constable Blessing making notes.

"You were asleep then, you say, Mrs. Vedrenya?"

"Yes. I have dat damn toothache and I took some laudanum earlier—"

"Earlier?"

"After supper. But it don't seem to help much, so I take one of dem pain pills—"

"What kind of pills?"

"The bottle don't say. Some codeine compound. The doctor, he get dem for my pain." In her nervousness she was forgetting her English. She held up her swollen fingers.

"Where'd you get them?"

"Holland get dem for me."

"Holland?"

"No, I mean Niles." She seemed flustered.

Niles spoke up. "I got the pills for Ada, Mr. Blessing. The prescription is from Dr. Brainard. At the Pequot Drugstore."

"Umm." Mr. Blessing rubbed his day's growth of beard thoughtfully, then addressed Ada again. "You took the pills and went straight to bed?"

"One pill. Niles bring me one pill with root beer."

"Is that correct, Niles?"

"Yes sir," he replied earnestly. "It was so hot, I brought root beer to everyone. With lemon."

"Everyone?"

"Yes sir. For my mother, and Ada, and for Aunt Vee."

"I see. Mrs. Vedrenya, what did you do after you took the pill?"

"I go to lie down and I must have fall asleep."

"Why did you leave the windows open? Didn't you realize a storm was coming?"

"I closed the windows," Niles said. "All of them, except in here. Aunt Vee was listening to the radio and she said she'd shut them if it started raining—but she didn't think it would."

"Then what?" He turned back to Ada.

"As I have said, I was laying down. I t'ink, I shall go to sleep if I do not get up, but I could not. The tooth pain stopped. I am asleep. The next thing,

Niles is shaking me. He says to wake up, Eugenia is gone."

"What time was that?"

"I don't know."

"It must have been after eleven," Niles pointed out, "because I remember I had the Maxwell House Coffee program on my crystal set and it was just going off the air when the rain started."

"Where was Mrs. Perry?"

"In the parlor, I thought."

"What do you mean, you thought? Wasn't she?"

"No, she was not." Ada was speaking. "It turned out she had walked up to Packard Lane to get some oil of cloves for me. For dat dam tooth. She stopped with friends during the rain."

"Where is Mrs. Perry now?"

Aunt Valeria had been on the phone, trying to get through to Torrie and Rider. The lines were down. After futile attempts she went upstairs to sit with Alexandra until Winnie got home from her sister's.

"I'd like a few words with your aunt," Mr. Blessing told Niles. He went upstairs and spoke with a near-hysterical Aunt Vee. When she had gone down to the parlor Niles went along the gallery and back to his own room. He was shivering, his teeth chattered from the cold and excitement; suddenly he felt burdened by fatigue. The search had continued on all night and now, raising one of the windows, he looked at a sky already tinged with a pearly glow, the meadow glistening with dew. Leaning on the window sill, he thought how the cloudless sky promised a beautiful day.

But the baby . . . where *was* it?

Ask Holland. Holland knew.
But Holland wasn't telling.

And since then all the days had been beautiful, beautiful and sorrowful and infinitely changed. Now Torrie remained hidden in her room and, close to her side, Rider, alternating between hope and despair. Now Uncle George was drinking more; he and Aunt Valeria could be heard behind their door, talking stridently. Now people came and went, tramping up and down stairs, questioning, recording, photographing, disturbing the already-disturbed household. People waking up hollering from nightmares. Now Winnie went from one room to another, trying to care for all, trying to smile, to be brave, to have faith, to keep the news from Alexandra . . .

But Mother knew, somehow.

Somehow she had learned—or sensed—the truth.

Poor Mother; it was terrible. They could scarcely keep her in her wheelchair: day and night she could be heard rolling angrily around her room in an agony of frustration, banging into things, knocking them over. She smashed her vanity mirror, then broke her tortoise-shell comb, then took scissors to her embroidered slippers. And then, two nights ago, when Niles had lain down—unfortunately on Holland's bed—listening to the crystal set, staring at the face in the ceiling, he had not heard the door open or the creak of the wheels, because of the earphones. When he looked up he saw his mother's face leaning above him. Oh, that face! Dead white, eyes ringed with black, the scarlet mouth opening, closing—it chilled him to think of it. Poor deluded Mother; how could

he make her understand that *he* was *Niles.* For Holland he accepted the furious rain of blows on his face, the silent curses heaped upon him. A natural enough error: she had taken him for his twin lying in his own bed. And now she was gone, put away from harm, and the house was more sorrowful than ever. *Babylon*
shadow hills

He tried to smile back at the Angel in the church window. What was it? Something she reminded him of—no, something he *wanted* to be reminded of . . . something he had forgotten . . .

A chuckle. Holland, close by in the pew, was sitting watching him.

"You can't remember, can you?"

Cripes! *How* he read his mind.

"Remember what?"

"You know." The enigmatic smile. Another chuckle, low, crafty like Achilles.

"What's so funny now?"

"I was just thinking."

"What?"

"You had another nightmare last night, didn't you? Yes you did. You pulled the sheets out all around your mattress. Something scared you."

Niles stiffened. "I was dreaming about the baby."

"What about the baby?"

Professor Lapineaux had left the organ loft. In a moment he would be coming to close up. Niles whispered hurriedly: "I was in this big house, and I kept getting lost. No matter where I turned I couldn't find my way. I walked for a long time, I walked and walked and then I heard it."

"What?" Holland's face was all colors, blue and

red and yellow and green, a kaleidoscope of hues from the stained glass.

"The baby. *Torrie's* baby. Crying, crying like it would break your heart, and I wanted to find it and bring it back to Torrie—"

"And that's when you woke up screaming. You're crazy, Niles."

"Holland?"

"What?"

"Where is it?"

"The baby?" Holland shrugged. "How should I know?"

"Yes you do."

"I said I don't. What else must I tell you?"

Niles could feel the muscles in his jaw working. "Holland, give it back."

"What, Niles?"

"The baby! Give it back—it isn't yours, it's Torrie's. It's her baby. You've got to give it back!" On and on and on, the entreaty becoming a litany, and Professor Lapineaux, watching from the shadows, shaking his head at the poor child, talking to himself.

"Ask the elves?" Niles was astonished at the airy remark. A threat was what was needed to shake some sense into him. "Holland, if you don't give it back— I'll tell."

A long, protracted silence. Then Holland said softly, "You'll tell what?"

"Everything. *Everything!*"

"You won't."

"I will!" he muttered through clenched teeth, gripping the turnings of the pew in front of him. He swore aloud and the Professor, taken aback by the language, stepped forward to bring the boy out into the daylight.

IV

She was across the street when he stepped from the vestibule onto the portico. Professor Lapineaux left him at the door and Niles skipped behind a pillar, then sneaked off down the sidewalk, tree to tree, confident he was unseen. Passing the wrought-iron gates, he went beyond the cemetery to the cornfield; he paused to take in the sweeping prospect. Stalks lay over the tired earth between bearded furrows. The westering sun glazed the russets, browns, and ochres of the field with a warm, coppery sheen, casting luminous shadows. Shocks of bound corn stood guarding the adjacent cemetery dead. The scarecrow, limp and tattered on a pole, straw-stuffed, straw-faced, looked back at him across the furrows.

From some vague distance came the annoyed caw of a crow; wind lightly stirred the papery corn; it seemed to whisper his name. *Niles . . . Niles . . .* His shoulders tensed. *Niles . . .* Dry, garrulous tongues, whispering . . . what? To remind him of— what? Of that which he had forgotten, that thing which the Angel had wanted to remind him of. What was it? What was wrong with his brain, why couldn't he remember? Ah well, it would come. A revelation, perhaps; but it would come. In one split second, like a lightning flash, it would be discovered, for after all, he had been born with the caul, hadn't he? Wasn't he half Russian? It would come.

Some lengths away, the burial was in progress. The mourners clustered around Arnie La Fever's open grave while Mr. Tuthill intoned the Twenty-third Psalm, as inevitably he did. Leaves, burnished red and gold, rustled above the narrow hole. Somewhere a bird sang. But of that group none seemed to mark the odd contrast between the entrancing birdsong and the pastor's doleful cadences. Niles observed how silently a stem detached itself from a twig: giving up its life—bright leaf, falling . . . falling . . . The leaf spiraled down to rest upon the lid of the casket. It looked like a hand, offering benediction.

Then he saw her again, at the edge of the field, beneath an umbrella-shaped tree, waiting, one hand on the thin trunk, her face shadowed, and it was as though she were shielding herself against the sun with a giant flaming parasol, her coat and hat and gloves all black under the fiery leaves. She crossed the turf, stepped over the furrows, and came along into the dead cornfield, her head nodding slightly, the faint, hopeful smile pulsing on her mouth.

He put his hands in his pockets and looked up at her. Again there was the outline around her head against the sky, that same white, vibrating line that reminded him of the halo around the Angel of the Brighter Day. Only in place of a lily she held in her hand a black glove.

"Child."

"What are you doing here?"

"I am walking, even as you."

"But what are you *doing?*" he pressed her. "Why aren't you home?"

"Should I be at home?"

"Tonight's the dinner."

"And there is much to do, yes. Winnie is seeing to it. And your uncle. I shall be there presently." She made a visible effort to soften the sternness of her features as she spoke. *"Douschka,"* she said—and it sounded to him like a beginning—"can you remember what we used to say about secrets?"

Sure, he remembered: everyone should have a secret.

"But sometimes it is not right to keep secrets." Her fingers brushed his hair, already darkening with the sun's cooling. "Isn't that so?"

"When?"

"When they hurt people. Then we must tell."

"You mean, give it up?" His hair dropped across his eyes, obscuring her look. He held his breath; hoped she wasn't going to ask the question.

"Niles, look at me." He raised his head, but did not look directly at her. He had a feeling. In a minute she would ask, he felt sure.

"You have a secret. Tell it to me. Tell it to Ada," she said kindly.

"I can't." He waited, head averted, letting the thatch of hair screen his eyes from her. He glanced over at the open grave, saw the casket being lowered, someone stepping forward to pluck the fallen leaf away, stooping for a handful of earth, sifting it into the hole.

"Child?"

He could feel her eyes on him still; sensed what she

was getting at; in another moment she would ask. Certainly she suspected. He knew that. Hadn't he told Holland? Over there, the mourners were leaving the cemetery, going down the roadway, out the gate.

"Niles."

Now it was coming. He recognized the no-nonsense tone. She would choose some words and say them, and together the words would form the question.

The moon pin glinted on her collar. "Does the secret have anything to do with the baby?"

See: doesn't *know;* suspects. "Yes," he answered dutifully.

"You must tell me." Still he refused. "Do you want Torrie to go on suffering the way she is?"

No. Certainly he didn't. He met her eyes, and now there lay between them the two things: her question, his answer. When she asked it, would he tell? He'd have to. *No. No, Holland. I won't. I was only kidding.* He felt his heart pounding, the blood singing in his ears. And the question lingered, like an unwelcome guest.

Those eyes, they seemed so old, so tired, so used up as she knelt, drew the boy into her arms. The moon pin felt cold against his cheek. He didn't want to cry, but the tears were not to be avoided. It hurt inside his chest where his heart pounded. And hers; he could feel it, faintly, through the material of her coat. Now, he knew, her arms holding him, her hands soothing, allowing no protest, the question would come; for this she had been following him, never letting him from her sight.

And it came; softly, hardly a question at all.

He twisted, tried to free himself. Her arms held him. "Don't ask me! I don't know!"

"Someone knows. You must say."

"I can't. I gave my word!"

"Yes you can."

"It's a secret. I promised."

"Promised who?"

"You know!"

"Say!"

"I promised *him!*"

He pulled away. A thin row of drops appeared along his cheek where the moon pin had scratched.

He took her handkerchief, walked a little way away from her, blowing his nose and looking out over the cornshocks, staring at the scarecrow, whose brittle, ragged form stirred in the lifting wind. On one shoulder, like an enormous black epaulette, perched a crow, its head cocked defiantly at him.

His eye upon the scarecrow's face, he saw, bit by bit, the face change, become another face. A face he would not recognize. Could, but would not. A face no longer straw and string, but lichen-spotted, decayed, the flesh shriveled, eyeless sockets, lips stretched away from withered gums pulled back from bare teeth, forever grinning in an ivoried skull. Yet, whose? *Whose?* Wait! *Oh Jesus!* Now he saw: the shock of blond hair, the gable-shaped brows, the mouth smiling as though hideously pleased to be staked out there among the cornshocks, mocking him.

"Niles, he is dead. *Holland is dead.*" She had come up beside him, took his hand, turned his face away from That Other face. "Remember, child? On his birthday? Holland? Come, you shall admit it now. It is not a game any longer. Do you understand?"

He shook his head, not wanting to give her this thing over him, this power which, he sensed, threatened him.

"Niles—" she began, then stopped, not knowing how to begin, torn by pity and fear; then, a final time, her question, she stopping his mouth when he said the words. "No, child; do not tell me to ask Holland—"

He had become a very imp, a sprite, horrid and ill-natured looking, his face a fury of maleficence, like the face of the doll-lamp. "Yes! Holland!" he accused; if she wanted the truth! Holland had taken the baby! Had come in the night and put the pills—*six* of them —in her root beer, had waited till she slept, had stolen the baby, had taken it away and put the doll-lamp in its place—little changeling baby.

"No, child—"

"Yes! He hates the baby! Because it's pretty, because we all love it! He hates it!" He ranted on, spilling out a contagion of ugliness and accusation. "I was afraid—I knew he would hurt the baby. I tried to protect her. I wanted to stop him. But I *couldn't.*" He caught his breath and plunged on. *"He* took the baby, *he* killed Russell—"

She gasped, her mind reeling as the revelations poured out, one after the other, nothing, nothing any longer kept from her. Yes, Russell saw the ring, so Holland put the pitchfork in the hay. Saw the *ring?* She was incredulous. *The ring?* He told her the entire story, of Holland's gift, of the difficulty he had procuring it, how with the aid of the rose shears—*"The*

rose shears?" "Yes, I put them back on the nail." And
Mrs. Rowe? "No, it was an accident, the Professor
was just going to scare her, honest!" Holland, Holland, Holland. Had flicked the wasp at Aunt Fan,
had poisoned Russell's rat, had done it all. And
Mother too, Mother snooping in the Chautauqua
desk . . . Mother down the steps.

Oh God, dear God. Niles. Niles.

Sorting out the horror, she watched him move
away, his back to the scarecrow, his face passionate,
guileless, thoughtful, indignant. What was to be
done, her expression said. To that question she must
come, sooner or later. *What was to be done?* She
stood looking through the oak branches, thinking,
the frail and feeble hands, black-gloved and swollen,
hands that all her life had found some business, some
concern, some task to fulfill, they now could only
clutch at one another, crabbed, ineffectual, helpless.

He went to her and tugged her sleeve to bring her
back.

Half musing, she shook her head; took him firmly
by the shoulders. "Say the words, child—say them
once and for all. Let that be the beginning."

He didn't want to understand. "What words?"

She forced his look around, across the field to the
cemetery and the family burial plot. "I want you to
say the words out loud so you will remember them."
He shrank into himself and like a willful pet eluded
her hands; they found him again and held him
tightly.

"Say the words."

"No."

"You must, child. Say them. Say, 'Holland is dead.' "

"He isn't," he sobbed.

"He is!"

"No! There isn't any grave! There wasn't any funeral! How could he be dead?"

"You were sick. You had been in bed, you were in your room in bed. Then we found you outside the barn, you were standing looking at the cupola, screaming names up at the weathervane. Never mind what sort—we understood. You took cold; while you were sick we brought Holland's coffin to the grave—"

"When?" Defiantly.

"In March. After your birthdays."

He shot her a triumphant look. "You see—it's a lie! In March the ground is still frozen—you couldn't have buried him!"

"This year there was an early thaw." Her voice was steel. "He is there, under the ground. See his gravestone."

His face reddened, contorted, nose and eyes wet and runny, he wrenched out the denial. "No!" He struck out at her; pain stabbed her belly, her shrunken breasts contracted further where he pounded his fists against her and cruelly twisted her fingers. Screaming, kicking, using fists and feet however he might, he could not defeat her; remorselessly she held him. Finally the words came sluicing out like water; he shouted them, loudly enough so that, over the field, in the graveyard, the sexton, digging, heard each separate one.

"He's dead, he's dead—*Holland is dead!*"

Her arms relaxed; she soothed and gentled him down, wiped his tears, held him, rocked him in her arms; Oh sweet, oh *douschka,* no more no more it shall be all right.

"But it was only a game, wasn't it?" he asked softly in her ear, his moist lips brushing her skin, his earnest voice causing hers to break.

"A—game. Yes, child, it was only a game. A game for us to play, you and me—"

"And Holland."

"And Holland," she repeated dully; then, refusing to give him this small victory over her, she took his face between her hands and peered into his eyes. "But it is all over now, do you understand?"—her fingers gripping harder—"There must be no more playing the game. It is—dangerous, do you see? It is wrong."

Wrong? How was it wrong? Had he done the wrong? Long in coming, her reply was desolate. "No, dearest child, *I* did. The wrong has been mine, all the while. I am an old woman at the end of her life, but I am not a wise one. I am a foolish woman for I could not see it. Perhaps I could, but I would not."

"Why?"

Now her whole being opened itself up to the awful realization that flooded in on her; she felt as though she were drowning; a huge wave of remorse buffeted her frail body. Now the truth was upon her and she reeled away from it; yet turn as she might the truth remained, not to be avoided, and for this truth she must dearly pay. She clenched her hands, unmindful of the pain it caused her. Through her brain poured a hundred accusations, and she lifted her fist as though to strike herself. Who has done this thing, she bitterly asked herself; and the answer mocked her: I. I have done this thing.

He repeated his question: "Why?"

"Because I did not wish to," she said, her voice steel again. No sooner steel than it wavered, softened. "But that is no excuse. It was wrong of me to permit it. But it broke my heart to see you sitting there by the pump, knowing what you were looking at, down in the water. It broke my heart to see you so unhappy, to think that because I loved you, I should be the cause of your unhappiness. I thought that in time you would outgrow it, do you see. Little boys grow into big boys and they leave such fancies behind, if they are fortunate, for they discover the real world then."

"Have I discovered the real world yet?"

"Oh, *douschka*." She caught her breath and, continuing, her voice was heavy and bleak. "Yes child, I see it now. Your world is very real—for you. Only—" She could not go on.

He stood without moving, waiting for her to finish her sentence, eyes wide in astonishment. He had never seen her cry before, not ever in his life, and he knew somehow that these were wondrously important moments passing here in the cornfield. She had turned away so that he should not see her tears. She stood looking along the rows of cornshocks, but instead of this she saw before her a plain, a field of sunflowers, not wilted merely, but dead, trampled, the flower-faces gray and withered, not lifted to the sun, but bent down toward the earth, all laid to waste.

And suddenly she felt very cold.

"—only I did not know how far it had gone," she finished, as though talking to herself, forcing her voice and body into control. "It was only because I loved you."

Still he returned her look. "Do you love me now?"

"Of course I love you."

"I am your beloved?" he asked with a child's innocence, the smile of an angel; and she had to answer it.

"Yes. In a manner of speaking."

"Then why can't it go on being the same?"

"The same?"

"Yes. You and me and Holland?"

Holland.

She pulled him to her. There was a long silence while she gathered her thoughts, then she spoke again. She had been thinking, she said, of how his father had died. That day, last November, carrying the baskets down to the apple cellar. What did he think about all that? About the *way* Father had died?

Forthright and unhesitating in his answer, he replied, "Holland was standing right by the trapdoor. I think he pushed it." There was an ease, an honesty to his words which she did not doubt. Her surmise was correct then: Holland, the *real* Holland, had killed his own father, had thrown down the trapdoor on top of him and actually destroyed him. Holland was his own father's murderer. This was no figment of Niles's imagination.

"Why?" she asked.

"He hated him."

"Did he? Did he say this to you? Did he tell you?"

"No; not in words. But I knew."

"How?"

"I think—I think it must have been my sixth or seventh sense. You know these things when you're twins with someone."

His sixth or seventh sense. She tightened her arms around him.

"But you didn't answer my question," he told her.

"I don't remember—"

"I said, why can't it go on, go on being the same?"

"Oh, my dear. Niles, you must listen to me. Carefully. Will you?"

"Yes."

"Things cannot ever be the same again. Not for any of us. Not any more. We sometimes reach a point in our lives where we can't ever go back again, we have to go on from there. All that was before is past now. It went too far. Everything has gone too far. It must stop, do you see? Now—it—must—stop."

"No more game?"

"No. No more game."

She shuddered as she looked at him, and he, absently thinking of a crow walking on her grave, seemed to read something in her expression that frightened him. Not something to do with Holland, because of what he had done to Father, but to do with him, Niles.

And he knew what she was thinking.

"Where are we going?" he asked as she took his hand—this atrocious child, whom even now she loved—and crossed the furrows, back to the cemetery lawn.

Where? Where indeed. Her hand to her heart as she walked, she let her mind guide her along to the logical conclusion. Well, they would go home. They would pass through the iron gates and leave the graveyard. They would go home and have supper in the kitchen, then join the selectmen for Granddaddy's Toast and then . . . and then . . . her mind faltered. Where would *he* go then?

What would be his punishment, she wondered, turning the alternatives over in her mind. What did they do to a child for such crimes? What child could *commit* such crimes? Where would they take him? To that barren place, that place of brick and iron bars, to be held there, like some dangerous animal?

"You're going to send me away," he said quietly, watching the toes of his shoes as he walked along beside her.

"Away?" she repeated, shocked that he had read her thoughts. "Why, where should you go, *douschka?*" With an abysmal attempt at a joke.

But he refused to answer, withdrawing then and refusing to speak of it any more, and she could tell that he knew, knew what she had been thinking, that his mind was picturing, as hers had, the dismal building of brick, red and grimy like Rose Rock, with iron bars and heavy screens, where Grandmother Perry had gone. That place, that *domicile*. No. No, that was not to be thought of. She would never consider such a thing, never such an end for her beloved. "No child, you shall not be sent away."

"All right," he said simply, squeezing her hand, and the look on his face was gentle and trustful. They were passing along the roadway, their feet making companionable sounds as they trod the gravel. She took heart once more. She had succeeded in part—

had persuaded him to say the words. Holland was dead. He had admitted that much at least: Holland was dead. If Holland was dead, then who was it that had done those dreadful things? Perhaps she could get him to face it somehow; and seeing, recognizing it, perhaps there was help at hand. Holland was dead; Niles alive. It was a beginning in any case, a first step. She would have to see how the others might follow. It would be like teaching a baby to walk.

A baby . . . *the* baby . . .

Pale and spent, she stopped in the roadway, faced him, and asked the question once more. "Niles, *where* is the baby?"

"The baby?"

"Yes. The baby of Torrie."

"Torrie's baby?" His face was reddening again. "I don't know."

"But you must, child. You *must!*"

"No! I don't!"

"Then who does?" she demanded.

His answer came, not so much as an answer, but as a scream.

"Holland knows! Ask Holland!"

Fast upon his scream she seemed to hear a voice, quite clearly and distinctly, warning: *Beware of mad dogs lurking, for lurking, they shall bite! And biting, shall bite again!*   SLAP

And now, no sooner did her hand strike the child's face than it flew to her open mouth. "Oh," she murmured, more stricken by her act than by any words of his. She stepped back, staring in horror at her palm. It was some moments before she could compose herself, and, her limp more pronounced, force

her trembling limbs to carry her along the roadway.
It was no good, she could tell. He would never give it
up, this incredible, this most monstrous delusion,
these *remains* he was obsessed with. It would be with
him for as long as he lived. She could see that now.
And this outburst she had just witnessed, so unlike
him, but so like . . . the Other . . . it was almost
as though . . .   *what thought*

She gave a shuddery gasp at the thought, and preceding him along the sidewalk by the church, unable
to look at him, she was unaware of how slowly the
red mark on his white cheek disappeared, unaware
too of his expression as he followed, staring with flat
opaque eyes from under gable-shaped brows at her
stiffened back. *HOLLAND!*

V

Usually the funny stories in the dining room never
stopped. If you listened at the door, you might hear
Mr. Pennyfeather telling a Mae West joke, or the one
about the Jewish man riding with the Pope—"Who's
det vit' Ginsboig?"—or Mr. Fenstermacher would re-
cite *Minnehaha.* You knew who was in the room just
from the sound of their laughter: Uncle George,
working to be jovial; Dr. Brainard, a deep chest rumble, like a truck starting up, ending in wct backfire;
Mr. Fenstermacher's, a high-pitched, nasal whine;
Mr. Foley, as befitted his occupation, laughing seldom. Tonight hardly anyone laughed at all. Talk was

sparse and subdued; you had a feeling everyone was in a hurry to get through the evening and leave.

As Winnie came through the swinging door from the pantry, the tinkle of ice and water splashing into goblets could be heard, and the clink of silverware upon china.

"Honest, Rider is hardly touching his plate," she said. "T'ain't right, Mr. Perry insisting on him being there." She jerked her head toward the dining room. "He could of eaten in here, or upstairs, on a tray, or out, like Mrs. Valeria." While Mr. Fenstermacher was being entertained at the Perrys', Valeria had been invited to dine with Mrs. Fenstermacher and then to go to a movie show.

Winnie poured hot coffee into the silver pot, and put it on a footed tray with the cream and sugar. "Winnie," Ada said, "when Mr. Angelini brings in the keg, put the tray in the center of the table so it shall not mar."

"Yes, Missus." Winnie banged her hip against the door and went through. Back turned at the sink, Ada's agitation showed itself as she scraped off the dinner plates.

Niles got up from his chair. He had a streak of mercurochrome on his cheek, a red crescent where the moon pin had scratched him. "Here, we can do that," he offered, signaling to Holland, standing a little way off by himself, his expression dreamy and faraway, with beads of perspiration across his lip, his eyes a bit filmy. The Asiatic Look again.

Rudely shaken from her thoughts, his grandmother looked back over her shoulder.

"Come on," Niles said, throwing a dish towel across the room to his twin, "I'll wash and you dry."

A dish clattered from Ada's hand into the sink. "Stop that at once!" she commanded, wiping a cheek with the back of her trembling hand. "Pick up that dish towel!"

Watching in the doorway while the towel was retrieved, Winnie went to the refrigerator and removed a bowl of whipped cream and spooned it onto the dessert. "Table's cleared," she announced, puzzled by the tension in the room. "Where's Leno?" she said, pretending to have seen nothing. "Mr. Perry wants you all to come in for the toast." Smoothing the cream with a spatula, she carried off the dessert. Niles looked at Ada, who had stopped her work and was silently clasping her hands. Finding the dishpan and Oxydol under the sink, he moved her gently aside, filled the pan with hot water, sudsed, and slid the plates in one at a time. *He has power*

The back-entryway door swung wide and in came Leno Angelini with the wine keg upright on one shoulder. At the same moment Winnie returned, with George behind her. "Grand dinner," he announced, eyes bright, and slurring his words a little. "Here's Leno, right on schedule. Take it in, Leno, take it in. Come along Ada, Niles. It's time." He held the door open. "You come too, Winnie. We want the whole family."

"George—" Ada demurred.

"Come on, come along in," he insisted in his heartiest manner. "It's a grand evening. It won't be a party without the toast, and it won't be a toast without the family." *including the baby*

As the others left, Winnie reached out and touched Ada. "What happened before?" she asked, bewildered. "Was Niles talking to himself?"

"No, my dear," Ada said with a weary shake of her head as she passed through the doorway. "It is only—a game."

Mystified, Winnie followed her through the pantry into the smoke-filled room, shimmering with candlelight. The table centerpiece, a three-tiered glass epergne, banked with fruit, had been removed to the sideboard amid an array of liquor bottles and waiting wine glasses. In its place on the footed silver tray stood Granddaddy Perry's wine keg, looking oddly out of place under Leno Angelini's impromptu covering of canvas, the frayed ends of the cord tied in a knot, and flanked by candles in pale fragile stalks of amethyst glass. As Ada came in, all the selectmen rose except Mr. Pennyfeather.

"Is that Ada?" he inquired from the foot of the table, near the pantry door. She went to touch his hand and kiss his cheek, and after greeting the others, politely refused Rider's seat and took a spare one away from the table beside the china cupboard. Leaving the chair on the opposite side of the cupboard for Holland, Niles stood against the wall, out of the light, directly across from Mr. Angelini, spruced up for the occasion.

When Winnie had distributed the glasses, George placed each in turn under the spigot and let the wine flow. Then, brimming, the glasses were passed around to each place. "And one for Winnie," George said, making a show, after he had handed Ada hers. "And one for Leno. Grand," he said. When Mr. Pennyfeather received his, he fingered the base and tapped the rim lightly with a spoon for attention. While the room fell silent he maneuvered his chair out and stood; stoop-shouldered and looking down at the table behind the smoked glasses that hid his blindness, he chose his words.

"Well," he began simply, "I guess we're all here now. Another year has passed, and once more we're gathered around Granddaddy Perry's table. It's been a sad year. The family has had a lot of sorrow, a lot of grief. When I was told that our annual gathering would take place tonight, I must admit I was surprised. And there are those others who may be even shocked—I don't know. But I'm glad we did meet, glad that George and Ada insisted. I think it has helped each of us lift our hearts a little." He turned his head in the direction of Rider, who nodded a slight assent. "Those of us, not members of the family, we're—well, in a sense we're representatives of this whole town and all the people in it. And we'd like to say we feel very much the suffering these folks have had to endure these past months. Too much suffering, some would say. But the Perrys are a strong people—always have been. And *I* know—we all know—that they'll find the strength to accept God's will."

"Amen," the others said.

His fingers slid cautiously along the cloth, groping for the wine glass. He located and lifted it and all the men rose again. "We would like," Mr. Pennyfeather continued, "to be the sort of friends to Granddaddy Perry's family that he was to the community, steadfast and kind-thinking. Pequot Landing had a good friend in Watson Perry, and once again we, all of us, are gathered here in his honor and to accept his generosity on behalf of the township. Ladies and gentlemen," he concluded with dignity, "shall we drink to the memory of John Watson Perry."

The name echoed around the table and glasses were lifted to the portrait above the sideboard in the traditional memorial toast. "Hear, hear," Niles repeated with the others, tasting his wine and lifting his glass to Holland, whose expression he could not read.

George accepted the toast and in return tendered the white envelope containing the check to Dr. Brainard, who passed it along to Mr. Fenstermacher, who handed it to Mr. Pennyfeather. The men sat down, and Winnie, draining her glass, began serving the dessert. Talk resumed. Mr. Pennyfeather chatted warmly with Mr. Angelini, who stood at his side and, embarrassed, accepted another glass of wine. Ada moved to slip quietly out through the pantry door and Winnie was passing the coffee when, suddenly, the hall doors at the opposite end of the room opened and all heads turned to see Torrie faltering on the threshold. Again the men stood while Rider hurried to his wife's side and tried to draw her from the room. *She has to be here*

"No—no, please. I—" She hung on his arm at the head of the table, looking around vacantly. She had dressed hastily: her sweater was misbuttoned, she hadn't bothered with stockings. She wore no makeup and her hair, pulled straight back, was caught carelessly with a piece of ribbon. In her arms she clutched the doll-lamp, whose cord trailed on the floor. She hesitated, surprised by all the faces. "I

why did she come

came—" She bit her lip, making it white in a visible effort to recall the reason for her appearance. "I came—" she began once more, with an anguished look to Rider.

"You came for the toast, wasn't that it, Torrie?" Uncle George suggested, an attempt to ease the awkward situation, and offered her his place. "Well, isn't this grand."

"Yes," she said vaguely. The lamp plug scraped along the bare floor behind her as she permitted herself to be seated. She rested the lamp on her lap and smoothed the skirt. In her bruised face the eyes were red-rimmed and puffy, their expression empty-looking. Her voice was tiny, and to Niles she wasn't Torrie at all, but some pitiful child-creature he scarcely recognized.

An embarrassed silence followed until Mr. Pennyfeather got up and said, "George, because Torrie has honored us with her company, I think we might have a second toast. Perhaps the Doctor would propose it."

Dr. Brainard cleared his throat and George motioned for another glass, while the selectmen coughed behind their hands, straightened their ties and tried to look anywhere but at Torrie, who sat rigid at the head of the table, watching expectantly as George leaned over, placed the glass under the spigot of the keg, and with an unsteady hand turned the tap.

Like blood from an open vein the wine began spurting into the glass, then slowed, flowed again for a moment, gurgled, dribbled away to nothing. Puzzled, George twisted the tap, set down the glass, and tilted the keg to it. Again, the slight trickle into the half-filled glass.

"Can't be empty," he mumbled, tapping the keg and rocking it on the silver footed tray. He listened, then looked over at Leno with a mystified shrug. "Damn thing's s'pose-a be full, right, Leno? 'Less someone's been at the wine, huh?" His tobacco-stained fingers had fumbled the knot loose; he pulled the canvas aside and by the light of a raised candle peered inside. Quickly he fumbled for his napkin, which he clapped over his mouth and, while Niles and Mr. Angelini kept their places, the others drew closer, Mr. Fenstermacher and Dr. Brainard, Mr. Foley, Ada as well, and together they stared. Mr. Fenstermacher was the first to break away, making awful retching sounds in his throat, Ada moaned aloud, and Torrie, rising, tottered forward, her arms flung wide, her screams beginning and Rider only half catching her as she crumpled, the doll-lamp rolling away to the baseboard, the bulb shattering.

"What is it?" Mr. Pennyfeather was demanding. "What is it?" He alone, seated behind smoked glasses at the foot of the table, was unable to see what the others plainly saw, what Niles, his eyes now on the wavering candlelight image of his twin, did not care to see—the little face that floated in the dark red wine, so like the baby in the bottle, hair waving, the eyes staring up at the ceiling, the mouth parted in a silent scream.

VI

Poor baby. Oh, the poor, poor baby, Torrie's little baby. His heart bled. Jesus, Holland, Christ, Holland, oh Christ, what a thing to do! What a terrible, awful thing to do to Torrie's little baby. Made your stomach heave to think about it. Holland must be crazy. Yes, that must be it, *Holland was crazy.* Anyone would *have* to be crazy to do a thing like that. He shivered; another crow. But there was this, he told himself, he'd been right all along. Holland had known where the baby was; certainly he had.

How quiet it was. Still, and deathly quiet. Usually the house was fairly cracking under the plaster, the walls, floorboards, ceiling stirring as though the place were about to collapse. But not now. Now, not a sound. Except the grandfather clock. *Tock*-tick, *tock*-tick. It was getting on his nerves, crouched as he was in the dark. How long was he going to have to stay here in the closet? He hated the dark so.

Changing his position slightly he struck an elbow against Uncle George's bag of golf clubs, grabbing them in time before they clattered to the floor. It smelled in there, old and stale. Must be either the galoshes or Father's leather coat, hanging on its hook. The closet was stifling. A tiny bit of light came through the crack where the door would not quite close. By putting his eye to the crack he could just see the landing at the top of the stairs. A while ago there had been frantic commotion up and down them, about what you'd expect under the circumstances. He himself had bolted from the dining room before anyone had realized he was gone—anyone, that was, except Ada, whose eye watched his every move, but she hadn't been quick enough, and before you knew it he was through the pantry, into the kitchen, then out the hall door and up the stairs and into the closet. Soon Uncle George came roaring up and into his room, evidently for the car keys, because Niles could hear something about Rider taking Torrie down to his mother's house on the green and calling Constable Blessing. Then he listened to the others leaving, the selectmen and the rest. When they had gone, he could make out Ada's and Winnie's voices, whispering at the bottom of the stairs, but even with his ear to the crack he couldn't understand what they were saying. After that it was pretty quiet, except you could tell people were walking around. Looking for him, he was sure. Then—silence. Except for the clock. *Tock*-tick *tock*-tick.

Now he heard another door open: Ada's, at the end of the hall. He recognized her footstep as she came along the gallery. Then she stepped into view at the head of the stairs. She had changed into her robe and her hair was unpinned and falling about her shoulders. On her face was a strange expression he couldn't read. She turned and started down the stairs, descending one step, then another, haltingly. Now she stopped, remaining stock still, listening, and doing something funny with her shoulders, hunching them, kind of, and Niles caught his breath and held it, not daring to move. Had she suddenly thought of the closet? No, she was continuing on. There was a loud click in the silence and in another moment the clock had begun to strike eleven slow, sonorous notes.

Now Ada had stopped halfway down the staircase and, with her back to the door, stood motionless, her shoulders slightly lifted as though the dying notes of the clock were reverberating against her bones, and, from the back, you could see her head making its little nodding motions. Then her head turned and he realized her eyes were closed, the brow furrowed, her hands clasped beneath her chin. Once or twice the muscle in her jaw twitched. She lifted her hair and let it fall, then laid her hand against her forehead, as if feeling for a fever. No, no, not a fever; she was concentrating! Her whole expression was one of deepest concentration; she was playing the game! Playing the game on him, to search him out.

Two times two is four. Two times four is eight. Two times eight is sixteen. Two times sixteen is thirty-two. Buzz me, Miz' Blue. Good evening, all you people out there in Radioland. No. It was no good. He couldn't stop her. Tried to think of other things; but couldn't stop her. Her eyes were open now, her body turned toward him and in another moment, with a rapid movement, she wheeled on the step and came back up, standing for a long, silent moment on the top landing, her eye not on the clock, but on the door, the damn door; cripes, why wouldn't it close! She took a step forward. And another. Stopping with each step as though, if there were someone hiding in the closet, she didn't want to discover him. Her hand emerged from the sleeve of her robe as she lifted it and reached out to seize the knob. He gasped as she threw the door open wide and the light from the hall fell on him.

"Get up," she ordered, and he obeyed, getting to his feet, then standing before her, unmoving, his eyes on hers, his body taut, panting like an animal, his head slightly tilted, staring from under dark, slanting brows, his eyes glazed.

"Come here." She put a hand out, the sleeve of her white robe falling away from her wrist in full folds. For a moment he remained where he stood, then brutally thrust out at her; she drew back, and he flung himself past her, out of the closet, savagely crashing down the stairs. At the bottom he glanced back to see her coming fast behind him, her hair streaming, her sleeves flapping like huge wings, neither calling his name nor yet stopping in her pursuit. Winnie, wild-eyed, jumped up from the kitchen table to block his way as he passed through the room. He ducked around her and pushed through the back-entryway and ran outside.

"No, leave me," he heard Ada cry to Winnie, "let me go!" And then: "Wait, Missus, I'll come—" "No! You shall stay here. This is for me to do, alone."

Niles scooted down the drive and under the breezeway; behind him the tiny figure fled over the gravel like a night moth. And as he slipped into the barn he saw the blur of white as it stopped at the corner of the carriage-house, where, disappearing into the weeds for a moment, it reappeared in the light, dragging behind the blue and yellow can of Richfield gasoline.

* * *

Red shadows cast by the flickering lantern overhead
tossed the apple cellar like a ship on an ocean of
blood. Niles eyed the other across from him. "God
damn you," he whispered, "God damn you to hell."
Hell hell hell, he heard his own voice come back to
him. "How could you do such a terrible thing?"
Thing thing thing. "Well, what have you got to say
for yourself? Can't you say something?" Again: *thing
thing thing.* The room rang with echoes. He waited
for an answer but there was only silence. Then he
heard:

"Peregrine for Perry."

"Yes," he replied, "Peregrine for Perry."

"Who is Peregrine?" Even the question was like an
echo.

"I am Peregrine," he replied. "The Peregrine is
me."

"Who are you?" the voice demanded cunningly.

"I'm me. Niles. Niles Perry."

"Are you? Are you really?" This with a sly
chuckle, light, mocking, eminently satisfied. Niles
was bewildered. Wasn't he? Really? Wasn't he Niles
Perry? If not, who then? Who else could he be? Why
the chuckle? What was so funny? What was the joke?

A grating sound came from above; he strained in
the scarlet darkness.

"Listen! Somebody's up there! Listen—hear?"

"You're crazy." Another chuckle.

"There is! I can hear them! I can!" And so he did;
really heard it: the grating of metal along the grav-
eled drive, the rusty creak of door hinges, the bump-
bump-bump of the can dragging over the wooden

floor; a moment's silence, then the heavy trapdoor lifting . . . upward . . . a slowly widening arc . . .

His shiver was exquisite horror. He would close his eyes and count to five, then open them and see who would be there.

One. Two.

He heard the low chuckle in the darkness. "It's not, you know."

"Not?" he echoed foolishly. He was to be disappointed, then?

He stared at the red walls, and in the dancing light saw, gathering out of nothingness, shapes hideously alluring, gigantically filling the room, saw, overhead, serpents, anaconda-long, never warm, half-sloughed skins like glittering chain mail, coiling undulent soft spotted wreaths around the beams, salmon tongues slicking into mortise and tenon. And Peregrine, Peregrine himself, amber-eyed Falcon Peregrine, come crying, cawing, swooping, brazen bird, audaciously rustling those pinions that were the measure of the boy's madness. He beat at the bird, striking it away, flailing, ducking, writhing, trying to cover eyes, ears, to smother, shut out sight and sound.

Remember.

He heard the word, and as it hung in the air, it broke apart into a chain of echoes—*remember—remember—rememberremember—*

"Don't you remember?" Holland was saying, his voice coldly demanding.

"What? Remember what?" Why did he suddenly feel doomed? *"Remember what?"*

Three. Four.

"Holland?" he implored. "Help. Help!"

"You forgot. Didn't you?" He sounded almost angry. *"You forgot."*

"Yes." Meekly he admitted it; he had forgotten. But what? What was it he had forgotten?

"It's all right, Niles Alexander," he heard Holland's voice, suddenly comforting as the trapdoor was at last thrown back. "We all have things that we forget, or"—very grave now, a little soothing, and not at all mocking—"things we would like to.

"Behold."

And Niles looked up and beheld.

She was standing there, just at the edge of the opening. A vision. That is to say, she appeared a vision: her pale form lighted by the lantern hanging below; her hair swinging about her shoulders, and the wings, the lofty white wings, rising and falling with the slow movement of her arms. He got up, moved toward her, as though walking in a dream, his eyes intent upon her face, her countenance so radiant, so serene, so peaceful, so—

No. Wait. Wait!

This wasn't the way it was supposed to be. Where was the radiant expression, the look of peace? Could this really be *her?* Her face was sad, its expression the most sorrowful, most pitiful, most wildly *penitent* imaginable; her eyes filled with tears, while she bent low above him; behind her fluttering wings—no, no radiance, no halo, only endless darkness there.

Her wings beat desperately. It seemed she beckoned him. Her tears fell faster; ah, but he would stop them, he thought, for now there could never be tears again, surely; somehow he must make her stop. But they continued, the tears, wetting his hands, soaking his uplifted face. Bitterly they stung, dropping like rain, drenching the red snow, running in rivulets, between the stones, drowning the room; and it came to him then, peering up into her eyes as she leaned toward the light, that the tears would never stop, they would flow on forever, like an everlasting river, like Acheron; and lo, the dream dissolved, became a nightmare.

Yet he was awake! Stop! What was she *doing?* The wings beat deliriously for the brief instant she hovered there. Stooping, she seized the lantern, and he, crying out, backed away to the wall while, in one explosive motion she hurled down the lantern, then in a swift, unlooked-for rush, wings rippling, shuddering, threw herself after, and the snow and the stones melted, the apple cellar itself surrendered its form, and the torrent of tears became one vast melting glow. Arms flung out against the blazing light, his back flat against the little door, he was suddenly reminded of that which he had forgotten, the one thing he had tried so hard to remember, and which in a split second, in this one particular moment, was disclosed to him. The fact was, he was going to die, and his dying wish, *that wish,* the very last thing he had desired to see, had been beheld: the Angel of the Brighter Day. "Niles" did die

It had come to pass. Verily, as though he had stood at Lourdes, he had seen a vision. And this is a very rare thing, for to see such a vision, to *know,* is not given to many in their lifetime; but who was there then to tell him it had come to him, this vision, not as she whom he awaited, but as the Angel of Death?

Truly, it was a revelation.

Miss DeGroot is quite late tonight. Unusual for her.

Do you notice how the lilac has deepened to blue, the blue to purple, the purple to black? *Ombré,* the French say, though I don't know where I got that word. I can no longer make out the stain on the ceiling, that rust-colored watermark with the familiar face peering down at me. Is that significant? I wonder what Miss DeGroot would say about that. Oh, I have remembered—Miss DeGroot thinks the stain is shaped like the Belgian Congo; imagine—though I know they probably have a new name for the Belgian Congo too these days. I can't keep up with the way they change the map, can you? I mean, given my choice, I have always preferred Leghorn to Livorno, Konigsberg to Kronstadt. But I'm not at all convinced that that blotch is like the Belgian Congo, whatever Miss DeGroot may say; to me it still looks like a face.

I know what you're thinking. You're not interested in Miss DeGroot, or the face on the ceiling. You're thinking about the old lady. You're thinking Ada could not have committed such horror, taking her own life that way in order to take that of the boy, appointing herself at once judge and executioner, dragging along the drive the heavy can of gasoline, summoning, God knew how, the strength to raise the

trapdoor, pouring the gasoline down into the apple
cellar—certainly a tinderbox with all that cattail stuff
around—crashing down the lantern, pitching herself
into the holocaust. How could she?

But she did.

Such was her will. People afterward said she was
crazy; and I agreed. Completely out of her mind to
do such a thing. Thinking back over that last, tragic
event, I am left with the thought of that wistful
phrase of hers about the heart's immolation; she was
her own Brünnhilde, and I have never doubted she
did it for love.

As it happened, her neck was broken in the fall to
the stone floor; she never felt the flames. Myself, I
was fortunate to have escaped. You may imagine the
terror I experienced, and my subsequent relief as I
backed away to the Slave Door, remembering only in
time that Uncle George's padlock, which secured the
hasp outside, had been sawed off with the hacksaw to
accommodate the Chan Yu disappearing trick. It's
true: of just such minor happenstances does our life
consist. Ironic, isn't it? You will perhaps understand
my being at pains to leave the Slave Door open behind me, that there might be sufficient draft drawn
through the trap and down into the room.

Afterward, I suggested to Mrs. Pennyfeather that
it might be fitting if Professor Lapineaux played
"Rock of Ages" at the funeral. Naturally, Mr. Tuthill
recited the Twenty-third Psalm.

Poor Ada.

With her death, I supposed that whatever story I
chose to tell would be believed. I must confess that it
was I who suggested that she must have been crazy,

and I *was* believed—up to a certain point. Soon after, however, thinking it safe to retrieve the contents of the Prince Albert tobacco tin—the ring, the finger, the glasses which had belonged to Russell, a ribbon from the baby's dress, the *evidence,* in short—from the toe of one of the rubber hip boots hanging on the tool-shed wall, where it had been safely hidden, I was surprised in this act by Mr. Angelini, he who had seen all from the very beginning, he who had been certain he'd hung his pitchfork back in its proper place on the wall.

And so it was Mr. Angelini who confided to Uncle George his discovery. Now it only remained for Uncle George to initiate the proper steps, which is how I came, in time, to this place.

Let me say I was not sorry to leave the house on Valley Hill Road. I found it, after a while, too large, too noiseless, too—dead. It seemed to be growing, enlarging and expanding, the whole house, and I felt its emptiness oppressive, as though conspiring against me, and I realized how much of my time was spent looking for someone, someone in the house, listening, waiting, seeking around corners, up a stairway, along a corridor, behind a door. But no. There was nothing. I was alone. Truly; though there were others in the house, I was alone. And lonely, let me admit it. I think it was then that I began to miss him, felt the lack of him, began to seek him out, to look for him, all through the house, the barn, the fields, down by the river. But he was gone, of course, he truly was dead then, he who I had been, the Other; and I became aware then how really alone I was. Sometimes I would think I saw him, a fleeting

glimpse only, a flash, just for a brief moment, standing there, there in the darkened corner of a closet, or
there, winding the grandfather clock as he used to, or
there, in the storeroom, wearing the pink shirt and
playing the old Victrola. But it wasn't really him.
Winnie saw to keeping the clock wound, for who else
could be bothered? The Victrola stood covered with
dust in the storeroom—that *silent* room—and no
corner of any closet harbored the Other. He was
gone; I could not conjure him up, as he had me. He
was gone, and, sadly, I missed him. I was alone then,
in the house, and I have been alone ever since.

Look. Do you see the moon? I was certain there
would be one. Lying here on my bed, I can see it
clearly. Interesting, how its light catches on the bars
outside my window, making them blacker and
thicker and so much more stern-looking. Hateful
place, this. But Miss DeGroot says I'm "family,"
meaning, I suppose, that I have been here that long.
That's Miss DeGroot's little joke; but I don't think
it's terribly funny.

With a moon tonight, perhaps there'll be a sun
tomorrow. I still remember that day when the moon
and sun both showed themselves together. I've never
seen it since. I hope the sun does come out. I do hope
it. As I hope for . . . well, no, not really, you know.
I don't hope. As I said, I have been lonely here, and
Miss DeGroot doesn't really count for very much.
The coldness, the grayness, the sink, the radiator—
what the hell. It's a terrible place, as I said, and I do
not care to have to do with the others who are here
also. I could, of course, if I chose, am in fact urged
to, but I do not, will not. They laugh at me in the

halls and downstairs, laugh at me behind the wire grill, annoy me; annoy me because they will not call me by my name as Miss DeGroot does. Call me his name—Niles; *Niles,* for God's sake, isn't that crazy? When I have told them, for years have told them, my name is Holland. Holland William Perry. But they are like that here in Babylon. (By coincidence, Miss DeGroot knew Grandmother Perry when she was sent here, so you know she's got to be pretty old, having been around all that time.) So I keep to myself. Mostly I like to watch the Shadow Hills buses end their route at the corner and turn around. Oh yes, they took the streetcars off years ago, but other than that nothing much has changed. It's still the end of the line.

TOTAL TRANSFER OF PERSONALITY TO HOLLAND — NILES HAS BEEN DRIVEN OUT OF NILES' BODY.